D0536577

19

MURDER AT THE CHASE

A Selection of Further Titles by Eric Brown

The Langham and Dupré Mysteries

MURDER BY THE BOOK *
MURDER AT THE CHASE *

Other Titles

DEVIL'S NEBULA
HELIX WARS
THE KINGS OF ETERNITY
NECROPATH
STARSHIP SUMMER
THRESHOLD SHIFT

* *available from Severn House*

MURDER AT THE CHASE

A Langham and Dupré mystery

Eric Brown

Severn House Large Print
London & New York

This first large print edition published 2016
in Great Britain and the USA by
SEVERN HOUSE PUBLISHERS LTD of
19 Cedar Road, Sutton, Surrey, England, SM2 5DA.
First world regular print edition published 2014 by
Severn House Publishers Ltd., London and New York.

British Library Cataloguing in Publication Data
A CIP catalogue record for this title is available from the British Library.

ISBN-13: 9780727894106

Except where actual historical events and characters are being described
for the storyline of this novel, all situations in this publication are fictitious
and any resemblance to living persons is purely coincidental.

Severn House Publishers support the Forest Stewardship Council™
[FSC™], the leading international forest certification organisation. All
our titles that are printed on FSC certified paper carry the FSC logo.

Typeset by Palimpsest Book Production Ltd.,
Falkirk, Stirlingshire, Scotland.
Printed and bound in Great Britain by
T J International, Padstow, Cornwall.

To Finn Sinclair, Tony Ballantyne, Keith Brooke, Beth Dunnett, Patrick Mahon and Phillip Vine, whose comments on early drafts of this novel were invaluable.

ONE

'Do you believe in ghosts, Donald?'

'What an odd question. No, of course not. Do you?'

Maria stood on the lawn with her legs crossed at the ankles, nursing a glass of Pimm's. She wore a jade-green summer dress which complemented her tanned skin, and a tiny lace hat that clung to the side of her head – and she looked, Langham thought, the very personification of elegance and beauty. Despite the gunshot wound to his chest that restricted his movements, he considered himself the luckiest man alive. What did a little scar tissue matter when he basked in the love and devotion of Maria Dupré?

The garden of his agent's Pimlico townhouse was thronged with the great and the good of the London literary world. Earlier Langham had spotted, like a bird-watcher, a Nobel laureate, an old poet of the Georgian school, three bestselling novelists and a recipient of the Hawthornden Prize. A dozen or so lesser species of novelist, like himself, were interspersed among the gathering like hedge sparrows. His agent, Charles Elder, moved from group to group, dispensing wit and charm in equal measure. His annual garden party for clients and friends was the high-point of his social calendar, and Langham wouldn't have missed it for the world.

He smiled up at Maria. 'Well, girl – do you believe in spooks, or not?'

She twisted her lips into a contemplative moue. 'I am not so sure, Donald. I think I sit upon the fence on this matter. I am agnostic.'

He squinted at her. 'You are strange. How can you be agnostic about ghosts? You either believe or disbelieve.'

'Ah, Donald – there you go with your certainties. Things are always black and white with you, no? There are no grey areas.'

He hoisted his empty glass. 'Guilty as charged. Makes life easier.'

'When I was a little girl,' she said, sitting down beside him on the garden seat and laying an elegant hand on his arm, 'living in Paris with my father, I thought I saw something.'

He stared at her, in thrall to her beauty and the cadence of her accent. He could listen to her all day. 'Go on. What was it?'

'We lived in a big penthouse suite in the centre of the city. My father was a minister in the newly formed government and we had just moved to a luxury apartment.' She gave a wonderfully theatrical shiver. 'I should have liked the suite perhaps, but it gave me the jeebie-heebies. What are you smiling at?' she said.

'The heebie-jeebies,' he said.

'Those too, Donald. Anyway, one room in particular frightened me, and I wouldn't go into it. It was the library, at the back of the apartment. It was always in shadow, and the atmosphere was . . . *terr-eeble*. One day, when I was hurrying past the open door, I glanced in and saw a figure.

2

An old man with grey hair, sitting by the window and looking out . . . Only,' she went on, staring at him with wide eyes, 'there was no one else in the apartment other than me and my father. Now, Donald, I went screaming to my father and told him about the mysterious figure, but of course when he investigated it was not there. *But*,' she said, squeezing his arm, 'a week later I overheard two of my father's guests talking one evening about the library . . . and they let it slip that fifty years earlier the owner of the apartment had been *shot dead* in that *very room*! Now, Donald, what do you think of that?'

He regarded her, trying not to smile. 'I think,' he said, 'that perhaps you heard the guests talking about the murder *before* you thought you saw the figure, and your overactive little girl's mind fabricated the apparition.'

She gave a genteel snort and slapped his forearm. 'You are a terrible man, Donald Langham! Anyway, I did not say that I definitely believe in ghosts, merely that I sit upon the fence. I certainly saw something that day, but I have never seen anything like it since.'

He just stared at her. While recuperating in hospital he'd decided that, at the first opportune moment, he would ask Maria Dupré to marry him. To that end he had suggested a break away in the country. Maria had agreed with alacrity, and Langham had found a small hotel tucked away in the depths of the countryside. They were to motor up to Suffolk on Monday, and later in the week he'd get down on bended knee – wound permitting – and pop the question.

She waved a hand before his eyes. 'Donald! Attention, please! You are miles away.'

'Sorry, just smitten by your beauty, Maria. Anyway, why all the talk of ghosts and ghouls?'

'I saw Alasdair Endicott over there, talking to Dame Amelia, and I was reminded of ghosts.'

Langham peered across the lawn at the willowy, rather effete young man paying polite attention to the dowager novelist. 'Yes, he does look rather pale and ghost-like, doesn't he?'

'Silly! He's just written a rather good novel about a haunting. I read it a while ago. I'm sure I told you at the time.'

'You read so much,' he said, 'and so fast.'

'And you were daydreaming about your next masterpiece, Donald. Do you know, you get that strange dreamy look in your eyes when you're plotting, and I can say any number of things and you don't hear a word.'

'I'm sorry, but I find that hard to believe. I hang on your every word.'

Someone stepped between Langham and the intense July sunlight, and he looked up to see Charles Elder. 'Donald!' Charles boomed. 'How remiss of me! Your glass is empty and here I am, putting the world to rights with Sir Peregrine and neglecting my guests!' He crossed to a nearby table and came back with a Pimm's.

'Now, what were you little lovebirds chattering about, if I might be so tactless as to enquire?'

'I was asking Donald if he believed in ghosts, Charles. Of course, being very English and very rational, he doesn't.'

4

Charles said, '"There are more things in heaven and earth, Horatio . . ."'

Charles was looking good, Langham thought, despite being released from hospital just a week ago – having suffered at the hands of the same gunman who was responsible for putting a hole through his own torso. His agent had lost a little weight, but was still gargantuan, and his porcine face was bright red in the afternoon heat. His luxuriant head of hair, snow white, stood up like whipped cream.

'But my dear Maria,' Charles continued, 'Donald is a materialist, and believes in nothing that he cannot grasp in his own two hands.'

'You do me a disservice, Charles,' Langham protested.

'I was telling Donald about Alasdair's novel, *The Haunting*,' Maria said.

'Aha!' Charles cried. 'Now if the experiences of young Alasdair aren't enough to convince the most hardened sceptic of life beyond, then I don't know what is.'

'I thought you said it was a novel, Maria?' Langham said.

'Oh, it is,' Charles said, 'but a novel based on his own experiences, apparently. I'll introduce you, and he can tell you all about it. A word of warning, though. Alasdair is a nice boy, but painfully shy.'

Charles sallied forth, waving the shooting stick he'd taken to using since leaving hospital, and buttonholed the young man.

Langham glanced at Maria. 'Have you met Alasdair Endicott?' he asked.

She nodded. 'And he's *very* strange. But here they come.'

Alasdair Endicott's face was gaunt and weak-chinned, and his resemblance to a goat was helped by a wispy moustache and feeble beard. Langham would not have been surprised to espy horns emerging from between the strands of his lank brown hair.

The young man bobbed his head as Charles made the introductions, his watery eyes flickering towards Donald and Maria and then away.

He offered a boneless hand to Langham in a limp shake. 'Delighted to meet you, Mr Langham,' he murmured with a flinching diffidence that spoke of a severe nervous disorder.

Charles clapped a meaty hand on Alasdair's shoulder, almost knocking him off his feet. 'Alasdair's novel landed on the doormat a couple of months ago, and if it were not for Maria's diligence in reading *everything* that passes over the threshold it might still be languishing there. Out later this year, from Gollancz,' he finished.

'Congratulations.' Langham smiled, unable to suppress a quick stab of jealousy.

Maria said, 'We were talking about ghosts, Alasdair. Donald here does not believe in them. But I told him that your novel was based on your own experiences, no?'

A pained look passed across the young man's features. 'That . . . that's correct, yes,' he stammered.

Maria shivered. 'I must tell you that I have never read anything more terrifying! Even M.R. James does not compare.'

6

Alasdair blushed.

'Your own experiences?' Langham prompted.

Charles mopped his face with a large bandana and suggested they beat a retreat from the direct sunlight. They made for the gazebo in the corner of the garden and seated themselves in the shade.

The young man seemed reluctant to speak about his experiences, so Langham pressed, 'If you don't mind enlightening a convinced sceptic . . . what exactly did you experience, Alasdair?'

'Ah . . . well.' Alasdair stared down at the floor-boards of the gazebo and looked distinctly uncomfortable. 'If you are a sceptic, Mr Langham, then I advise you to remain so.'

Maria leaned forward, wide-eyed. 'In the opening of the novel the hero is present when a demon is summoned at a séance . . .'

Alasdair laughed nervously and waved a limp hand, like a pale fish that had lost the will to live. 'I had a . . . a strange experience while living in America as a child.'

'A séance, my boy?' said Charles. 'Do tell!'

'A séance, yes.' Alasdair swallowed, and his prominent Adam's apple bobbed. 'Before the war I lived with my father in Hollywood. He was a screenwriter, and one evening he . . . he hired the services of a medium.'

'What happened?' Maria asked.

Alasdair coloured under her attention and stammered, 'Pretty much what I described in the novel.'

Maria explained. 'In the first scene, our sceptical hero is convinced when the medium manifests the spirit of his dead wife . . .'

'And you witnessed this?' Langham asked.

The young man coloured to the roots of his hair and murmured, 'Unfortunately, yes.' He smiled shyly at Langham and, as if unhappy with the topic of conversation, changed the subject. 'But I understand you once knew my father – Edward Endicott, the mystery novelist.'

Langham sat back, surprised. Edward Endicott was a tall, robust man in his sixties, an ex-Hollywood screenwriter who penned mystery thrillers under the byline of E.L. Endicott: a more complete contrast to his diffident son could not be imagined.

'And how is Edward?' Langham asked. 'I haven't seen him for years.'

'Well . . . He was working on his mystery novels until a month or so ago.'

'Was?' Langham echoed. 'But no longer?' He always felt uneasy when he heard that fellow writers were suffering from writer's block – as if it were a malady he himself might catch.

'A few weeks ago he became obsessed with a new subject, and decided to write a book about him.'

'Him?' Maria asked.

The young man hesitated under the trio's scrutiny. 'One Vivian Stafford,' he said.

Langham repeated the name. 'I'm sorry, I've never heard of him.'

Charles was massaging his considerable chin. 'Wait a minute! By Jove, I do think the name rings a bell. Just a moment . . . Wasn't Stafford some kind of satanist, way back in Victorian times? Contemporary of Crowley, Mathers and all that crowd?'

Alasdair nodded. 'Stafford led his own coven and dabbled in the dark arts. He was, in his own words, a confidant of the Devil himself.'

Maria looked at Langham and hugged herself with delicious fright.

'My father met the man a few weeks ago and became interested in him,' Alasdair said. 'Then a week or two ago he . . . he experienced some kind of occult evening at which Stafford exhibited his . . . powers.'

'How fascinating!' Maria declared.

Langham was about to press the young man for further details when Sir Peregrine Carstairs appeared at the entrance to the gazebo and boomed, 'So this is where you're hiding yourself, Elder! Out with you, man! I have Williams and Frobisher and the rest, wanting all the gory details of the attack. I've never known you pass up the opportunity to tell a good story.' Carstairs nodded to the company. 'Excuse me while I steal the old man!'

Charles put up a vain protest, but allowed himself to be led back across the lawn to where his audience awaited.

'Now, where were we?' Langham said, turning back to Alasdair Endicott – or rather to the seat which, just seconds ago, the young man had occupied.

He appeared to have slipped away – as elusive as one of his ghosts, Langham thought.

'Did you see where he went?' he asked Maria.

She pointed across the garden to the path which led along the side of the house. Langham was just in time to see Endicott junior making good his escape through the gate.

9

'Well . . . what do you make of that?' he asked.

'As Charles said,' Maria said, tucking in her chin and imitating Charles's baritone, '"There are more things in heaven and earth, Horatio . . ."'

Langham laughed. 'Damned odd, if you ask me. I've met Edward Endicott quite a few times. Splendid chap. No nonsense, down-to-earth type. Not the sort who'd get mixed up in all that satanist rubbish.'

Maria shrugged. 'Well, you heard what Alasdair said. His father seems quite obsessed.'

Langham frowned, unsettled at the thought of Edward Endicott wasting his time writing about a sham satanist. He glanced at his wristwatch.

Maria grabbed his arm and whispered into his ear, 'Let's escape! You did say you'd treat me one night to a meal at *Le Moulin Bleu*.'

'I did, didn't I? Well, seeing as it's you . . .'

'And you did get paid by Worley and Greenwood last week.'

'That's the trouble with falling in love with your agent's deputy,' Langham bewailed. 'She knows exactly when and what you've been paid!' He made a swipe for her derrière as she laughed and danced out of the gazebo.

He climbed to his feet, wincing at the sharp pain in his chest, lit his pipe and followed Maria across the lawn to say his goodbyes to Charles and his guests.

TWO

Caroline Dequincy bought a pair of sunglasses and three new lipsticks from the cosmetics counter at Harrods, then treated herself to coffee and cake at the café on the third floor. The latter was an indulgence which she succumbed to every time she left the sleepy village of Humble Barton and took the train up to London. Heaven knew, she deserved the occasional treat. Her life since leaving the States after the war and settling in England had been, on the surface, a smooth transition from the hectic and meretricious lifestyle of Hollywood to the quiet peacefulness of English country life. She didn't miss Los Angeles, or the movie business, in the slightest – and her infrequent American visitors just *loved* her little thatched cottage tucked away down a leafy Suffolk lane. What people failed to discern was the truth that dwelled just beneath the tranquil surface of her existence. We are all prisoners of our past, she was fond of reminding herself; prisoners of our mistakes which we cannot undo and which we must therefore live with. She had lived with her big mistake for over thirty years now, but only in the past few weeks had it returned to haunt her.

And on top of that there was all this business with Edward . . .

She watched a couple seated at a table across the café. They were middle-aged, perhaps a few

11

years her junior, and obviously lovers. She imagined that they had snatched time away from their respective spouses to rendezvous like this, and they reminded Caroline of a scene from *Brief Encounter* – the way they held hands across the table and spoke quickly, confidingly. She lit a cigarette – a Du Maurier, another small indulgence – and snorted a billow of smoke like an angry dragon. That's what I probably look like, she thought: an angry old dragon resentful of the happiness of others.

Oh, but how she hated herself for her running after Edward as she did! He was clearly not interested – had even told her so, though not so bluntly. And yet she harboured a faint hope that one day . . . She buckled her cigarette, brutally, in the glass ashtray, and seconds later lit another. She recalled a line from a Graham Greene story she had read last year, referring to 'optimism more appalling than despair', and applied it to herself. Her optimism was appalling for being hopeless – it would be far nobler simply to give in to despair. Really, she should cut her losses, get out of Humble Barton and leave Edward to get on with his life in peace.

She knew she would do nothing of the kind, because what she had now with Edward – friendship, coffee, the occasional dinner – was better than living a life without any contact with the man whatsoever.

She finished her second cigarette, drained her coffee and hurried from the café. She dallied in the dress department, admiring the latest Paris fashions and half toying with the idea of buying a knee-length silk summer dress, but decided against it. The hemline was too high and the neckline too low for a woman of her advancing years. Fifty-seven in August, and showing every pucker and wrinkle . . . She spent a lot of money on the very best cosmetics with which to plaster up the crevices, and she found that large sunglasses helped, though only in summer. If she wore them in winter they only served to draw attention to what she was attempting to conceal.

As she stepped from Harrods and approached the taxi rank, she slipped on her new glasses and felt an immediate relief from the glare. There had been a period, on arriving in London after the war, when she had worn sunglasses every time she ventured out – even in winter. Then it had been a necessity, as it seemed that every other passer-by recognized her and wanted her autograph. Her films had been shown regularly at London cinemas during the war, and her celebrity had undergone something of a minor resurgence. That was ten years ago now, and strangers rarely stopped her in the street with that strange combination of diffidence and admiration and asked if she really was *the* Caroline Dequincy.

She slipped into the back of a taxi cab and said to the driver, 'Liverpool Street Station, please.'

In her shopping bag she had Harrods' own specially milled white flour – which she used for all the baking – some smoked salmon pâté and three bottles of burgundy. She was having a little 'at home' on Monday, a gathering to which she hoped Edward would come, and she liked to serve something special from time to time. She had considered buying a small jar of caviar for her own consumption, but talked herself out of it. She had to be careful these days, especially considering . . .

No, she told herself, don't even think about it – not today, a beautiful sunlit July Saturday, with the pleasure of the 'at home' to look forward to, and maybe dinner with Edward later in the week. Don't spoil things.

But by then, of course, she could think of nothing else.

The big mistake of her past, to which she was shackled like a prisoner.

She had been so young, and immature, and desperate to get on . . . And she had been unable to foresee the consequences; indeed, she had hardly thought of the future, and still less that someone, more than thirty years down the line, might learn of her indiscretion and use it against her.

She stared out of the window at the passing streets and tried to think of other things.

London had changed a lot since her arrival ten years ago. Then it had been a city on its knees, the people colourless and impoverished – or seeming so after the glitter and affluence of Hollywood. London itself had been a bombsite, and it had seemed to Caroline, as she tried desperately to find accommodation in the bitter November of 1945, that every street bore testimony to the diligence of the Luftwaffe. Her recollection of life in Maida Vale was of food shortages, startling gaps in the skyline where buildings should have been, and a bent, grey populace scrabbling around for food and fuel. She had been relatively well off back then, and had felt guilty at being able to afford the little luxuries that made life bearable. She smiled to herself. It seemed that her life had always consisted, in one way or another, of feeling guilty.

And then Edward had bought the rambling Chase in rural Suffolk, had invited her up one weekend, and she had fallen in love with the village.

Not long after that, a delightful thatched cottage had come on to the market at a price well within Caroline's budget, and she had snapped it up. Over the years she had worked to make the garden the finest in the area, and worked too to win over Edward Endicott . . . though needless to say she had been more successful at the former than the latter.

She recalled Edward's reaction when she had told him she was buying Rosebud Cottage. With typical English reserve he had smiled and said, 'Why, that's capital, old girl. Save me the train fare of going up to London to meet you for those dashed expensive coffees you insist on.'

At Liverpool Street she paid the taxi driver and made her way to platform three. She had a couple of minutes before her train was due to leave. She stepped through the barrier and hurried towards the train.

A dozen or so individuals were pacing along the platform before her – and her heart sank as she made out a tall, familiar figure. She felt an insistent revulsion, and the sight of him was enough to make her feel terror and impotent rage.

She had hoped that she might never set eyes

on him again. The last time had been just a week ago when he had been a guest of Edward's at the Chase. They had spoken briefly, exchanged bland platitudes, and then Caroline had excused herself and escaped.

Now she slowed down so that Stafford would get well ahead of her. She waited until he climbed into a carriage twenty yards down the platform, and then boarded the train herself. As she moved along the corridor, looking for a vacant compartment, she considered the man and the fact that he was on the train: it could only mean that he was bound for Bury St Edmunds, and thence to Humble Barton, surely? She wondered how long he might stay, impressing Edward with his evil genius and giving away a little more of his life story to his eager biographer. It would mean, of course, that the Chase would be out of bounds to her for the next few days. Even if Stafford stayed at the Three Horseshoes, which he was wont to do when he came to the village, there was no telling when he'd be at the Chase . . . and she really didn't want to bump into him and be forced to indulge in polite chatter. The thought of being civil to the man who . . .

She shut out the thought and concentrated on finding a quiet seat where she could read her novel uninterrupted.

The carriage was full of travellers no doubt making the most of the good weather and heading into the country. She stepped through the sliding door to the next carriage and peered through the glass into each compartment. At last she found one that appeared empty and slid open the door.

She stopped on the threshold, her breath catching. 'Oh,' she gasped.

Stafford must have found the forward carriages full and moved back along the train until arriving at the vacant compartment. There he sat, as stiff and upright and black-clad as some desiccated undertaker. He looked up, blinked in surprised recognition, and seemed to undergo a subtle transformation – like an actor assuming a role. He gave his trademark rictus smile and said, 'Why, Miss Dequincy, what a pleasant surprise.'

She had no idea then, or thinking about the encounter later, what came over her. She felt a hot flush of anger, of welling rage – and all her fear of the man was swept suddenly aside and was replaced by anger and indignation. 'You!' she said.

His smile hardly faltered. He indicated the vacant seat opposite. 'Would you care to . . .?'

She stood on the threshold, clutching the door-frame for support. Her knees felt weak and she found her voice with difficulty.

'What are you doing?'

A shadow seemed to pass over his face. 'Why, merely visiting Edward, of course.'

'Why can't you just leave us . . . *me* . . . alone?'

Stafford blinked in bewilderment. He seemed, for a second, almost human. 'But my dear Caroline, I don't begin to understand . . .'

At his use of her first name she felt her gorge rise.

'And don't call me Caroline, you hypocrite!' She stopped, staring at him, then said suddenly, surprising herself, 'How do you know about . . .?'

17

'Know?' He stared at her, his black eyes flinty. 'Know about what?'

She shook her head. 'Why can't you just leave me alone?' She hated herself for the desperation, the pleading, in her tone.

'Could it be the little "event" at the hall?' he mused. 'I seem to have ruffled a few feathers then.'

Stafford rose to his considerable height, his cadaverous face peering at her. He reached out a thin, corpse-pale hand and said, 'I honestly don't know quite what you are getting at, Miss Dequincy. But perhaps, if you'd care to join me, we could discuss . . .?'

'Get off me!' she cried as his cold fingers touched her hand.

She fled, sobbing, and hurried down the corridor. She looked back, and felt a surge of relief when she saw that he wasn't following.

She barged into the next carriage, slowed her headlong flight and attempted to calm herself. She moved along the carriage until she found a compartment all to herself and took refuge as the train raced out of London. She pulled out her compact and powdered her face, drying her tears and sniffing.

She tried to read, but found it hard to concentrate; even Muriel Spark's lucid prose failed to hold her attention. What had she done? In a moment of thoughtless anger she had alerted Stafford to the fact that she was on to him.

She had to change trains for Bury St Edmunds at Ipswich. As she alighted she saw Stafford cross the platform to the waiting room. She had ten minutes to wait for the connecting train, and stood beside the WH Smith bookstall for the duration. When the engine panted into the station, she remained concealed beside the stall until Stafford moved from the waiting room towards the second carriage. Relieved, Caroline watched him climb aboard, then hurried to the final carriage. She found a seat in an empty compartment and opened her book. This time she did manage to lose herself in the story.

Almost three hours after leaving London, the train steamed into Bury St Edmunds and Caroline alighted warily.

If she hurried from the station and caught a taxi before him . . . Or she could hold back, wait until he'd boarded a taxi and departed for the village. She looked along the length of the platform and saw that she was one of the first passengers to alight. She hurried across the platform, through the exit and out into the forecourt. She was approaching the taxi rank and the first cab in line when she heard a voice behind her.

'Miss Dequincy . . . I rather think there has been some misunderstanding. If only we might—'

His cadaverous hand reached out for hers again, and his touch was like ice.

She whipped around and said, 'Leave me alone!'

His hand fell away, and his gaze became hostile. 'If only you would explain . . .'

His duplicity, his unwillingness to admit his crime, enraged her. She said, 'I know it's you, Stafford, and I'll tell you this. If you don't stop . . . don't stop your little game, by God I'll kill you!'

And so saying – and wondering where the threat had come from – she pulled open the taxi door and ducked inside. Seconds later she was speeding away from the station and the dark figure of Vivian Stafford towards the safety of Humble Barton and Rosebud Cottage.

She arrived home thirty minutes later and was relieved to find that Molly, her maid, had departed, leaving a shepherd's pie to be warmed up.

She ate a little, forking through the meal half-heartedly and going over and over her encounter with Stafford. She felt by turns elated at the strength she had shown in confronting him and then anger at herself for doing so. She believed in the man's propensity for evil, after everything Edward had told her about him. He had powers, special powers, and if he should choose to use them against her she would be unable to resist.

Perhaps, as she was a friend of Edward's, Stafford would restrain himself from punishing her little outburst.

After dinner, as the sun was going down, she poured herself a gin and tonic and drank it down in one, followed by another.

In the morning she would go for a long walk through the woods and then call in on Edward at the Chase. Yes, she would do that – get there before Stafford and take Edward for a stroll through the meadows. She couldn't open up and tell Edward her fears, of course – she couldn't admit to him the mistakes of her past – but it would be a comfort to hold on to his arm and bask in his reassuring company.

She smiled to herself and poured another drink.

THREE

The soldier appeared briefly on the ridge, silhouetted against the bloody Madagascan sunrise. He raised a hand, and Langham made out the distinct shape of a grenade poised to be lobbed into the ditch where Ralph Ryland lay, pinned down by gunfire. Instinctively Langham raised his submachine gun and fired. He heard a sharp cry and the Vichy French soldier fell back. Seconds later the grenade, unpinned and primed, exploded.

Langham came awake with a cry and sat up.

He was breathing hard, drenched in sweat. He knew from experience that the panic would subside in time and be replaced with a constant sense of gnawing guilt.

He had killed a man, and no amount of retroactive rationalization would alter the fact. It was all very well to say that he had saved a comrade's life – and very likely his own – by shooting the Frenchman dead, and while his rational mind acknowledged this, on some primal level what he had done still felt wrong. He had killed a fellow human being and he would live with this until his dying day.

He wished Maria were with him, sharing his bed, sharing every minute of his life. With her he forgot everything unpleasant and could lose himself in his love for the young woman. Once or twice during the past couple of weeks, since his discharge from hospital, he had almost brought himself to ask Maria if she would care to spend the night with him – but something, some innate reserve or lack of confidence, had stayed his tongue. He wondered now at his hesitation. It had been so long since he'd been intimate with another, and to escalate the terms of their relationship might, he thought, spoil everything. He knew that this was ridiculous, but even so he was reluctant to ask in case Maria should think that all he wanted from her was physical intimacy.

Cursing himself, he jumped out of bed, bathed and then dried himself before the two-bar electric fire in the bedroom. For all that it was high summer, it was still nippy in the early mornings. Maria had laughed and called him soft when she saw the fire, and now he smiled at the recollection. Even her gentle admonitions pleased him.

He ate a slice of toast and marmalade washed down with a mug of Earl Grey. This afternoon he was meeting Maria for a stroll across Hampstead Heath and tea at the café there, and tomorrow morning they would motor down to Suffolk.

After breakfast he tried to finish off a short story he'd begun in hospital. He wrote five hundred words on his Underwood typewriter and then halted, struck by a thought. Why wait until they were in Suffolk to ask Maria if she would marry him? That would make the next few days, as he tried to manufacture the perfect moment, an excruciating period of anticipation that would spoil his enjoyment of their holiday. Why not, he thought, relighting his pipe and puffing away, take the bull by the horns and ask her outright this afternoon? By Jove, he would do just that. No shilly-shallying; he'd wait until they were quite alone on the heath, tell her that he loved her madly and ask if she would consent to marry him.

He smiled at the idea and fell to tapping away at the keyboard.

At twelve he jumped into his Austin Healey and motored from Notting Hill through the Sunday-quiet streets to Kensington.

Outside Maria's apartment he tooted the horn a couple of times. A minute later she tapped down the steps, slid into the passenger seat and leaned over to kiss his cheek. Her perfume engulfed him.

'Donald! And how was your night? No dreams, I hope?'

He pulled into the road and accelerated north. ''Fraid so. Same one. Always the same one.'

Her hand found his arm and squeezed. 'I'm sorry, Donald. How do you feel now?'

'All the better for seeing you. It's strange . . .' he began.

She tipped her head. 'What is strange?'

'Over the past ten years I've had the dream about three times. Yet since the shooting, it's been every other night.'

'Well, there you are. The shooting is responsible, no? It brought all the memories flooding back.'

'Well, I damn well wish they'd return to where they came from.'

23

She was silent for a time, staring at him. He felt her eyes on him and turned to smile at her. 'What?'

'They say that sharing past events always helps, Donald.'

'I must have gone over what happened with you a dozen times. You must be sick of the whole story.'

'I never get sick of listening to you talk about the past. You know that.'

'Thank you. That means a lot.'

'But when I said you should share past events, I meant—'

He interrupted. 'I'm not seeing a quack, if that's what you're suggesting.'

She laughed prettily. 'Of course not, Donald. What I meant is that you should *write* about what happened, no? Incorporate the incident, and your feelings, into a story or novel. That way you can exorcise your feelings, your guilt.'

He rocked his head, considering the idea. 'I don't know. Does that kind of thing work?'

'Oh, you are so old fashioned and English. Have you never read Jung?'

'Daniel Young, the crime writer?'

She hit his shoulder with the heel of her hand. 'Be serious! Carl Gustav Jung,' she said. 'And of course writing about it will help. You shouldn't keep these things bottled up.'

'But I don't. I talk to you about them.'

'Yes, but if you were to write them down, you would perhaps delve deeper into your feelings, I think.'

'Well, I could incorporate the incident into the

24

next Sam Brooke novel, have a character who was in the war.'

'*Voilà!* Do that, Donald.'

They arrived at Hampstead Heath, left the car on Highgate Road and strolled along hand in hand. It was another sweltering summer's day, and Langham rolled up his shirtsleeves and took a deep breath.

'How is your chest, Donald?'

'Getting better every day. And you should see the scar. It's an absolute corker.'

'And your leg?'

The gunman, before shooting him in the chest, had grazed his calf with a bullet. Langham kicked out his right leg. 'Oh, it's fine. Not even a limp to show for it.'

'You're collecting battle scars.' She reached up and traced the scar on his forehead, courtesy of a bullet in 1942.

'Well, it's the quiet life for me from now on.'

The heath was busy with strolling couples and dog-walkers. They passed the pond, where boys and girls sailed model boats and ducks noisily demanded bread from passers-by.

'Do you know something, Donald – I think we should get a dog.'

He looked at her, his heart kicking. Such talk of shared possessions fostered in him thoughts of domesticity and intimacy. 'A dog?'

She smiled. 'I would like . . . I think a poodle, Donald.'

'A poodle? Horrid little things.'

She twisted her lips. 'Well, what kind of dog would you like?'

25

'Never really thought about it, Maria. They're lots of work. I don't know. How about a red setter? They're good-looking animals.'

'Yes, I like red setters, too. Maybe one day.'

He smiled and wondered if a little later, perhaps – after they'd had tea and were sitting on a quiet hill overlooking London – he should broach the subject of their future.

They headed through a copse towards the café. 'What did you make of Alasdair Endicott yesterday?' Langham asked.

'Alasdair? What made you mention him?'

'He just popped into my mind. I know – his father, Edward, has a red setter.'

She considered the question. 'I think he was reluctant to tell us much about his experiences, Donald. He turned the conversation towards his father, no?'

'What's his novel like?'

She shivered. 'The strange thing about it is that its subject is so fantastical – hauntings and possessions and so on – and yet he makes you believe in it because he writes with such naturalism, and his characters feel real. I *believed* in what he was writing about.'

'I'll have to read it.' He steered Maria through the picket gate of the café and found a vacant table.

They ordered egg and cress sandwiches and Darjeeling tea, and Maria said, 'Tell me about the story you're working on, Donald.'

So he told her the plot of the story, and for the next hour they chatted about his work and Maria's, and the novels she'd read recently, both for pleasure and for the agency. She told him about an old schoolfriend she'd bumped into recently, and the latest gossip from literary London. Langham listened, enthralled; he was sure that he could spend hours like this, listening to her mellifluous French accent and staring at her big caramel eyes and full lips.

They finished their lunch, left the café and strolled up the hill. Langham felt replete, contented. They came to the crest of the hill and gazed around them. All London lay at their feet, coruscating in the heat haze. He realized, suddenly, that they were quite alone.

'Stop,' he said.

She turned to face him. By God, she was beautiful. 'Come here.'

They embraced. The weight of her against him, her perfume, the scent of her skin . . . He wanted to laugh out loud like a maniac and tell her that he loved her wildly and would she marry him there and then, on the spot, with the sun as their witness . . .

'Maria.'

She stared at him with moist eyes. 'Oh, Donald, I'm so happy.'

He knew that now was the moment, that everything conspired to make these seconds propitious: he would ask her to marry him and she would melt into his arms and say yes, yes.

The sudden yapping of a dog shattered his thoughts. A furry black creature danced around the couple, pawing at Langham's trousers with intemperate canine urgency.

A plummy voice, almost as loud as the dog's

barks, called out, 'What a happy coincidence, my dears! Fancy happening upon my favourite couple on this wonderful afternoon!'

Maria manufactured a smile. 'Why, Dame Amelia. How lovely.'

Dame Amelia Hampstead bore down on them, her large face rather red with the exertion of climbing the hill. She wore a voluminous grey dress the shade of a storm cloud, and – Langham thought uncharitably – almost as vast. She called to her mutt to stop pestering the couple, and the hyperactive Belgian Schipperke – Poirot, by name – obeyed instantly and came to heel.

'You're looking well, Dame Amelia,' Langham said politely.

'Never better, young man.' She beamed from him to Maria and said conspiratorially, 'I don't mind sharing this with you, my children – *I'm in love.*'

Langham was startled by the pronouncement. 'You are?'

'Indeed. And I know what you're thinking – that a turkey so old should hardly be indulging in affairs of the heart.'

'Nothing of the sort!' he protested.

'And who is the lucky man?' Maria asked.

'My new editor at Collins. No spring chicken himself. Widower, ex-RAF. And such a gentleman. We hit it off from the word go.'

She gestured with her walking stick, and all three set off down the hill. 'In fact,' Dame Amelia went on, 'I'm late for our little assignation. I wonder if you would be so good as to assist me down to the café? I always find walking up hills no trouble at all, but walking downhill plays havoc with one's knees.'

'My pleasure,' Langham said, taking her arm and raising his eyebrows at Maria.

They proceeded down the incline at a snail's pace and Dame Amelia said, 'I do hope I didn't interrupt anything, Donald.'

He managed a winning smile and said, 'Not at all, Dame Amelia.'

They came to the café and said their farewells. 'I think I'm a little early, but not to worry. Here, Poirot! Come here and we'll wait for your favourite uncle.' She moved off, vast and sedate, like the storm cloud she so resembled.

The simile, Langham thought, as they took the path back to the road, was apposite. He kicked a stone.

Maria took his hand and tugged at him. 'Don't be so glum, Donald. I have an idea. Do you still have the wine I bought you for your birthday?'

'Mmm.'

'Well, perhaps we should go back to your flat, snuggle down on the settee, listen to the wireless and share the wine, no?'

He brightened. 'Capital idea,' he said, and led the way back to the car.

The wine was like velvet.

Maria curled up next to him on his ancient, spavined sofa. Dance band music played softly on the wireless, interspersed occasionally with the announcer's mellow tones. She laid a hand on top of his and they spoke almost in whispers.

29

'Charles seemed in good form yesterday,' he said.

'He's bearing up well.'

'Lost a bit of weight, too.'

She laughed. 'Oh, you should have heard him complain about the hospital's food. Anyone would think he had been lodged at the Ritz and was expecting a *cordon bleu* menu!'

'He hasn't said anything to you about the trial?'

She pursed her lips around a mouthful of wine, swallowed and shook her head. 'Not a word. He must be apprehensive, of course.'

'Well, we'll visit him regularly.'

Charles Elder was due to be tried, in one month, for the crime of homosexual indecency. His lawyer expected him to receive up to six months in gaol, which struck Langham as an outrage. He only hoped that his agent would bear the travail with his usual high spirits and optimism.

Langham finished his wine and Maria poured him another. He felt a little tipsy, and not a little elated. His usual tipple was beer, but since meeting Maria he'd developed a taste for French red wine – only fitting, he thought, in the circumstances.

He turned to her and stroked a stray strand of dark hair from her cheek. Her lips were slightly parted, her eyes shining. He kissed her, and she responded, working a hand around his neck and pulling him to her. He stroked her flank, feeling the corrugation of her ribs beneath her silk blouse.

Across the room, the telephone bell shrilled.

30

'Dammit!' He stared at the hunched, bakelite monstrosity with loathing. 'Who the hell can that be?'

'Tell them to go away, Donald, and never to ring again!'

'I'll jolly well do that,' he said and crossed to the phone.

'Yes,' he snapped, snatching up the receiver. 'Who is it?'

A hesitant voice enquired, 'Is that Donald Langham?'

'Speaking. Who is it?'

He looked back at Maria. She reposed on the settee like Venus, smiling at him. The caller said his name, but Langham failed to catch it. 'I'm sorry. Who is it?'

'This is Alasdair Endicott. We met yesterday, at Charles Elder's garden party. I'm awfully sorry to bother you like this, but . . .'

The young man's tone was so apologetic that Langham immediately regretted his peremptory tone. He sat down on the arm of a chair and lodged the phone on his lap. 'That's all right. How can I help you?'

He looked across at Maria. Her broad brow was furrowed in a who-is-it expression.

'Well . . . I have read a number of your books, Mr Langham,' Alasdair began. He fell silent, and Langham prompted, 'Yes?'

'And I read, in the biographical information at the back of one of them, that you ran a detective agency.'

Langham sighed. That line had been the poetic licence of someone at Worley and Greenwood who had gilded the lily in the hope of increased publicity.

'Well, I didn't exactly run the agency, Alasdair,' he said – and caught Maria's quizzical expression. 'I worked at a friend's agency part time for a couple of years. But I don't see . . .'

'The thing is, Mr Langham, I don't quite know what to do.'

'About what?'

'Well, I arrived here this afternoon – at my father's place in Humble Barton. I come up every month or so for dinner, and have done for a number of years. Only this time . . .' Silence again, which stretched, until Langham said, 'Yes?'

'Well, when I arrived, my father wasn't here. He's always in his study – always, without fail, working on a book.'

'What time was this, Alasdair?'

'A little before one o'clock.'

'Perhaps he had to pop out unexpectedly—'

'No. He wouldn't do that. At least, not without leaving a note. And also . . .'

'Yes?'

'It's very strange, and I know you'll find it hard to believe what I'm about to tell you.'

Langham sighed, exasperated. 'Try me.'

'He is always in his study, *always*, without fail. And he was this time, before he vanished.'

Langham rubbed his eyes, uncomprehending. He wondered if it had been Alasdair Endicott who'd been hitting the wine. 'What on earth are you talking about?' he asked.

Maria was sitting upright now, leaning forward

32

with her knees pressed together and frowning as she followed the one-sided conversation.

Alasdair said, 'You see, the study door was locked from the inside, and there was no other way he could have left the room. I had to break down the door. But . . . but you see, he wasn't in there.'

'Well, perhaps he was never in the room, Alasdair?'

'But he was! Otherwise, how was it that the door was locked *from the inside*!'

Langham considered what the young man had told him. 'Have you informed the police?'

'Of course. The local constable lives just down the lane. I reported my father's disappearance to him and explained the situation.'

'And?'

'And he said that there was little he could do until my father had been missing for a number of days.' A silence, followed by a nervous, 'So that's why I rang you, Mr Langham. I found your number in my father's address book.'

'I see.'

'I was wondering . . . That is, I was hoping that I'd be able to hire your services. I mean . . . if you're free at the moment.'

Langham sighed and slipped from the arm of the chair and on to the cushion. 'Well, I was just about to go on holiday.'

'Oh, I say. I'm awfully sorry.'

Langham thought about it. 'Just a tick. Where did you say your father lived?'

'A small village called Humble Barton, Suffolk. It's ten miles north of Bury St Edmunds.'

33

'Hold on a minute, would you?'

He cupped a hand over the mouthpiece and said to Maria, 'Could you be a sweetheart and fetch the map-book from the study? It's on top of the pile of manuscripts next to the desk.'

She hurried from the room and returned seconds later with the gazetteer. She mouthed: *What is it?*

Still cupping the mouthpiece, he said, 'Alasdair's father's gone AWOL. He's in a bit of a flap.'

He opened the map-book to Suffolk and found the relevant page. He located the market town of Bury St Edmunds, ran a finger due north and found the village of Humble Barton.

Five miles south of the village was Brampton Friars, where he'd booked the hotel.

He said into the phone, 'Alasdair?'

'Hello?'

'You're in luck. We're actually staying not too far away from you for a couple of days. Look, I could drop in to see you later tonight. I can't promise anything. If your father fails to show up, then it'll be a police matter. But I do know someone who might be able to help if Edward doesn't turn up soonish.'

'You don't know how grateful I am, Mr Langham.'

'If I can take your address . . .'

He found a notepad and pencil and scribbled down the address and phone number, then reassured the young man that in all probability Edward would turn up, hale and hearty, sooner rather than later.

Alasdair thanked him again and rang off.

34

'What was all that about?' Maria asked when he returned to the settee.

He shook his head. 'Probably something or nothing.' He recounted the details, then added, 'The odd thing was he was convinced that Edward had vanished from *inside* his locked study.' He reported what Alasdair had said, word for word, and smiled at Maria's increasingly incredulous expression.

'Perhaps,' she said at last, 'the young man has gone around the bend, as you say.'

'Perhaps he has at that,' Langham said. 'Hell, I feel quite sober now.'

'And me too.' She looked at the tiny watch on her wrist and said, 'I have to pop around and see my father before we set off. I will ring for a taxi.'

'Don't bother, I'll drive you home.'

'Donald.' She hoisted the empty wine bottle. 'You might *feel* sober, but I'd rather take a taxi.'

He rang for a cab and, five minutes later, cursing his luck for the second time that day, escorted her outside. They kissed in the late afternoon sun.

'I'll pick you up at seven,' he said as she slipped into the back of the taxi. She kissed her fingers and waved as the taxi pulled from the kerb.

Langham retraced his steps up to his flat and sat down on the sofa, inhaling Maria's perfume and looking forward to the break in leafy Suffolk. He said her name aloud, and smiled at what a love-sick fool he was.

Then he fetched a bottle of Fuller's bitter from the larder, returned to the settee, and wondered what might have happened to Edward Endicott.

FOUR

Maria drove her Sunbeam saloon from Kensington to her father's house overlooking Hampstead Heath.

He had phoned her on Saturday morning asking if she would care to visit him soon, his tone barely disguising his disappointment that she had not called in for well over a week. 'But then I expect you're very busy at the agency these days,' he had said, 'and with seeing that young man of yours.'

She had bit her lip guiltily, admitted that she was seeing Donald on both Saturday and Sunday, but could call round briefly on Sunday.

'That would be delightful, *ma chérie*,' he'd said, with not a little irony.

Now she pulled up before the three-storey townhouse and jumped from the car. It was a perfect summer's day and Maria had never been happier. She contrasted her fortunes now with what she had had six months ago. Then she had been bored with her job – before Charles offered her the partnership in the agency – and lonely. Now, as if by magic, all that had changed. She practically ran the agency while Charles took time off to recuperate from his wounds, and she was in love with a wonderful man.

She rang the bell and her father's maid, Sabine,

36

answered the door and showed Maria up to the drawing room.

'Maria!' her father exclaimed, rising to his feet and embracing her. 'You are looking more beautiful every time I see you . . . which is not that frequent these days.'

They kissed cheeks. 'I'm sorry, Father. You know how busy I am.'

'Of course. How is the agency? Tea?'

'Darjeeling, please.'

Her father relayed instructions to Sabine and sat back on the window seat. The French cultural attaché to London was in his early sixties, slim, debonair and silver-haired. He had never remarried after the death of Maria's mother almost twenty-five years ago, but she knew that he had a string of admirers in Paris and London.

'I'm so busy you wouldn't believe it!' she said.

'And do you think you'll cope when Charles is . . .?'

'Of course, and anyway, Charles said that he'll employ some part-time help for the duration.'

Her father sipped his tea and said, 'I suppose it's a foregone conclusion that Charles will face a lengthy sentence?'

That, she thought, was the only cloud that dulled her sunny days: the fact that Charles would be jailed, and how he might cope with incarceration. He was a man who loved the luxurious things in life, and the privations of Her Majesty's prisons would hit him hard.

'According to his solicitor he faces a term of at least six months, maybe even a year.'

He shook his head. 'The English, so cultivated

in many ways, can be so barbarous in others.'

She smiled brightly. 'But let's not talk of all that,' she said.

'Of course not,' he said. 'And Donald?'

'He's well, plotting his next novel.'

'And when will I meet him? Soon, I hope?'

She tipped her head and said, 'I'm sorry about last time. Donald so wanted to come over but I just couldn't get away from the office.'

'Well, how about I make another date – for next weekend, perhaps, when you have got back from Suffolk, yes? Dinner, here, just the three of us.'

'That would be wonderful.'

He sipped his tea, looking at her speculatively. 'If you don't mind my asking, Maria, how serious is he . . .?'

'Serious? About . . .?'

He smiled. 'About you, of course.'

'Father . . . I've told you. I'm so happy with Donald—'

'Which is not, *ma chérie*, what I asked. How serious is *he* about *you*? He has not yet . . . proposed?'

She smiled and sipped her tea. She was sure that Donald, in his own leisurely, reserved, round-about fashion, was working up the nerve to ask her to marry him. In fact, there had been one or two occasions lately when she had thought that he had been on the verge of doing so – only to be thwarted by the collywobbles or some silly interruption. She just hoped he'd get a move on and ask her.

She said, 'Not yet.'

'And if he did?'

'Then I would accept.'

'It is the done thing, as they say over here, for the *prospective* groom to ask permission of the *prospective* father-in-law beforehand, is it not?'

She felt herself redden. 'Father . . . I'm not sure Donald is the kind of man to stand on ceremony like that. I mean, Donald doesn't like "fuss and palaver", as he calls it. And anyway, isn't that all rather old fashioned these days?'

Her father frowned. 'Well, it would be good manners.'

'Very well, I will mention it to him.'

Her father nodded and sipped his tea. 'Oh, by the way, I have read one of his novels.'

'And?'

'And, to be honest, it was not quite what I was expecting.'

She felt disappointed. 'In what way?'

'Well . . . it was not as stylish as I was expecting.'

'Expecting, or hoped? Father, Donald writes thrillers set in the underworld. The content dictates the form.'

'And they are rather violent.'

She smiled to herself. 'They are nothing like the man himself, if that's what is bothering you. Donald is the most gentle, quiet, un-violent man you could wish to meet.' She felt herself glowing even as she thought about his English reserve, his calm, strong, reassuring presence. 'As you will find out when you meet him.'

He smiled. 'I will look forward to that.'

'Anyway, enough of me,' she said. 'What have

39

you been doing of late? How was the reception for Mauriac?'

The Nobel prize-winning writer had flown into London last week for a series of talks in London, Cambridge and Oxford, and her father had thrown a dinner party for him at the French embassy.

'He was charming, as ever, witty and erudite. I invited Philippe to attend.'

Her breath caught. 'Philippe?'

'Why, Philippe Delacroix, or have you forgotten?'

'No, no, of course not.'

She busied herself by refilling her cup and asking her father if he wanted more. As she poured, she wondered why he had dropped Delacroix's name into the conversation.

'He asked after you,' he said, watching her closely.

'He did? And what did you say?'

'I said that you were doing well in your work, and still single . . .'

She felt a sudden flare of anger at her father's presumption. 'And how is he?' she said with what she hoped sounded like off-handedness.

'He is extremely successful these days, as you no doubt know. His paintings are becoming increasingly sought-after. He still . . . he still thinks the world of you, Maria.'

She gritted her teeth, then said, 'Well, isn't he the little hypocrite? If he felt anything for me he wouldn't have walked out when he did!'

'But my dear, five years ago he was under considerable pressure. His father was still alive, and you know how old Delacroix and I never saw eye to eye. We were opposed politically and . . .'

'And he forbade his son to marry me,' she said. She felt her hand shaking, and placed her cup in its saucer. 'And now that his father is dead?'

He smiled, shrugged. 'He asked after you, asked if perhaps I might arrange a meeting.'

She leaned forward and stared at her father. 'No! I will not accept this! You have no idea . . . no idea at all! If he had been even *half* a man, any kind of man at all, then Philippe would have told his father that he loved me, regardless of your enmity with him. But, oh, no, Philippe, the coward – Philippe who I *thought* I loved at the time – tells me that . . . that what we had was impossible and we had to part . . . And now he waltzes back on to the scene and demands you arrange a meeting!' She stopped, almost choking with rage. 'I say no, no, this is unacceptable!'

Her father dabbed his lips with a napkin and said, 'I understand your sentiments, my dear, but all I can say is that Philippe's intentions are honourable, and if it is any consolation at all, he told me to convey to you that he was as distraught as you were about what happened.'

She snorted. '"What happened"? He makes it sound as if it were an act of God! We were engaged to be married, after all, and he walked out on me because his father said that he would disinherit him if he married the daughter of "that Socialist Dupré"! And Philippe, like the coward he was, simply buckled under the pressure and agreed. If he'd loved me, if he'd *really* loved me,

41

then he would have told his fascist father to go to hell!'

'Maria . . .'

'And now that his father is dead, he comes crawling back thinking that everything will be as it was, that I will forget his betrayal and melt into his arms. Well, no, no! You can tell him from me that he can rot in hell!'

She stood and moved to the window, staring out over the heath without seeing a thing.

Her father said, quietly, 'I think your protestations are less due to righteous rage than to the realization that—'

She whirled around. 'Yes?'

'That you still harbour . . . feelings, let's say . . . for Philippe.'

She smiled icily, crossed to where her father was standing, and kissed him on the cheeks. 'I really must be going now, Father. Donald is driving me to Suffolk where we will have a wonderful break. *Á bientôt.*'

She hurried from the house, slipped in behind the wheel of her car and drove at speed back to Kensington.

FIVE

Langham collected Maria from her Kensington flat at seven o'clock and motored north. The sun dazzled in a cloudless sky and the forecast on the wireless predicted a few days of continued good weather with temperatures in the seventies. Langham had never felt better. His chest wound was no longer giving him gyp, he was in love with a beautiful girl, and he'd thought of a good twist for the short story he was working on.

He smiled across at Maria. She had been a little quiet as they drove through the London suburbs and he wondered why. 'How's your father keeping?' he asked.

'Oh, as ever. He is well, and very busy.'

'Still attempting to educate the English in the ways of the French?'

She smiled. 'Something like that. But let's not talk of him, Donald,' she said gaily.

She changed the subject and told him about the agency and her plans to expand the business by exploring the European rights market for her authors. She even claimed that she was excited about solving, as she called it, the Mystery of the Missing Writer.

'I don't think it'll be that much of a mystery,' Langham said. 'No doubt he'll have turned up by the time we arrive.'

'But how did he simply *vanish* from a locked room, Donald?'

'I think there'll be some perfectly obvious explanation, mark my words.'

As they drove towards the countryside Maria seemed herself again, smiling and laughing as she told him a funny story about one of her writers.

At one point she said, 'Oh, my father has invited us for dinner. This Saturday. He really wants to meet you, Donald.'

'Well, this time we'll make it, hmm? No importuning authors keeping you busy at the office. Ah, here we are. Brampton Friars, three miles. Nearly there.'

The Old Rectory Hotel proved to be a large sixteenth-century building with a thatched roof set in a riotous garden in the centre of the busy village. 'Oh, isn't it delightful?' Maria exclaimed as Langham braked in the gravelled drive.

The bells of the neighbouring church peeled as they carried their cases into the warped, darkened timber entrance hall. They were shown to a pair of cosy rooms at the back of the hotel overlooking a long, lawned garden, and the maid asked them if they would care for some dinner, which was being served in the dining room.

They ate at a table next to a window which was thrown open to admit the heady scent of wisteria and the cool evening air.

Maria reached across the table and clutched his hand in excitement. 'This is wonderful, Donald! It's a pity we are here for two days only.'

'It is rather divine, isn't it? Look here, perhaps

we'll be able to extend our stay for a few days? Charles will be able to hold the fort till Friday, won't he?'

'That would be wonderful, yes!'

At ten o'clock Langham glanced at his watch and sighed. 'Well, I suppose we really should be pushing off to see old Alasdair. He'll get himself into a right old tizzy if we don't show up.'

'And perhaps you will be proved right, and his father will have turned up already.'

'I'd better ring him before we set off.' He gestured across the village green to a half-timbered public house, the Five Jolly Butchers. 'And we could dine there one evening. Postgate gave it a decent write-up in a recent *Good Food* guide.'

They found a phonebox beside the lychgate of the church and Langham got through to Alasdair Endicott.

'Oh, thanks awfully for calling, Mr Langham.'

'I take it there's no sign of your father?'

''Fraid not . . .'

'In that case we'll be right over.'

Alasdair gave directions to the house and rang off.

Humble Barton proved to be a smaller version of Brampton Friars, a quaint collection of cottages convened around a village green (which still boasted a set of medieval stocks, Maria pointed out), with a honey-coloured Norman church, a public house called the Three Horseshoes, and a post office-cum-general store.

The driveway to Endicott's Chase burrowed

through an overgrown tunnel of rhododendron and holly, and the house itself proved to be a rambling, late-Elizabethan pile. As Langham eased his Austin towards the ivy-clad building, Maria leaned forward and commented, 'It looks just the place where a reclusive writer would shut out the world and concentrate on his masterpiece.'

'It does quite, doesn't it?' Langham said as he pulled up beside a battered silver Wolseley.

Alasdair Endicott greeted them on the threshold. Garbed in his old-fashioned tweeds he appeared, against the background of the dim hallway, less of a fish out of water than he had seemed at the garden party. 'I'm delighted you could make it, Mr Langham, Miss Dupré,' he said as he led them inside.

Maria peered around at the oak-panelled hallway and the oil paintings of the Suffolk landscape. 'What a wonderful place!'

'Isn't it? My father moved here just after the war,' Alasdair said. 'This way; I'll show you to the study.'

He led the way along a twisted, oak-timbered passage to a room at the rear of the house. The door stood open, the timber frame splintered. Langham looked at Alasdair, and the latter explained rather sheepishly, 'It didn't take that much forcing, actually. The door itself is as solid as rock, but the lock – or rather the timber jamb – wasn't.'

'And you're quite sure that the door was locked from the inside?' Langham asked.

'Oh, quite, yes. Look.' Alasdair indicated the

big, square locking mechanism on the inside of the door. The head of a big iron key protruded.

Langham stepped into the study and looked around. The room was long, low and packed with bookcases overflowing with books and loose manuscripts. Moonlight cascaded through the French windows at the far end of the study, illuminating a desk scattered with papers.

Langham said, 'You said you arrived today at one? But what made you suspect that your father was missing and break down the door?'

Alasdair shrugged his slight shoulders, looking uncomfortable. 'Well, you see . . . I'd phoned my father on Friday, but there was no reply. I was a little concerned, as he's normally at home at five when I ring. I feared he might have . . . I don't know, collapsed.'

'So he might have been missing for a couple of days when you arrived today?' Maria asked.

Alasdair bobbed his head. 'Which is why I took the rather intemperate-seeming measure of . . .' He indicated the door.

'And other than the main door and the French windows, there are no other entrances to the room?' Langham asked.

'None, and the French windows were securely fastened, again from the inside.'

Langham moved to the French windows and took a handkerchief from his breast pocket. Covering his hand with it, he tried the handle. The door was not locked, but a catch above the handle was fastened.

He turned to Alasdair, who was still hovering nervously beside the door. 'Very well,' Langham said. 'What do you think happened to your father?'

Maria turned from a large eighteenth-century globe she had been examining and stared at the young man. He blushed, bobbed his head, and said, 'It seems obvious to me that he was in his study when he vanished. The door was locked from the inside, and the French windows were fastened. How might he have locked and fastened them if he *hadn't been* in the room?'

Langham cleared his throat. 'That doesn't really answer my question, Alasdair. How do you think he disappeared?'

The young man coloured instantly, and Langham found himself wishing he'd phrased the question a little more diplomatically.

'Mr Langham,' Alasdair said, sounding almost pained, 'my father is investigating the life of a man whose powers of the occult are legendary. Stafford is . . . some have said that he is evil. I think, perhaps, that he might be responsible for my father's disappearance. You see, I suspect Stafford might have been angered in some way by my father's investigations.'

Langham strode to the chimney breast, his face averted from the young man in order to conceal his scepticism. He knelt and peered up the chimney: it was a working fire as embers still reposed in the hearth, but the soot-pelted flue was not wide enough to admit the bulk of a grown man.

He straightened up. 'Just a tick. Yesterday Charles said this Stafford cove was alive back in Victorian times, a cohort of Crowley and company.'

48

Alasdair swallowed nervously. 'That's right, he was. You see, he was born in 1835.'

Langham laughed. 'Hold on . . . that'd make him around a hundred and twenty.' He stared at Alasdair. 'Are you seriously trying to tell me that the man your father met and the Victorian satanist are one and the same?'

'Well, my father thinks so. You see, he discovered a photograph up at Stafford Hall – the old house where Stafford lived back in the last century.'

Alasdair crossed to the big oak desk beside the French windows, opened the top drawer to the right of the knee-hole and took out a photograph, which he passed to Langham.

The photograph showed the head and shoulders of a severe-looking, bald-headed man with the thin, pinched face of a misanthropic vulture. He wore a high Victorian collar and carried a brass-topped cane, and the photograph itself was sepia-tinted and clearly very old.

'Vivian Stafford,' Alasdair said. He reached into the desk and produced a second photograph. 'This one is more recent, and taken by my father on the green outside the Three Horseshoes a few weeks ago.'

Langham examined the recent snapshot of three people seated around a table in the open air. The figure in the foreground was the subject of the older picture – Stafford, if Alasdair was to be believed. He was the spitting image, right down to the hooked nose and the hunched, vulture-like posture. He even carried an identical brass-topped cane. There were two other people in the picture, a man and a woman. On the table between them was a wine bottle and several empty glasses.

'It looks like the same man, Donald,' Maria said.

Langham considered the first photograph, and then the second again, frowning.

'What do you think, Mr Langham?' Alasdair enquired.

'I need to think about this,' Langham said. 'Look, I wonder if you could make a pot of tea?'

'How remiss of me. I do apologise. My father would call me a poor host. How do you take it?'

'Don't suppose you have any Earl Grey?'

'My father's favourite.'

'In that case black, no sugar.'

'And the same for me, Alasdair,' Maria said.

When the young man hurried off, Maria turned to Langham and began, 'Why—?'

'Just to get him out of the room so we can talk,' Langham said.

Maria tipped her head, lips pursed, and said, 'You think he is bats-in-the-belfry, no?'

'Well, that's one way of putting it,' he said. 'Look here.' He tapped the photographs. 'This really doesn't prove a thing, you know?'

'But they appear to be of the very same person, Donald.'

'I dare say. But my argument is that this photo' – he indicated the supposed Victorian print – 'could have been mocked up and made to look old. It's not proof, just because it looks old.'

She rocked her head. 'Agreed,' she said, but sounded dubious.

Alasdair returned with a silver tray bearing

three china cups and a teapot. He poured the tea and asked hesitantly, 'Interesting, don't you think?'

'I think the resemblance is remarkable, Alasdair. But that doesn't mean to say that, even *if* the photographs are genuinely separated by over fifty years, they're of the same man.'

'But I've seen Vivian Stafford, Mr Langham! I've *met* him. Stafford came back to the village a few weeks ago to visit his old family seat – Stafford Hall, owned by the artist Haverford Dent. Dent's a chum of my father's and it's through Dent that my father met Stafford. And I met him at a do at the Three Horseshoes just last week.'

You've met someone *claiming* to be the Victorian satanist Vivian Stafford, Langham thought. 'You mentioned that Stafford might have been angered in some way by your father's writing about him?'

'That is only my supposition, Mr Langham. You see, I suspect that Stafford might not want the world at large to know that he is still alive, or the extent of his . . . practices.'

Maria raised an eyebrow. 'Which are?'

Alasdair sighed. 'My father told me about Stafford shortly after he first met the man. He'd read up on Stafford and described the Satanic rites he practised back in Victorian times.'

'And you think Stafford might have taken against your father for what he was writing, and this, you believe, might have led to Edward's disappearance?' He was unable to keep the scepticism from his voice.

51

Alasdair nodded. 'That's right. You see, the ledger that my father was writing in, and the loose notes he kept relating to Stafford, are missing.'

'You've searched the room?'

'My father kept his ledger on the desk. It was his habit, almost a ritual. He never moved it and would fly into a rage if the cleaner so much as touched it, and the same with his notes.'

'So you think Stafford had your father, *and* his manuscript and notes . . . removed?'

The young man bobbed his head diffidently. 'I do, Mr Langham.'

Langham blew out a hefty, sceptical sigh and moved around the room, examining watercolours, old books, and a collection of wooden peg dolls lined up in a mahogany case. He moved to the French windows and stared out across the lawn.

There was a rational explanation for all this, of course. People did not simply vanish without a trace from locked rooms. He transferred his attention to the French windows and stared at the frame for some time before his attention was caught by the catch. It was a simple lever attached to the frame, which in the perpendicular position allowed the French windows to open, and when turned to the horizontal position fastened it.

'Hold on a minute.'

Maria was at his side. 'What is it?'

He pointed. 'The catch. Now, if I'm right . . .'

He took out his handkerchief again and turned the handle. As he had hoped, it moved easily and he pushed open the door.

'Now,' he said, looking from Maria to Alasdair, 'watch.'

He ensured that the handle of the catch was standing vertically, then took hold of the door and pulled it towards him, snatching his hand smartly away so as not to have it trapped.

The door banged shut and, as he'd suspected, the handle fell from the vertical with the impact and lay horizontally, securely fastening the door as it did so.

'You see, the fitting is sloppy. I'll do it again to prove . . .'

He opened the door and pulled it shut. Again the handle dropped and fastened the door.

'So there you have it. Nothing supernatural at all. That's how it *appeared* that Edward had vanished from a room locked from the inside. He left the room through the French windows and either slammed the door shut or it blew shut in the wind.'

'But the missing ledger and his notes?' Alasdair asked.

Langham shrugged. 'That, of course, is another matter entirely.'

He strode to the far end of the study, deep in thought. He realized that he'd pulled his empty pipe from his jacket pocket and was gripping it between his teeth, something he did when working on the plot of a novel.

'As far as I can see, there are three possible explanations,' he said, taking the pipe from his mouth and pointing it at Alasdair. 'The first is that he wanted – for reasons known only to himself – to create a mystery. So he took his ledger and notes, locked the study door from the inside, then stepped outside and closed the French windows. *Voilà!*, as you would say, Maria.'

'And the second explanation?' she asked.

'It was simply an accident. Edward decided to set off for a day or so and took his work with him. He locked the study door and stepped through the French windows, which blew shut in the wind. Unlikely, I admit – but far more likely than any occult explanation.'

'And the third possibility?' Alasdair asked.

Langham replaced his pipe and said around the stem, 'Third – and in my opinion the least likely scenario of them all – someone did want him out of the way. But not this hundred-and-twenty-year-old Stafford, I hasten to add. They lured him from the house on some pretext, then returned to take his ledger and notes, locked the door and left through the French windows, slamming them shut behind them.'

'But why would they do that?' Maria protested.

Langham shrugged. 'Why else? To create the air of occult mystery that some people have more than willingly subscribed to.' He stared at Alasdair as he said this, and the young man coloured to the roots of his wispy hair.

Maria asked, 'Do you know of anyone who might have wished misfortune upon your father?'

Alasdair shrugged his sloping shoulders. 'My father doesn't have an enemy in the world,' he murmured.

'And Edward was not in the habit of going away unannounced, taking his work with him?' she asked.

'Sometimes he did take himself off on hikes, but he would always tell me when he would be away.'

Langham said, 'We'll give it a day or two, and if he still hasn't turned up I'll contact the friend of mine who runs the detective agency. He's thorough, and his rates are reasonable.'

Alasdair smiled wanly. 'I'd appreciate that, Mr Langham.'

'And let's leave off the formality, agreed? I'm Donald from now on.'

Maria said, 'And I'm Maria.'

Langham was about to suggest they make tracks – cheered by the thought of a quiet drink in the snuggery – when the insistent barking of a dog sounded from beyond the French windows.

'Hello, I think you have company.'

A magnificent red setter bounded into view, straining against a taut leash and dragging in its wake a woman who, at first glance, bore an uncanny human resemblance to her canine counterpart. She was tall, graceful, red-headed – and, despite being dragged along by the hound, managed to maintain a certain graceful elegance even in duress.

'Rasputin!' Alasdair exclaimed.

Langham looked at Maria. 'The woman? What an odd name . . .' he said, and Maria playfully cuffed his ear.

Alasdair opened the French windows and stepped out. Langham and Maria followed, and the dog bounded up to the young man and reared on its hind legs, favouring him with a slavering tongue.

The woman handed Alasdair the lead and arranged her hair. She wore a smart, two-piece navy trouser suit and lodged a hand on her hip as she smiled indulgently at Alasdair and the hound.

'I was walking along the river just now and I came across Rasputin sniffing around by the folly,' she said in a pronounced American accent. 'I wondered what Edward was doing letting him out.'

She turned a dazzling smile on Langham and Maria and swept a tress of hair from her broad brow. She was a shade under six feet tall and emanated an aura of faded glamour. Langham thought that she looked familiar – then realized that he recognized her from the photograph of Stafford and the other people sitting around the table on the village green.

'But I wouldn't have intruded if I'd known you had guests.' She advanced with an outstretched hand. 'I'm Caroline. Caroline Dequincy, and you have my apologies for gatecrashing you people like this.'

As Langham took her hand, he was aware of two things: the strength of her grip and the miasma of gin on her breath. 'Not at all,' he responded, introducing himself and Maria.

Maria was wide-eyed. 'Caroline Dequincy? *The* Caroline Dequincy?'

The woman smiled modestly. 'I'm afraid so . . .'

'But I have seen many of your films! Before the war I watched *Silent Sunset* and *California Sweet*. They were wonderful.'

'That's awfully sweet of you to say so. But my,

56

doesn't that just show my age? They were made way back in the early thirties! I'm getting old.'

She looked past the trio and into the study. 'I don't suppose Edward is around, is he?'

Langham said, 'Actually, he had to pop out briefly.'

She waved. 'Oh, it doesn't matter. Only I'm throwing an "at home" tomorrow afternoon. All in aid of St John Ambulance, but really' – she went on in a stage whisper –'just an excuse for an afternoon drink. I was going to invite Edward along. But say, why don't you all come, too? The more the merrier.'

Langham said, 'We'd be delighted, wouldn't we, Maria?'

Maria hugged herself. 'Wait until I tell my father that I've met you, Caroline. He is also a big fan of yours.'

The actress waved away the compliment with a modest gesture. 'Go on with you. That's a lot of water under the bridge. Anyway, I'm glad Rasputin's back where he belongs. And I'll see you folks tomorrow afternoon, OK? 'Bye, Rasputin, you naughty hound!'

Langham moved back into the study and crossed to the desk. He picked up the photograph showing the people around the table and passed it to Maria, indicating the red-haired woman.

Alasdair came in, followed by the dog.

'I thought it was Dequincy,' Langham said. 'Was she friendly with Stafford, do you know?' he asked Alasdair.

'Well, I think they met a few times. Caroline and my father are quite close.'

Maria pointed out the bloodhound seated at Dequincy's feet. 'Is the dog hers?' she asked Alasdair.

'That's Boardman, Caroline's faithful companion. He and Rasputin are as thick as thieves.'

'I'd like to ask Dequincy about this Stafford character,' Langham said. 'Do you recognize the other person in the snap?'

Alasdair peered at the photograph. 'He's our vicar, Marcus Denbigh. More than likely he'll be at Caroline's tomorrow.'

'Do you mind if I hang on to the photos for a while?'

'Not at all.'

'Well, perhaps tomorrow we will have the chance to ask Caroline, and the vicar, all about the mysterious man in the picture,' Maria said.

Five minutes later they took their leave and motored back to Brampton Friars.

SIX

The following morning at breakfast, Maria said, 'Why is it, Donald, that you English like these muffins so much? They are actually quite revolting. Heavy and soggy. Ugh!'

'Try the toast,' he said, buttering another round. 'It's excellent, especially with Marmite.'

'Ah, Marmite!' She wrinkled her nose. 'Another strange English delicacy.' She picked up the jar and examined it as if it were a grenade. 'I wonder why it has a French name?'

He looked at her. '"Marmite" is French?'

'Of course. It means a small cauldron or cooking pot, the same shape as the jar.'

'Well, you learn something every day.'

'When I was a girl,' she said dreamily, 'we had a cook who made the most wonderful croissants for breakfast. I remember sitting on the balcony of our apartment in Paris, in the sunlight, eating croissants with apricot *confiture*.'

She buttered a slice of toast and applied a thick coating of raspberry jam. 'Mmm . . . You're right, Donald. The toast is very good – but I still find it odd, even after all the years I've lived in England, to cook bread until it is almost burned.'

'You don't have toast in France?'

'*Non*. Why would we, when we have croissants?'

He watched her across the table as she nibbled at the slice of toast and sipped her tea. 'I'll enquire at reception, shall I, and see if I can book the rooms for another few days? How long would you like to stay?'

She gave him a gleeful grin. 'Would it be terrible if we stayed until Friday?'

'Of course not. I'll ask.' And after breakfast, he thought, they could stroll around the village. Yesterday he'd noticed a grassy earthworks beyond the church; there would be a magnificent view of the surrounding countryside from the summit. It would be a fitting place to pop the question; they could visit the village in years to come, and laugh at how circumstances had intervened again and again to postpone the inevitable.

'I have never been to a . . . what did Dequincy call it, Donald? An "at home"? What exactly is an "at home"?'

He waved the remains of his toast. 'Oh, it's just a posh name for morning or afternoon tea. The host will be "at home" to receive visitors over a period of a few hours. You bring things to be sold to fellow guests, or give a donation – cakes and baking and so forth. It's usually in aid of a good cause.'

'Another quaint English custom?'

He laughed. 'Like morris dancing, Marmite and toast.'

She tipped her head to one side and regarded him. 'Don't you think it strange, Donald, that a famous Hollywood movie star should be living in a sleepy English village?'

60

'On the contrary. From what I've read about Hollywood, it's a wonder that more folk don't escape its craziness and seek refuge in the relative sanity of rural England.'

'Have you seen any of her films?'

'Not to my knowledge. Were they good?'

'I loved them when I was young. She was a glamorous star and played the . . . how do you say? The "love interest", mainly. But I recall one film in which she had the leading role as a British spy in the First World War.'

'She's retired now?'

Maria shrugged. 'I don't really know. I would like to find out more about her. I'm looking forward to meeting her again. I've been thinking . . . Her films were made in the late twenties and early thirties – and she must have been in her thirties then. Which would mean she's in her mid-fifties now.'

'You're joking. I had her down as no older than forty-five.'

After breakfast they returned upstairs briefly to wash, then Langham descended to reception and enquired about the possibility of extending their stay.

When Maria joined him five minutes later, he had to report the bad news that their rooms were booked for the rest of the week after tonight, and that all the other rooms were taken too.

'Bother!' she exclaimed as they strode out into the sunlight. 'Well, Donald, we shall have to look elsewhere in the area, no?'

'Let's do that,' he said. 'But don't let it put the kibosh on things, old girl. We'll find somewhere just as pleasant, mark my words.'

She laughed at him. '"Kibosh"? What on earth is "kibosh"?'

'Do you know something?' he admitted. 'I haven't a clue.'

They were stepping through the gate, between sprays of fragrant wisteria, when the receptionist rushed from the hotel and called out, 'Oh, Mr Langham!'

He turned, expecting to be told that a mistake had been made and that there were rooms spare, after all.

'Mr Langham,' she said. 'You're wanted on the phone.'

'Did the caller give you his name?' Langham asked.

'A Mr Endicott, sir, from Humble Barton.'

He said to Maria, 'Probably ringing to tell us that his father's returned safe and sound.' He followed the receptionist back inside.

'Hello? Alasdair?'

'Mr Langham,' Alasdair stammered.

'Edward's turned up?'

'No. No, Mr Langham. I . . . that is . . . Look, I wonder if you could come over?'

'What is it?' he asked. Alasdair sounded distressed, to say the least.

'I . . . I've found something. I've called the police.'

'Found something?'

'If you could come over, *please*,' Alasdair repeated with mounting desperation.

'Right-ho. We're on our way.' He replaced the receiver, thanked the receptionist and hurried from the hotel. So much for a leisurely stroll up the earthworks and a declaration of his love at the summit.

'Donald?'

He repeated his brief conversation with Alasdair as they hurried to the car.

'But what do you think he has found?'

'I dread to think. He sounded quite upset.'

They jumped into the Austin and drove through the leafy lanes to Humble Barton.

The front door of the Chase stood open. Langham led the way into the gloom of the hallway and turned right down the oak-panelled passage that led to Edward Endicott's study. He expected to find Alasdair there in a flap, but on entering the room he discovered it was empty. The French windows were flung wide to admit the warm summer breeze and the scent of honeysuckle.

Langham stepped through and called Alasdair's name.

In response, a dog barked. Rasputin came bounding down the length of the garden and jumped up at him, fully intent on laundering Langham's face with his sopping tongue. 'Down boy, down! Now, where's Alasdair, hey?'

The lawn extended for a hundred yards, flanked by flowering borders, and ended in a tangled copse. He was about to turn back when a figure emerged from the trees at the end of the garden and called out, 'Here, Mr Langham!'

They hurried across the lawn to where Alasdair Endicott stood, hugging himself in a visible state of agitation. Oblivious, Rasputin lolloped after them.

Alasdair appeared dishevelled, his shirt collar torn open and his hair in disarray, as if he'd slept the night in his clothes. Langham took his shoulder. 'Alasdair?'

His watery eyes seemed to focus on Langham without seeing him. 'I was out with Rasputin. Took him for his morning walk. This way . . .'

He strode along the worn path that disappeared into the shady copse, and Langham and Maria followed him. The transition from baking sunlight to cool shadow was instant.

Rasputin stopped dead and, his tail wagging like a manic metronome, applied his muzzle to the ground.

'Look,' Alasdair said, pointing.

Langham pulled the dog away and knelt, Maria crouching down beside him.

She whispered, 'It looks like blood, Donald.'

'And it's not fresh, by the look of it.'

The fluid had spilled across the sandy path and dried, but more had splashed some dock leaves to the left of the path, coating the plants with a dark red patina.

He looked up at Alasdair. 'You said you've called the police?'

'They should be here at any minute.'

'When did you discover this?'

'A little after nine.' He hesitated. 'It is blood, isn't it, Mr Langham?'

'I'd say so, yes,' he said, standing up. 'But we don't want to jump to conclusions. It might be from any number of things. There are foxes in the area, I take it?'

The young man nodded. 'My father used to keep chickens years ago, but packed it in after a fox savaged the lot.'

'There you are then. A fox might have got a rabbit or something.'

He scanned the undergrowth for any evidence of an obliging carcass, without any real hope of finding one.

He returned his attention to the blood, judging that perhaps half a cupful had been spilled. Which, he thought, suggested a pretty severe wound. He examined the worn path for footprints, but the passage of Rasputin back and forth had scuppered that possibility.

They turned as someone called out from the house. A uniformed constable propped his bicycle against the wall and approached. Alasdair hurried off to meet him.

Maria said, 'What do you think, Donald?'

'I don't know . . . It *might* be something a fox has savaged.'

'But you don't think so?'

'To be honest, no. I think there'd be more evidence of a scrap.'

Alasdair and the constable joined them, and after brief introductions PC Thomson hitched up his trousers and knelt to examine the blood. He was a tall, slim man in his fifties, with thinning grey hair and a careworn face.

He looked up. 'And you say Edward's been missing since Friday?'

'Well, I phoned him from London on Friday and there was no reply. As I told Mr Langham, that was unusual as my father is always in during the day. But it wasn't until Sunday that I came up and found him missing.'

PC Thomson stood up, his gaunt face drawn into a frown. 'I don't like the look of this. I'd best contact my super and he'll call in a crime team from Bury St Edmunds as likely as not. If I could use your phone, Mr Endicott? And if you don't mind me saying, you look as if you could do with a stiff brandy.'

As the pair were about to set off for the house, Langham said, 'Alasdair, would you mind if I took Rasputin for the walk that was interrupted this morning?'

'Of course,' Alasdair said distractedly. He fished the lead from the pocket of his jacket, passed it to Langham and accompanied PC Thomson from the copse.

Langham bent to fix the leash to the dog's collar. 'Lead the way, boy.'

'Donald?' Maria said, hurrying after Langham as he was pulled along by the canine traction engine that was Rasputin.

'Keep a sharp eye on the path, Maria. If Edward was coshed there'll be more blood. And with Rasputin here we might strike lucky.'

The dog tugged on the lead, and Langham restrained him to a slow walking pace as he cast his eyes across the rutted path and the under-growth. Sunlight dappled the ground, illumi-nating vortices of dust motes. The air was sultry, and from far off a cuckoo sounded its evocative, muffled double-note.

'My word,' Langham said in an attempt to lighten the mood. 'This brings back memories.'

'You had a dog as a child?'

'Not me. But a friend of mine had a spaniel. We took it for long walks through the woods next to our village.' He smiled at the recollection.

'My father is a cat person,' Maria said. 'We

never had a dog. That is why I'd like one, when . . .'

He glanced at her, but she looked away; he felt a sudden swelling in his heart, and wondered fleetingly why the hell he was being led by a hound through woodland when he could be on top of an earthwork – or better still in a pub garden somewhere – plighting his troth to the woman he loved.

She said, 'Donald, I hope we don't find . . .' She let the sentence hang.

Hauled along by Rasputin, Langham struggled not to break into a run as he scanned the path and the flanking undergrowth.

Minutes later he heard the chuckling of a river and made out the glint of water through the foliage. The footpath emerged from the trees and branched right and left, skirting the bank of a river. They paused to admire the view.

'But how beautiful!' Maria exclaimed.

The water was overhung with willow and elm, and silver fish glittered in the still, cool shallows.

'Look, Donald,' she said, pointing.

A little way to their right a hunchbacked timber bridge gave access to meadows on the far side. A circular stone building with a conical tiled roof stood amid what looked like a vegetable garden.

'I wonder if it belongs to the Chase?' she said. 'Did you notice the painting of it in the hallway?'

Langham admitted that he'd missed it. 'It looks as if it's used if the veg patch is anything to go by.'

'Should we take a closer look, do you think?'

Rasputin tugged at the lead, eager to be on his way again. 'I think the hound has other ideas,' Langham said, and allowed himself to be drawn along the riverbank path away from the bridge.

Rasputin jogged along, nose to the ground, tail wagging. 'Do you think he's on to something?' Maria called as she hurried to keep pace.

'I don't know,' Langham replied. 'Are you, boy?'

The worn footpath moved away from the river, cut through the woodland again, and minutes later emerged through a hedge on to a narrow lane. Langham and Maria paused for breath. Maria hooked a finger into the front of her blouse and blew to cool herself. 'Phewee! It is so hot!'

'Positively Mediterranean,' Langham said. He was jolted from the perpendicular as Rasputin took off again. They gave chase, eyeing the patched macadam for telltale spots of blood.

The lane wound towards the centre of the village, and minutes later the ridge of a thatched roof came into sight above the hedge. Ahead, a white picket gate was set into a bank of privet, and it was towards the gate that the dog made its way.

'Ah,' Langham laughed. 'All is revealed . . .'

A dolorous bloodhound sat on the other side of the gate, staring out at them like a sombre hanging judge that had somehow found himself behind bars. Rasputin bounded up to the gate and attempted to lick the bloodhound's nose. The latter forbore the attention with admirable stoicism.

'Ah, so this must be Caroline's bloodhound, Boardman,' Maria said.

Langham looked up the garden path. A rambling lime-washed cottage stood in an extensive garden, its thatched roof shaped around its tiny upper windows like beetling brows.

A long lawn was dotted with tables, and servants in black moved among them laying napkins, plates and cutlery. There was no sign of Caroline Dequincy.

'At least now we know where to come for Caroline's "at home",' Langham said, attempting to haul Rasputin away from the gate and the inscrutable hound beyond.

Maria pointed down the lane. 'I think if we follow the lane and turn left we should arrive back at the Chase.'

They set off, dragging a reluctant Rasputin.

Minutes later they came to the heart of the village, turned left and crossed the green. Langham recognized the lane that led to the Chase: a virtual tunnel between stands of ash and sycamore. Not that they would have had difficulty in finding their way back as Rasputin was now leading the charge, no doubt anticipating the reward of a feed on his return.

It was a relief to be out of the direct sunlight as they passed into the shade of the trees, and very soon they arrived at the gravelled drive. Langham expected to see a police car drawn up beside his own car and Edward Endicott's ramshackle Wolseley, but the drive was otherwise empty.

Alasdair Endicott pulled open the front door as

they approached, and looked from Langham to Maria expectantly. 'Anything?'

Langham said, 'Rasputin seemed more intent on leading us a merry dance to see his old chum – Caroline's bloodhound.'

As they passed down the darkened hallway, Maria said, 'This is the painting I was talking about, Donald.'

They stopped to examine the small oil, and Alasdair switched on a wall light.

'Endicott's Folly,' he said. 'It belongs to the house. My father uses it in summer to write and potter about the vegetable garden.'

'I suppose you checked that he wasn't . . .?' Langham began.

'It was the first place I looked, after searching the house. It was quite empty.'

They moved to a long sitting room, its dark furnishings and dour oil paintings thrown into relief by the intense sunlight pouring in through the French windows at the far end of the room.

Rasputin trotted off, his claws tapping on the polished floorboards. He stood by the door to the hallway and gave a peremptory bark, which Alasdair ignored.

'It's some place your father has, Alasdair,' Langham said as he and Maria collapsed into the springless embrace of an old sofa. 'Hollywood must have paid well.'

Alasdair looked from Langham to Maria. 'He was only in Hollywood for five years before the war, working to pay off debts accrued in London in the early thirties. Between you and me, he returned to Blighty down on his uppers, so to speak. For the past few years he's been churning out his thrillers.' He smiled wanly. 'He rubs along somehow, but don't ask me how.'

Langham nodded diplomatically, surprised. On their brief meetings, Edward Endicott had always striven to give the impression that Hollywood had been a cross between Aladdin's cave and a bottomless well full of dollars for the taking.

'Did Edward know Caroline in Hollywood?' Maria asked.

'That's where they met. She worked on a couple of films he scripted.'

'I wonder why she left America and settled here?' she said.

Alasdair shook his head. 'She never speaks about that period of her life. At least, not to me. She is rather a private person.'

'Perhaps that is not so surprising,' Maria said, 'given that much of her life until now must have been conducted in the glare of publicity.'

'I have the impression that Caroline wants a quiet life,' Alasdair said. 'I know that a reporter was snooping around a few months ago, wanting Caroline's opinion of some director who'd just died. She fled Rosebud Cottage and took refuge here for a few days.'

'If she and your father are close,' Langham said, 'I won't mention the fact that he's missing. And I'd better not mention the blood.' He shook his head. 'All this business about Stafford and the occult . . . Speaking as a dyed-in-the-wool rationalist, I find it hard to swallow.'

Alasdair hesitated, nervously fingering his threadbare goatee, then said, 'A couple of weeks

71

ago Stafford held a séance up at Stafford Hall. He must have approached Dent, the artist, for his permission to use the venue. By all accounts it terrified a few of the people present.'

'And you too?' Langham asked.

'I didn't attend,' Alasdair said. 'But I did experience another incident.' His nervy glance flicked away, eyed the floor and returned to regard Langham shyly. He took a long breath, looking uncomfortable. 'A few days after their first meeting, my father invited Stafford to stay. While he was here, he . . .' He looked at Langham, an uncharacteristic challenge in his gaze, '. . . he brought forth various spirits, apparitions. The Chase is haunted, you know? I was aware of the story when my father first bought the place, but I must admit that I never experienced anything myself. Until, that is, after Stafford had been here.'

'And then?' Maria said.

'And then I experienced a truly terrifying . . .' He stopped. 'I'm sorry. I can tell that you don't believe a word I'm saying.'

Langham shook his head. 'I believe that you were convinced by what you experienced. I'd like to hear what happened.'

Alasdair took a deep breath. 'Well, apparently there was a murder committed in the Chase a long time ago. Around 1750. A fight between father and son about an inheritance. It ended in the son stabbing the father to death and, a little later, taking his own life. He killed his father in what is now my father's study, and hanged himself from the beam in the hallway.'

Maria murmured, 'And what did you see?'

'I had a phone call from my father while I was in London. He was beside himself with excitement. He said that he'd seen an apparition, brought forth by Stafford. He exhorted me to come back and corroborate what he'd seen.'

'And you came back?' Maria was wide-eyed.

'I must admit I thought that my father had been hitting the whisky. I saw nothing the first night, even though I stayed up with my father until well after two. But on the second night . . .'

'Yes?'

'I left my bedroom to go to the bathroom. I was walking along the corridor to the west wing, which passes the hallway, and I thought I heard something.' He swallowed, his prominent Adam's apple bobbing. 'I heard a strangling sound. I thought at first that it was my father. I rushed towards the stairs.' He smiled at Maria and Langham. 'I saw a figure in doublet and hose, swinging from a rope attached to the beam in the hall. I have never seen so frightening a sight in my life. It was so real, yet at the same time insubstantial. The young man swung, and as he did so he turned to face me and I swear that, as he saw me looking down on him, he reached out to appeal to me, a ghastly rictus on his face.' He stopped and closed his eyes. 'I might have been able to convince myself that I'd been dreaming, given time . . . But as the apparition vanished and I stared at where it had hung, I saw my father. He'd emerged from his study and was staring up at me, a look of vindication on his face.'

Langham sat back on the sofa, wondering how

to respond. He was saved from doing so when a grandfather clock whirred and struck one at the far end of the room, its note echoing. Rasputin jumped to his feet and gave a loud bark.

'OK, boy,' Alasdair said. 'I'd better feed the beast.'

'And we'd better think about setting off for Caroline's,' Langham said.

Maria laid a hand on his arm. 'But we have nothing to take. Perhaps as we pass through the village I could pop into the shop?'

Alasdair said, 'I have the very thing. My father keeps a rather good wine cellar. I'm sure he wouldn't mind your appropriating a bottle of Chardonnay. I'll feed Rasputin and fetch one.'

As he hurried from the room, the dog on his heels, Maria turned to Langham and said, 'Well, what do you think of that?'

'Very generous of him,' he said, 'though I can't stand Chardonnay myself.'

Maria batted his shoulder. 'What do you think of his story, silly!'

'Oh, that? Well, as he said – given time, he'd probably have convinced himself that he was dreaming.'

'But his *father* saw it too, Donald!'

Langham gestured. 'It's rather like those ghost stories one is told around the camp fire as a boy scout,' he said. 'There's never a shred of actual proof, just so much hearsay. The mind can convince itself of anything, if it so desires. Or,' he went on, 'people can, for reasons known only to themselves, lie.'

Maria snorted, and was about to say something

when Alasdair returned bearing a dusty bottle of white wine. He passed it to Langham. 'I'll try to make it later, when the police have been.'

They thanked him, said their goodbyes and made their way from the room. As they passed through the hallway, Langham looked up at the thick, blackened oak beam.

Despite himself, he shivered.

SEVEN

Caroline had only a hazy recollection of the past day.

She had succumbed to the sedative of the Gordon's just after midday on Sunday, and had spent the next twelve hours pretty much blotto. She had woken this morning with a pounding head and the sudden realization that today was the day she was supposed to be hosting her 'at home'. Fortunately Molly, the little dear, was beavering away in the kitchen when Caroline struggled out of bed at ten. She had even got rid of the evidence, in the form of the gin bottles, and had a mug of black coffee waiting when Caroline eventually emerged from the bathroom.

She recalled a period of sobriety yesterday evening when she had delivered Rasputin to Alasdair, and met the charming couple just up from London. She wondered if they had detected the reek of gin on her breath or noticed her shaking hands. Then, the minute she returned home, she'd hit the bottle again. Alasdair had said that his father had had to 'pop out' for a while, which was a bore as she would have liked to have spent a little time with Edward. The worrying thing was that on Sunday, when she'd called at noon to see Edward, there had been no sign of him. She tried to convince herself that he'd taken himself off on one of his occasional hikes without informing a soul.

At eleven she made a vast rum punch and had her first drink of the day. Molly was in the garden, setting up the tables and parasols, and Caroline took the opportunity to help herself to a swift, fortifying double rum to steady her fraying nerves.

She poured herself a second glass, carried it out to the kitchen garden and sat in the shade. She had spent the last hour preparing the vol-au-vents and nibbles, both the rum punch and the fruit punch, and now she could sit back for an hour and enjoy the summer's morning. The waiters she had hired – four young men from the Midland Hotel at Bury St Edmunds – were not due to arrive until one, so she would not be on call to show them the ropes until then.

She experienced a vivid flashback, a quick vision that lingered in her mind's eye, of Vivian Stafford's long, cadaverous face.

She tried to shut out all thoughts of the man and took another drink.

She concentrated on her 'at home' instead. She held one every couple of months during the spring and summer, with all proceeds going to a worthy cause. She enjoyed entertaining and being the centre of attention. It was the one thing she missed from her old life in Hollywood – the parties where she had often been the star attraction, and played up to the attention paid to her by the young, handsome, would-be actors drawn to the sticky and often deadly fly-paper that was Hollywood. She smiled bitterly at the recollection; then she had had the looks to carry off the leading role at soirées on Sunset Boulevard. Now she had lost her looks and was reduced to playing host to garden parties in rural Suffolk . . . But she was being unfair to herself. She had chosen this quiet life, this retreat, and for the most part she liked playing the ageing, semi-reclusive, one-time star, and looked forward to these occasional gatherings, especially when there were new people to talk to.

She was looking forward to meeting Alasdair's friends, Donald and Maria. They were the kind of people, relatively young, beautiful – well, in Langham's case handsome – that the village was missing. The youngest person in the locality at the moment was the Reverend Denbigh, and Caroline found the vicar insipid. She bore his company only because he was great chums with Alasdair.

Great chums . . . Well, that was one way of putting it.

Edward had popped over a couple of weeks ago on the pretext that he'd been passing with Rasputin, and had hemmed and hawed for an age before coming out with what was bothering him.

'Ah . . . I don't know what to think of Alasdair these days, Carrie.'

'What on earth do you mean?'

'Dash it. His friendship with that damned vicar. 'Scuse me French.'

'I'm sure Alasdair is perfectly capable of choosing his own friends,' she had said, a little ambiguously.

'You know what Denbigh is, of course.'

78

'I've heard rumours . . . Not that I take any notice of tittle-tattle.'

He'd looked uncomfortable. 'Well, he and Alasdair have been seeing rather a lot of each other, y'know? Whenever he's up from London he's always round at the vicarage.'

'Edward, Denbigh is the only person remotely close to Alasdair's age in the village. It's perfectly natural that they should strike up a . . . a friendship.'

'Hmm.' Edward had cleared his throat, reddening. 'It's just that Alasdair's almost twenty-five now and there hasn't been sight nor sound of a young filly on the horizon.'

She'd laughed at his phrasing, which made him sound like an Indian colonel in his dotage. She had wanted, then, to cross the room and take him in her arms, reassure him that he should accept his son for what Alasdair was, not for what he wanted him to be. She had almost done that, but had stopped herself just in time. Her show of affection would have unsettled Edward even further, and he wouldn't have shown his face at the cottage for a month or more.

'Penny for them, Caroline.'

'Oh.' She jumped at the sudden voice, and looked up to see Haverford Dent leaning against the lime-washed wall. He must have been there for some time, watching her.

She tried not to show her resentment at being spied upon as she said, 'Dent! You gave me a turn.'

His smile slipped into the nearest thing to a leer. 'Well, I'd *like* to give you a turn, Caroline.'

Dent was in his sixties, his long face ravaged by a life of debauchery and drink – and God knew what else. He wore tatty tweeds that would have been old before the last war, and smoked a foul-smelling meerschaum pipe. Caroline had found the old goat intriguing when she'd first arrived at the village, but the attraction had soon worn off. Dent was an ego-maniac – even if he was also a talented artist, or perhaps *because* he was. Edward had warned her, years ago, that sooner or later Dent would attempt to 'press his charms' on her – and she had tried not to laugh at his quaint phraseology.

A few months ago Dent had tried just that – made a clumsy pass at her in the public bar of the Three Horseshoes – but Caroline had slapped his face and called him a drunken fool. They hadn't spoken since, which was fine as far as she was concerned.

'I'm surprised you have the bare-faced audacity to show up here.'

'As if I'd let our little misunderstanding come between us, Caroline.'

She sighed. 'If you've come for the "at home", Dent, you're an hour early.'

'Well, y'know what they say about the early bird?'

Did his every utterance have to be an innuendo? It made the slightest encounter with the man a tiresome battle.

'Why not come back at one, when the do begins?'

He smiled. 'Smelled the booze from miles away,' he said. 'Thought to myself that'll be

80

Caroline mixing the plonk, and no doubt helping herself to a snifter while she's at it. So I thought why let her drink all alone, and wended my way down the old hill . . .' He moved his right hand from behind his back, where he'd been hiding it, and Caroline saw that he was clutching a glass of rum punch.

He caught her expression and explained, 'Molly, she's an obliging lass and no mistake. How could she refuse when I asked her so nicely?'

'You should leave the girl alone.'

He nipped a shred of tobacco from the tip of his tongue and flicked it on to the grass. 'Anyway,' he said, 'what's all this about old Edward?'

She sat up. 'What about him?' she said, rather too quickly.

Dent smiled. 'Word is he's missing.'

'Missing?'

'Gone since Friday, according to some.'

'He's no doubt taken himself off with his tent,' she said.

'Alasdair's in a bit of a state about it. That's why he called in the detective writer chappie.'

She stared at him. 'I don't have the faintest idea what you're talking about.'

'Bumped into Alasdair this morning with that hound of Edward's. He asks me if I've seen Edward, then tells me he's gone. Vanished. So I said, "Perhaps that occultist chappie, Stafford, has magicked him away." And you know something, Caroline, I think I hit a nerve. Young Alasdair turns white, stammers something and skedaddles.'

'Edward will be back in a day or so, mark my words,' she said.

'Let's hope so,' Dent said, staring at her with what she thought might be a calculating look. 'And word is that Stafford's in town again. At least according to old Harry, who saw him leave the train at Bury on Saturday evening.'

'Is that so?' she said airily.

'So even if he does turn up you won't be seeing much of Edward for a few days, now that his muse has descended.'

Sometimes Dent, with his superior jibes, his veiled hints, was insufferable. She wished there was some way of shutting the man up, but he responded to anything she said – no matter how cutting or caustic – with an arrogant smile and a knowing twinkle in his eye. And he was always ready with some pithy put down or acute observation. How she hated the man!

He pushed himself away from the wall and held up his glass. 'That slipped down a treat. Now to see if Molly will fill me up. Excuse me – Bacchus calls.'

He moved around the corner to the kitchen door, and a minute later Caroline heard him sweet-talking her maid.

She sat for a while, expecting his imminent return, but he must have tired of baiting her and gone off in search of other prey: a couple of local girls had arrived to set up tables on the lawn, and members of the Women's Institute were erecting their table and chairs near the gate.

Caroline sipped her drink and tried not to think about Vivian Stafford.

'Ma'am, the waiters have arrived,' Molly said from the kitchen window.

82

Caroline gathered herself and went inside. She poured a large glass of rum punch and, taking a breath like the actress of old preparing to step out before the cameras, she fixed a smile and emerged from the cottage. Heads turned and stared at her as she sailed across the lawn and addressed the waiters, and she did her best to push all thoughts of Vivian Stafford from her mind and enjoy the next few hours.

She was determined to do so, even if she had to drink herself silly in the process.

EIGHT

'Oh, hello there.'

Langham and Maria turned. A thin young man with a battered straw hat and a clerical collar was making heavy weather of pedalling a bicycle along the lane. He applied the brakes, juddered to a halt and dismounted.

He offered a diffident hand. 'Marcus Denbigh, vicar at St Andrew's. And you must be Alasdair's friends from London?'

They shook hands. 'Word travels fast,' Langham said, introducing himself and Maria.

'Village telegraph,' Denbigh said. 'Alasdair mentioned you to Mr Jones this morning. Mr Jones is my verger – my eyes and ears on the world of Humble Barton, you might say.'

Langham put the Reverend Denbigh at no more than thirty; he was balding which, far from giving him the gravitas of years, served only to emphasize his youth. His dog collar hung loose on his thin neck, its parabola matching his hesitant smile.

They continued strolling along the lane.

'Are you going to Caroline Dequincy's "at home", too?' Maria asked, pointing to a large cake tin in the bicycle's wicker basket.

'One must show willing,' Denbigh said, 'and Caroline doesn't do things by half. She brings a little Hollywood into our lives, you might say, and she bakes awfully good cakes. Are you up for long?'

'We might be around for a day or two yet,' Langham said.

'Well, if you have time, do pop in to a service one morning.'

While Langham was casting about for a suitable reply, Maria smiled and said, 'That would be lovely, yes.'

Denbigh was pensive for a second or two, biting his lip before asking diffidently, 'I hope you don't mind my enquiring – village telegraph again – but everything's OK at the Chase, isn't it? Only Mr Jones saw a police car pull into the drive a little while ago, and as we haven't seen old Edward around for a few days . . .'

Maria glanced at Langham, who said, 'Between you, me and the gatepost, Edward Endicott's gone AWOL. But don't breathe a word of it to Caroline, agreed?'

'Mum's the word. I say, but what do you think might've happened?'

'Chances are he had to dash off to London and forgot to let people know,' Langham said, electing not to mention the blood. 'Is Edward popular in the village?'

Denbigh pulled off his straw hat and fanned himself with the vigour of a punkawallah. 'Well, he isn't unpopular. He keeps himself to himself, writing his books.'

'Do you know what he's working on?'

Langham looked at the young vicar as a shadow seemed to pass across his face. He shook his head. 'Not specifically, no.'

'He's good friends with Caroline, I hear? They met in Hollywood.'

'Yes, they're very close, despite the age difference.'

Maria looked at him. 'Age difference?'

'Well, Edward is well over sixty and Caroline can't be a day over forty,' he said.

'But I watched her films in Paris when I was a little girl,' Maria said. 'I was calculating just this morning – wasn't I, Donald? – that Caroline must be in her mid-fifties.'

'Amazing!' Denbigh exclaimed. 'Rumours about the monkey glands must be right.'

'Monkey glands?' Maria said.

'Village gossip has it that she goes up to London every month to a specialist in Harley Street who injects her with monkey glands.'

Above the hedge to their left, Rosebud Cottage came into view. The scene was almost too quintessentially English for words, Langham thought, and on cue a trio of swallows dipped and veered along the lane before them.

He said, 'I hear you've made the acquaintance of Edward Endicott's friend, Vivian Stafford.'

At the mention of the man's name, Denbigh stiffened. 'I've met him very briefly once or twice, but I can't say I know him. You'd be better off asking friends of Edward . . . Ah,' he said, brightening. 'Here we are.'

The white picket gate was open, and a cherubic old dear sat at a small table taking donations in return for raffle tickets. Langham bought a couple of strips for sixpence and strolled up the garden path towards the lawn, set out with shaded tables and chairs.

Caroline Dequincy was holding forth to a

gaggle of villagers at the far side of the garden, her bloodhound at her heel. A waiter circulated and Langham and Maria accepted a rum punch each, Denbigh a barley water. Langham calculated that perhaps thirty people thronged the lawn, some seated and many standing in small groups; a hubbub of polite conversation filled the summer air.

'Allow me to point out the leading lights of our village,' Denbigh said. 'Now, there's Mr Jones – already mentioned; and the tall lady in the feathery hat, that's Mrs Lorrimer – big in the WI. Beside her is Major Travers, retired, who despite his rank is a tub-thumping socialist.'

'Good for him!' Maria laughed.

Langham said, 'I don't suppose a fellow by the name of Dent is here? Haverford Dent, the artist?'

'Ah, you've heard of our infamous Son of the Canvas, have you?' Denbigh said with ill-concealed distaste.

'He's a friend of Edward Endicott, isn't he?' Langham asked.

Denbigh twined his index and forefinger. 'They're like this,' he said. 'Which surprises me as I should have thought that the pair would have had nothing at all in common.'

He scanned the crowd. 'There he is, the rather gaunt, dishevelled character in tweeds sweet-talking Daisy Sommers who, by the by, is young enough to be his granddaughter.'

Maria said, with a twinkle in her eye, 'You don't approve of Mr Dent?'

Denbigh pursed his lips and regarded his barley water. 'Let's just say that Mr Dent plays up to the caricature of the dissolute artist. People are of the opinion that he rather enjoys shocking the bourgeoisie.'

'Oh, in what way?'

Denbigh gave a thin smile. 'In every way. It seems to be his personal crusade to work his way through the ten commandments and take great delight in breaking them all, one by one.'

Langham eyed the vicar. 'Even murder?'

Denbigh muttered, 'Well, I wouldn't say that.' He paused, then went on: 'He certainly hasn't quailed at adultery, though, and the parties he occasionally throws at the hall are positively bacchanalian, or so I'm told.'

'Is Dent married?'

'Was. His wife ran off just after the war, so I believe.'

Langham sipped his punch. 'Didn't he hold some kind of séance at the hall not so long ago, at which Stafford presided?'

The vicar's expression tightened, and not for the first time Langham received the distinct impression that Denbigh was holding something back. He pressed, 'You've heard about that?'

Denbigh shot him a bitter look and said, 'I happened to be there, Mr Langham.'

'You were?'

Denbigh sighed. 'I thought it incumbent upon me to attend the 'Evening of the Occult', as Stafford termed it in his invitation, to ensure that the . . . let us say . . . more gentle souls among my parishioners didn't come to any harm.'

Maria said, 'And did they?'

Denbigh coloured. 'I must admit that, to my

shame, I failed in my duties. I left before the proceedings really got under way.'

'What offended you, if I may ask?' Langham enquired.

Denbigh opened his mouth to reply, if with reluctance, but was saved from doing so when Caroline Dequincy disengaged herself from her admirers and strode across the lawn, Boardman at her side.

'Ah,' Denbigh said, 'here's our host. You've met, I take it?'

Maria murmured that they had, and Denbigh said, 'In that case introductions are surplus to requirements. Please excuse me while I circulate.' He smiled at Langham and Maria and murmured, 'Caroline,' as he moved off towards the nearest knot of locals.

'I hope young Denbigh wasn't boring you too much?' Caroline said. 'He can be rather puppy-like with newcomers to the village. He's still a little wet behind the ears.'

'He was telling us about the locals,' Maria said.

'Ah . . .' the actress laughed. 'No doubt dispensing his Christian prejudices with abandon.'

Seen closer to, her made-up face bore telltale crow's feet around her green eyes and small lines, like grammatical brackets, around her mouth. Still, Langham found it hard to credit that she was in her mid-fifties.

'There seems to be little love lost between him and Dent,' he said.

'What do you expect? Young pup just a few years out of the cloistered seminary and a repro-bate like Dent whose morals are on the far side of loose? Dent isn't Christian and makes no bones about it. I'd call him . . . pagan, myself.'

'And what do you think of Dent?' Maria asked.

Caroline laughed again – a flash of perfect Californian teeth – and laid beautifully manicured fingers on Maria's arm. 'Listen, honey, I lived in LA for twenty years, so nothing shocks me any more. As to what I think of him . . .' She twisted her full lips around a mouthful of rum punch, considering. 'I don't care for Dent, his work or his person. He's a figurative painter whose images are often shocking. He also sculpts, and creates strange mechanical inventions which make little sense to me. But I think he's at his most objectionable when he extends his crusade to shock beyond the confines of his art.'

'In what way?' Maria asked.

A calculating look entered Caroline's jade eyes, and after a slight hesitation she said, 'God knows I'm no prude, but Dent's proclivities are way beyond acceptable.'

Langham glanced across the lawn to where the rangy artist, who struck him as some kind of satanic hybrid of shambling camel and predatory wolf, was still hanging over the virginal Daisy Sommers.

Caroline laughed. 'And I'm not talking about his one-man crusade to bed every woman in the village between the ages of fifteen and sixty,' she said. She leaned closer and said in a stage whisper, 'You heard it here first: his activities verge on the de Sadean.'

Langham glanced at Maria and raised an eyebrow.

'But you've finished your drinks.' Caroline gestured, and an attendant waiter hovered at their side and dispensed fresh glasses of punch.

'Oh,' Langham said, proffering the wine. 'This is from Endicott's cellar.'

'How sweet.' She took the bottle and looked from Maria to Langham. 'But no Alasdair?'

'Ah . . .' Langham said. 'He's a little busy at the moment. He said he'll be along later.'

The actress looked from Langham to Maria. 'And what's all this talk flying around concerning Edward?'

Langham cleared his throat. 'What have you heard?'

'Dent says he's not been at home for a couple of days, and just an hour ago a police car was seen in the drive. Come on, I can see that you two know more than you're saying.'

'Well,' Langham said, 'Alasdair drove up on Sunday and found his father missing. He'd arranged to stay with him over the weekend, so of course he was worried.'

'But what do you think's happened to him?' Caroline asked.

'I must admit that I have absolutely no idea, but I suspect he's popped down to London for a few days.'

Caroline frowned. 'I rather think he would have told me, if that were the case.' She gestured to a vacant shaded table and they sat down. 'But Edward does go off hiking from time to time; it's possible that he forgot about his arrangement with Alasdair and took himself off into the wilds.'

'Would he have taken his work with him?'

Langham asked. 'You see, his ledger and notes were missing.'

'I don't know. Perhaps.'

Maria said, 'And you found Rasputin, Caroline. Surely had he gone hiking he would have taken the dog with him?'

'That's right,' Caroline said, 'though Rasputin does have a mind of his own and has been known to give Edward the slip. How is Alasdair taking it?'

'He's worried, as I mentioned.' Langham hesitated, then continued, 'He seems to think that someone called Vivian Stafford is mixed up in all of this.'

He watched the actress closely as he said the name, and witnessed a quick narrowing of her eyes – almost a wince – at the mention of Stafford. She said, 'And why does Alasdair think Stafford might be involved?'

'As you no doubt know, Edward is working on a book about the man. Alasdair thinks that Stafford objected to the idea . . .' He shrugged. 'All this is mere speculation on Alasdair's part, of course.'

'Of course.'

'He also thinks that this Stafford is the same man who was alive over one hundred years ago,' he went on. 'I understand that you've met him?'

She drew herself upright in her seat and gave a dazzling smile. 'That's right. We have met a few times.'

'And what do you think?'

'About?'

'About Alasdair's – and Edward's – idea that

the Vivian Stafford from the Victorian era and the man claiming to be the same person are, indeed, one and the same?'

From the corner of his eye, he noticed Maria pause with her glass an inch from her mouth, her eyes intent on the American. Caroline seemed to consider his words for a time; she picked up a tray of canapés from the table and offered one first to Langham, who declined, and then to Maria, who took a vol-au-vent and popped it into her mouth without taking her eyes from Caroline.

The American drew a deep breath, looked from Langham to Maria and back again, and smiled. 'You might think me crazy, both of you, but on the matter of Vivian Stafford I find myself in complete agreement with Edward and Alasdair.'

Langham tried not to let his incredulity show. 'And what makes you think . . .?'

She looked away. He noticed that the actress had clasped her hands tightly in her lap. She seemed to be debating with herself whether to tell him something. At last she said, 'It's rather a long story.'

Langham said, 'I understand that Stafford recently held an occult event up at the hall. Did you attend?'

She nodded. 'It was the first of two. He's due to hold another in a week or so. Stafford called it an "Evening of the Occult" and claimed that he would be in contact with the dead. And before you laugh, you would have believed him too. He has a certain macabre delivery, and along with his rather corpse-like appearance . . . Well, let's just say that he was convincing.'

'I can just imagine the scene,' Langham said. 'The drawing room of a great hall, thronged with a gaggle of curious locals . . .' Under the table, Maria prodded him with the toe of her shoe.

Caroline pointedly, though with good humour, addressed the attentive Maria. 'To begin with, Stafford addressed the gathering in the library. He explained who he was – without mentioning his antecedents – and for an hour he held us spellbound as he recounted some of his exploits, and the various hauntings he'd experienced up and down the country.' She paused, her gaze distant as if reliving the night itself. 'After that he gave us a short tour of the hall. And I must say that for someone who isn't all that interested in times past, I found it fascinating. At one point he went into a trance, and when he came to his senses he claimed to have made contact with the other side.'

She hesitated, the consummate actress pausing for effect. Maria was leaning forward, hanging on Caroline's every word. 'What happened when Stafford "made contact with the other side"?' she asked, so wide-eyed that Langham almost laughed at her expression.

'You must first appreciate that we were in the east wing of the hall, which apparently had been shut down for the better part of a century. Dustcovers shrouded most of the furnishings and cobwebs festooned the candelabras and walls.'

'Sounds like the set of a horror film,' Langham said.

Caroline smiled. 'Oh, it was far creepier, let me tell you, than the set of any horror movie.

And I speak from experience. The only illumination in this part of the hall was gaslight, and it was feeble.'

'And then?' Maria said.

'And then Stafford opened his golf-ball eyes, announced that he was in contact with a spirit and asked us, one by one, if we would care to witness a . . . "manifestation", as he called it. We were petrified, but at the same time spellbound. I found Edward's hand and held on for dear life.'

She paused again. 'Stafford gave a cry – a series of commands in what sounded like a foreign language, perhaps Latin. He flung back his head and cried out at the top of his voice, and all of a sudden – and I know you'll find this hard to believe, but ask anyone who was there – the temperature in the room seemed to plummet. I was freezing. And then we heard a sound . . .'

Langham had to admit that, despite his scepticism, he was drawn into the actress's story.

'I must say that it scared us silly. I know I jumped a mile; young Daisy Sommers shrieked and almost fainted, which of course was the cue for the old goat Dent to play the gallant and escort the girl to a chaise longue . . .'

'But the sound?' Maria asked, breathless. 'What was it?'

'A moan, a low, continuous moaning like nothing I'd ever heard before – or ever want to hear again. It was like something from the depths of hell.'

Langham concealed a smile behind his raised glass.

Caroline continued, 'If that had been the extent

of the "manifestation", then I think we would have been convinced anyway. But there was more to come. I'd hardly recovered my wits when something flew across the room and vanished through, *through*, the far wall. I only caught a fleeting glimpse, but I was thankful for that.'

'What was it?' Maria murmured.

'I know what you're thinking – some white, spectral, stereotypical ghost, like a Halloween bedsheet . . .' She shook her head. 'It was terrifying.' She leaned forward, a frown buckling her forehead as she recalled what she'd witnessed.

'It was more grey than white, and insubstantial; human in form, but tattered, shredded. And its expression . . .' She closed her eyes, lost in the recollection, and Langham had to admit that her performance was award-winning. 'What terrified me most was that its expression was one of abject terror, as if it were fleeing from the legions of hell itself. I recall turning to Edward, to ask if he'd seen it . . . But his expression said it all: he looked appalled. The others were horror-stricken, too.'

Maria said, 'Did Stafford explain what the apparition was?'

'Apparently that wing of the hall had suffered an extensive fire at some point in the 1820s. A servant girl was burned to death, trapped in an upper room. Her spirit, still trapped, is said to haunt the hall to this day. Stafford said that what we'd witnessed was the girl's tormented soul.'

Maria caught Langham's eye and pulled a frightened face.

Caroline smiled. 'That was merely the start,'

she said. 'Next, Stafford said he had a greater surprise awaiting us in the grounds of the hall. By this time the event had proved too much for Major Travers and Daisy. The major said he'd see the girl home, and it says a lot for Dent's interest in what was going on that he didn't try to muscle in and insist on escorting the girl himself. For all his scepticism, he was hooked.' She looked pointedly at Langham and said, 'But I've noticed that about sceptics: when push comes to shove, they're as vulnerable to fear as the next man.'

He raised his glass. 'In the heat of the moment, Caroline, I don't deny that what you've described would have given me the willies, too. But in the cold light of day, with the aid of logic unhampered by suggestibility, I would have sought a rational explanation to what had happened.'

'Such as?' the actress asked.

Langham shrugged. 'I've no idea. I wasn't there. But I know there would be a logical answer to what the charlatan was doing.'

Maria said, 'Will you please *shush*, Donald!' She propped her elbows on the table and cupped her face in her hands, staring at Caroline with massive eyes. 'I want to hear the rest of the story.'

The actress said, 'So where was I?'

'Stafford was leading you all towards a rendezvous with eldritch ghouls,' Langham supplied.

'Thank you. Just so. We followed Stafford from the hall. It was getting on for midnight. A full moon was out—'

'But how could it *not* be?' he murmured to himself.

'We made our way to the mere, and Stafford stood at the water's edge and told a story – which Dent later corroborated – about a beast that was said to roam the countryside in search of stray travellers. The Brampton Hound. They still talk about it in the Three Horseshoes, though it hasn't been seen for well over fifty years.'

She paused, then went on: 'Standing there, a ghostly figure himself beside the water, Stafford claimed that he could summon it forth.'

'And no doubt proceeded to do just that,' Langham said.

'He called out, and it was as if his cry was the command for the clouds to draw a veil over the full moon. What had been, until seconds before, a scene etched in silver, became suddenly pitch black. The silence was absolute. Then we heard a growl from the woods at our backs, a slavering, howling noise that grew in volume as whatever it was drew closer.'

'You saw it?' Maria exclaimed.

'By this time Edward and I, and the others, were high-tailing it back to the hall. Fortunately I didn't see a thing. Back at the hall, Edward swore he'd seen a wolf-shaped creature at the edge of the woods . . . I'd had enough, but Edward wanted to take part in the culmination of the night's events – the séance – so I went along with him.'

'And what happened?' Maria wanted to know.

'There were perhaps ten of us seated around the table as Stafford went into a trance. He summoned his go-between, who would provide the link between this world and the next.'

'A Red Indian, I take it?' Langham quipped.

Caroline smiled. 'In this instance, Donald, the spirit of a girl who had passed on a hundred years earlier. It was, believe me, eerily unnerving to hear this man speaking in the high-pitched voice of a little girl.'

'And what did it say?' Maria whispered.

'It invited questions about the relatives of those around the table who had passed on, and Mrs Kent asked it about an aunt of hers who'd died just a few months previously. The girl – through Stafford – made contact with the dead aunt and told Mrs Kent that her aunt was with her, and wanted to tell Mrs Kent that she was not to worry about her niece in Australia, as financial help was at hand. A detail, might I add, that none there other than Mrs Kent knew about.'

Beside Langham, Maria shivered.

'And the séance finished with what proved to be the scariest incident of the evening.'

'More scary even than the slavering beast?' Langham asked.

Caroline stared at him seriously. 'Far more, Donald. You see, the child, through Stafford, said that one of us around the table would, before a calendar year had passed, fall victim to a killer.'

Langham said, 'But she didn't specify who?'

'No,' Caroline said, 'which was the most unsettling thing about the pronouncement. The evening broke up after that. Stafford took his leave in a swirl of his black velvet cape – I almost expected him to vanish into thin air – and we made our way back to the village.'

From across the lawn, Langham noticed the

approach of Haverford Dent. Caroline looked up in irritation at the looming figure.

'Caroline! No good hogging the guests all to yourself, y'know? Well, are you going to introduce the charming couple?'

Dent smiled from Langham to Maria, his gaze lingering on the latter. He exuded a distinct odour of perspiration and tobacco smoke, and cut a dishevelled figure in his baggy tweeds. His face was long and in colouration resembled the tallow shade of the meerschaum pipe he clutched in his gnarled right hand. Langham thought he resembled one of those crusty, rambunctious old English character actors who were always cropping up these days in Ealing comedies; he judged the man to be in his early sixties.

Without waiting to be invited, Dent grabbed a chair, reversed it and sat down with his arms lodged along the back.

Caroline said, 'Dent needs no introduction – his fame has spread to Bury St Edmunds, and even perhaps beyond. Dent, meet Donald Langham and Maria Dupré.'

He took their hands. 'Charmed,' he smiled. 'Langham? The writer chappie? Edward mentioned you when he saw one or two books of yours up at the hall. I recognized you across the lawn from the snap on the jacket of *Murder at Sea*. Decent yarn, I must say. Don't mind the odd whodunit. A distraction from me work, y'see. Said to myself that I must have a natter to this chap and his beautiful companion . . .'

He turned to Maria. 'And what do you do,

100

m'dear? No, don't tell me. Let me guess. You work in films, mm? If not, you should.'

She smiled frostily. 'I work as a literary agent, Mr Dent.'

'Ah, Miss Ten Percent?'

'Seven and a half, actually.'

He laughed. 'Surely her services are worth much more than that, eh, Langham?'

Caroline looked across the lawn and said, 'Ah, new arrivals. Do excuse me while I play the host.' She smiled at Langham and Maria, then turned to the artist and said, 'And do behave yourself with my friends, Dent.'

The artist watched her cross the lawn, Boardman obediently at her heel. He shook his head. 'How'd you get on with the old Ice Maiden? And I say "old" advisedly. We're very near the same age, would you believe? Difference is our Caroline looks after herself.' He barked a laugh. 'I *enjoy* life too much!'

'Your fame precedes you,' Langham said, not believing for a second that Caroline Dequincy and Dent were anything near the same age.

'Don't believe half of what you hear about me, young man. Villagers hate my guts. Bunch of insular little Englanders.'

Maria smiled, without warmth. 'But you cannot call Caroline that, Mr Dent.'

'Oh, our Caroline is far from insular, m'dear. Behind the glamour dwells a keen mind. Damaged, mark my words. But who wouldn't be after twenty-odd years working in Hollywood? That's why I call her the Ice Maiden – her hauteur is a reaction to years of psychological, and perhaps even physical abuse.'

101

Maria surprised Langham by saying, 'You are rather outspoken, if you don't mind my saying, Mr Dent.'

He barked a laugh. 'I don't mind anyone saying *anything*, m'dear. That's what's wrong with the country these days – no one really says what they mean. We live in an age of polite inconsequential-ities, a throwback to an earlier era. Well, all that'll change, mark my words. Social upheaval is on the horizon. So of course I'm bloody well outspoken, and I don't care who says so.'

He looked around impatiently, gestured to a waiter, grabbed two glasses of rum punch and poured one into the other. 'Now that's what I call a decent measure,' he said, downing half a glass in one swallow. 'So what are you two lovebirds doing in this neck of the woods?'

Maria leaned back and gazed coolly around the gathering, effectively absenting herself from the conversation. Langham considered Dent's description of them, and wondered if they did publicly exhibit their mutual affection – or if Dent was just very observant.

'We're friends of Alasdair Endicott,' he said. 'I understand you know his father?'

'Edward's a good friend. A fool, but a good friend.'

'A fool?'

'A bloody fool, and I'm not saying anything behind his back that I wouldn't say to his face. I've told Edward time and again that I think he's wasting his time.'

'In what way?'

'This blasted book he's started writing about that charlatan, Stafford.'

'Ah . . .' Langham took a mouthful of punch. 'So you don't think Vivian Stafford is really a hundred and twenty years old?'

Dent closed one rheumy eye and regarded Langham with its sceptical partner. 'Of course I bloody well don't! Do you?'

'No, I don't. But Edward and Alasdair seem to be taken in by . . . whoever Stafford is.'

'That's because both father and son are gullible. See a few party tricks and they're smitten, taken in by the fellow's smooth patter.'

'How did Edward become involved with Stafford?'

Dent pulled at his nose, reflecting. 'A month ago this odd-looking cove turns up at the hall. Introduced himself as Stafford and said he'd just dropped in to look at his old country pile . . . The stranger made no claims to be the *actual* Vivian Stafford – the Victorian satanist who owned the hall back in the last century – at the time. I knew about Stafford, of course. Had all the gen from the agent when I bought the pile twenty years ago. Anyway, I assumed the old vulture was some long-lost descendant. We got talking and I suggested we repair to the Three Horseshoes, and who should we bump into there but old Edward. Well, one drink turned into five or six, the way it does, and chucking out time came and went. Then Stafford says he's in touch with the departed. Y'understand, we'd had a few by this time, and I was game for a laugh. So I asked him what the bloody hell he was on about, and he said he was a practitioner of the black arts. He claimed that the bar was haunted – and I made some quip about spirits aplenty, which didn't go down well. He also said that Endicott's Chase was the abode of spectres and told some tale about a murder there in the 1750s. So Edward arranged for Stafford to visit the Chase and *commune* with the spooks.'

Langham nodded. 'Alasdair told us about it.'

He noticed that Maria had tipped her head to one side, listening to Dent's tale while trying to appear uninterested.

'I declined the invitation for the following week, but heard all about it from Edward. Then Stafford retreated from the scene for a day or so, and the next thing I know he'd been in contact with Edward who's babbling about the Victorian satanist and this Stafford being one and the bloody same. Next I find out he's writing a book about the man. Then a couple of weeks ago, Stafford turns up and he asks if I'd be amenable to staging an "event" up at the hall – his old stamping ground, as it were. Well, I thought the old vulture a charlatan, but I was game for anything.' He quaffed his punch and called for more from a passing waiter.

'Caroline told us all about the evening,' Langham said.

Dent grabbed two glasses, combined them, and took a swallow. 'It was a riot! My God, half a dozen of those who attended were scared witless! And the evening culminated in a midnight séance, where he manifested a spook.'

'And you remained sceptical?'

Dent squinted at him. 'Verily, sir. Smoke and mirrors. Stagecraft. Legerdemain. I'll give the charlatan this – he's a bloody good magician, but a medium or a satanist or whatever, he ain't.'

He looked from Langham to Maria. 'Of course, the event only served to increase Edward's obsession. Talked about nothing else, holed himself up at the Chase and scribbled his bloody book. We hardly see him these days, and his presence at the bar of the Three Horseshoes is sorely missed, I can tell you. Once upon a time he propped up the bar *every* night.'

'Intriguing . . .' Langham said. 'It's good to meet someone who shares my rationalist leanings.'

Dent winked. 'We *create*, sir. We know fact from fantasy. And speaking of fantasies . . .' He was suddenly alert, as tense as a gun dog as he stared across the garden towards a young woman in a flowing white dress who was talking to the Reverend Denbigh.

'That's young Lizzy Carstairs. Didn't know she'd be here. Better save her from being bored to death by the parson. Someone has to do it.' He smiled at Langham. 'Look here, I have an exhibition of my work up at the hall, starting Wednesday. I'm throwing a bit of a garden party and what have you. Why not come along and take a gander? In the interim . . . do excuse me.' He almost leapt from his chair and loped across the lawn towards the angelic Lizzy, his gait bordering on the vulpine.

Maria watched him go. 'What a peculiar man,' she said.

Langham laughed. 'I don't know . . . I found his openness a trifle refreshing. Talk about calling a spade a spade. And I'm curious about his work. I think I'd like to attend this garden party-cum-exhibition of his.'

'I must admit, I did wonder what his art might be like.' She hiccupped, leaned across the table and took his hand. 'This punch is rather good, isn't it? I do think I'm rather drunk.'

He smiled at her. 'I do know you're rather beautiful, Maria. Dent's eyes almost popped from his head when he saw you.'

'Yes, and I wish he'd kept his eyes to himself,' she said. 'I felt like something in a butcher's shop window.'

Langham looked across the lawn to where the incorrigible Dent was elbowing the vicar aside and bearing down on the young woman like a predatory animal. At that moment Caroline Dequincy breezed up to the couple, spoke briefly to Lizzy Carstairs and eased her away from the artist's company. Dent looked around for his next nubile victim, found none, and consoled himself with another double punch from a passing waiter. He shuffled over to a seat beneath a rose-choked bower, flung himself down and sulked.

'The artist thwarted,' Langham murmured.

They moved from the shade of the table, secured glasses of non-alcoholic punch this time, and spent the next hour wandering around the garden, admiring the flowering borders and fruit trees and chatting to villagers. Their presence as newcomers in the village was commented upon again and again, and the fact that they were

106

holidaying in the area and not moving to Humble Barton was greeted with disappointment.

'What we need,' said one old woman, 'is more young blood in the village!'

They came to a swing on the bough of an ancient flowering apple tree, and Maria sat down and swung back and forth, kicking her bare legs. Langham leaned against the knobbled bole, lit his pipe and puffed contentedly.

'Would you like to move into the country, Donald?'

'Do you know something? I don't think I would. I mean to say, it's very beautiful and all that, but I don't think I could live here. Wonderful to come out for a break, though. I think I've lived in the Smoke for too long. You?'

She kicked out, swinging high. 'I think I would like to own a cottage in the country. So that we could come away from time to time when London becomes just too much. That would be nice, wouldn't it?'

He nodded, his heart swelling. 'That would be wonderful. I'll ask Caroline if she has any contacts in Hollywood who might offer me a thousand for the rights to one of my books. Then I'll buy you a little thatched place down a quiet country lane.'

She quickly hunched her shoulders at the thought and smiled at him.

'Hello,' he said, pushing himself from the tree trunk. 'I think that's young Alasdair.'

Maria jumped from the swing and landed like a gymnast, knees bent. Langham slipped an arm around her waist and they made their way towards the new arrival.

NINE

Alasdair waved as they approached. He looked exhausted, as if he'd sprinted all the way from Endicott's Chase. Langham suggested they sit in the shade and fetched a fruit punch for the young man.

'Well?' Langham asked. 'Any news?'

Alasdair took a long drink. 'They came an hour ago, a whole team of police bods in overalls. I showed them where the blood was and they found quite a bit more.'

Maria winced and found Langham's hand beneath the table.

So much for Rasputin's credentials as a bloodhound, Langham thought.

'They were painstaking about it,' Alasdair went on. 'They went over the garden with a fine-toothed comb and grilled me pretty severely into the bargain. Anyone would have thought that *I'd* bashed my father on the head, the way the inspector set about the questioning.'

'They've got to be thorough and dispassionate in their line of work, Alasdair. They'd quiz everyone in the same way, believe me.'

The young man smiled wanly. 'They asked all about his recent movements, which of course I knew nothing of . . .' He shrugged. 'It's odd that, even though I know I've done nothing, they made me feel quite guilty.'

'Did you mention Stafford and your theories?' Langham enquired.

Alasdair nodded. 'I thought it best.'

'And how did they take it?'

'I think "scathingly" is the correct word. They looked at me as if I were a fool.' He sighed. 'I wasn't going to come along here. Didn't feel much like socializing, given the circumstances. But . . . I've just had a phone call from the inspector. You see, my father was a blood donor at the hospital in Bury St Edmunds. They were able to match the sample they took. Or, rather, not match it.'

Langham stared at him. 'What?'

Alasdair shrugged again, as if he didn't believe it himself. 'The blood I discovered in the garden, and the other samples they found further along towards the river . . . well, none of it was my father's.'

'But that's capital news!' Langham said.

'Yes, it is rather, isn't it? It begs the question whose blood is it, though, and what on earth has happened to my father?'

Maria shook her head. 'The mystery deepens, but at least you know now that Edward is not injured. That can only be a good thing.'

Alasdair nodded abstractedly. 'But not *knowing* what happened is so . . . so damnably frustrating.'

'I know what you mean,' Langham said. 'But try to look at this turn of events as positive.'

Alasdair glanced at Langham and Maria, mute appeal in his eyes. 'How long are you staying around here?'

Maria said, 'We had hoped to stay a few more days, but the hotel has no more vacancies.'

'Could you recommend anywhere local?' Langham asked.

'Look here . . . I'm sure my father wouldn't mind if you lodged at the Chase for a few days. Why don't you? You'd be very welcome. I can't promise anything special in the way of breakfast but we have seven rooms to choose from.' He smiled at them. 'And it would be good to have you around. If, that is, you don't mind the odd ghost.'

Langham looked at Maria, who said with a theatrical shiver, 'I've always wanted to stay in a haunted house, Donald. Let's!'

'I think I can tolerate sharing the place with a few putative spooks,' he said. 'We'll bring our cases over tomorrow morning after breakfast.'

'Excellent.' Alasdair looked across the lawn and smiled. 'Dent, the old goat, putting on the charm with Mrs Lorrimer of the WI. I shouldn't think he'd make much progress in that department.'

'We've made the acquaintance of the infamous Dent,' Langham said. 'The word "eccentric" might've been invented to describe him.'

'I cannot say I was very much taken with the man,' Maria opined.

'He has that effect on people,' Alasdair said.

'Caroline certainly didn't have a good word to say about him,' she said.

'That's because . . . between you and me . . . she would have nothing to do with his advances, and told him so in no uncertain terms in the Three

Horseshoes not so long ago. She slapped his face in front of a full bar – made quite a fool of him, by all accounts.'

'Ah,' Langham said, 'now his sobriquet for her is explained. The Ice Maiden.'

'That's unfair on Caroline,' Alasdair said. 'She's a very nice person. My father thinks the world of her.'

Maria asked, 'And what is your opinion of Mr Dent, Alasdair?'

He shrugged. 'When there's no women about, he can be good company. I've had a few interesting conversations with him in the Three Horseshoes. But I must admit that he can be something of a pain with his continual running after . . .' He came to a halt, blushing.

Maria looked up and smiled as Caroline approached their table and sat down. Boardman flopped on to the grass beside her feet. 'Alasdair,' she said, 'I'm so pleased you could make it. You look positively pooped.'

Alasdair smiled. 'Well, that's one way to describe it. I've just taken Rasputin for his afternoon romp, then hurried straight over here.'

Caroline refreshed their glasses and said, 'I do wish Edward had said where he was taking himself off to.'

Langham stopped himself from quipping that perhaps they should get Stafford to help locate him.

Alasdair looked up. 'I was considerably more worried before the blood—' he began.

The actress looked up quickly. 'What blood?'

'Ah,' Alasdair said, colouring. He explained

about the blood Rasputin had discovered in the back garden. 'But according to the inspector who quizzed me earlier, it isn't my father's.'

Caroline shook her head, shocked. 'Are they sure?'

'Apparently. That's what they told me, anyway.'

'Then whose blood could it be?' she said, more to herself.

Maria said, 'We borrowed Rasputin, Donald and I, in the hope that he might trace . . .' She shrugged.

'But he proved useless,' Langham continued. 'He just led us on a wild goose chase to your garden gate and Boardman.'

At the sound of his name, the dog lifted a lethargic ear and opened a bloodshot eye.

Langham sat up. 'By Jove, here's a thought. How about we try again, but this time with Boardman? He's a bloodhound, after all.'

Caroline looked at him. 'You mean . . .?'

'We take Boardman on a walk through the copse and see if he comes across anything . . .'

'I don't know.' Caroline sounded dubious. 'Surely if there were anything more to be found the police would have done so.'

'There can be no harm in trying,' Maria said. 'We could meet up in the morning.'

'I don't know whether I'll be up to a long walk in the morning.' Caroline laughed and hoisted her glass. 'This isn't the first.'

Langham said, 'Well, if you don't feel like it, maybe we could borrow Boardman?'

The actress looked at him, lost in thought, then said, 'No. No, I'm sure I'll be fine.'

'Excellent,' he said. 'How about we meet at the Chase around eleven?'

A short while later Caroline excused herself and announced the drawing of the raffle.

The jeroboam of champagne was won by none other than the Reverend Denbigh, who blushed and stuttered as he accepted the prize, then promptly handed it back to the actress to be re-raffled.

Langham leaned over to Maria and said, 'It'd be ironic if Dent won the thing.'

Caroline shook the brown paper bag containing the tickets and a little girl drew the winner. Caroline unfolded the ticket and called out, 'Yellow, 333!'

'Half the number of the beast,' Langham laughed. 'Well, blow me down,' he said as Haverford Dent, clutching the winning ticket above his head, jigged across the lawn towards the actress. He accepted the jeroboam like a cup final captain being awarded the trophy and kissed it to polite, if restrained, applause from the assembled villagers.

A little later Langham and Maria made their farewells and drove back to Brampton Friars.

TEN

The following morning after breakfast Langham and Maria checked out of the hotel, loaded their cases into the Austin and motored the five miles to Humble Barton.

It was another hot summer's day with not a cloud in the sky. The forested folds of Suffolk undulated east and west, hazy in the morning light. The occasional church steeple indicated where sleepy villages were tucked away down winding lanes as overgrown as rabbit-runs, and at one point muffled church bells pealed ten o'clock.

What with the hectic social whirl of the past day or so, Langham had had little chance to ask Maria the all-important question, but he was sure there would be ample opportunity to do so over the course of the next few days.

'Isn't it wonderful to be away from London?' Maria said. 'Do you know, I don't feel in the least bit guilty about not working.'

'That's quite unlike you. It's a wonder you haven't brought along a pile of manuscripts.'

'It's a quiet month,' she said. 'Everyone's on holiday.'

'I was wondering how long we should stay at Alasdair's? We don't want to overstay our welcome.'

'How about we leave on Friday? He did invite

114

us, after all, and he seemed pretty keen to have us stay.'

'That's true,' Langham said. 'It would be a shame to go back to London before then.'

She looked at him, a wicked glint in her eye. 'You don't mind staying in a haunted house? You won't get the . . . the "heebie-jeebies", will you, Donald?'

'I should jolly well think not. Anyway, if Alasdair's as free with his father's wine as he has been so far, I'll be so drunk I'll sleep right through any ghostly visitations. Ah, here we go . . .'

Ahead, a jouncing tractor that had slowed them down for a couple of miles turned through a farm gate, its trailer spilling gobbets of manure. Langham accelerated, an ordure-laden breeze blowing in through the open window.

Five minutes later they pulled into the drive of Endicott's Chase.

Alasdair opened the front door and blinked at them; he appeared a little worse for wear. 'Ah, come in. Would you mind awfully if I'm far from sociable this morning? I had one too many at the Three Horseshoes last night.'

Maria looked solicitous. 'Are you all right, Alasdair?'

'I'll be fine. This way – I'll show you to your rooms.'

Langham carried their cases up the wide oak-panelled staircase. At the top a corridor ran right and left to each wing of the house. Alasdair indicated left, along a passage whose timbers had, over the centuries, warped and shifted to create a quirkily uneven obstacle course. Langham almost tripped over an odd step – which Alasdair told him was the result of an extension to this wing in the 1830s – then ducked beneath three low oak beams, before Alasdair indicated the first room. 'This is yours, Maria.'

Langham left her case just inside the door and followed Alasdair to the next room. 'I hope you're comfortable,' Alasdair said. 'I think I might go and lie down for a while. Perhaps a spot of lunch at one?'

'Only if you're up for it.'

When Alasdair retreated, Langham admired the room. A small window looked out over the driveway. The outer wall sloped out from the ceiling to the floorboards, the result of the room being tucked under the steeply bevelled thatch.

He heard a playful tapping sound to his left, and a communicating door opened. Maria ducked through. 'Isn't this lovely, Donald!'

'I'll say. Much nicer than the hotel room.'

She came to him and they hugged. She whispered, 'And I'll leave the door open so that if you're frightened in the night . . .'

She nuzzled his shoulder and he kissed the crown of her head, wondering at her offer.

He was spared further consideration of her invitation by a sudden cacophony of barking dogs. Rasputin started up in the lower reaches of the house, and Boardman – lolloping up the drive – responded in kind.

Langham and Maria peered through the tiny window, saw Caroline and chuckled at the sight of the rangy American actress holding on for dear life as Boardman hauled her towards the Chase.

They left the room and descended to meet her.

Langham opened the front door and the dogs almost collided in their enthusiasm. Barking their greeting, tails wagging furiously, they trotted off into the house.

'Whew!' Caroline exclaimed. 'I feel as if I've been dragged here by a whirlwind. But he does so love Rasputin.' She looked around. 'No Alasdair?'

'The worse for a hangover. He's resting. I see you're suffering too,' he said, pointing at the huge pair of sunglasses that obscured half of the actress's face.

'The gathering went on rather late last night,' she said, 'and I think I rather overindulged.' She lifted her glasses and lodged them high on her forehead, pinning back stray tresses of auburn hair in the process. 'Look, do you really think this is a good idea? I mean, if the police couldn't find anything . . .'

Langham said, 'Go and lie down in a dark room, Caroline. But I'd still like to take Boardman.'

The actress smiled unsurely. 'No, I'm sure I'll be fine.'

Langham led the way through the house and out into the back garden. He thought the actress was looking more her age this morning: the parenthetical lines about her mouth seemed deeper in the cruel light of the sun. He recalled Haverford Dent's assertion that Caroline Dequincy was almost as old as him – which would make her over sixty – and dismissed the idea as absurd.

Rasputin and Boardman came trotting from the kitchen. 'Here they are,' Langham said. 'You ready to do a bit of sleuthing, Boardman?' He looked at Caroline. 'Perhaps we'd better take both dogs,' he suggested. 'Now that they've found each other, I don't think they'd take too kindly to being separated.'

'Perhaps Boardman can give Rasputin lessons on how to follow a trail,' Maria said.

They walked across the lawn, preceded by the dogs.

'Where did you say the blood was?' Caroline asked.

'A little further along here,' Langham said.

Caroline pulled on Boardman's lead with a strong arm. 'I don't understand what's going on,' she said. 'Isn't it just too coincidental? I mean, Edward vanishing like this, and then the spilled blood . . .?'

'It is a little strange, no?' Maria said.

Langham said, 'You heard what the police said – the blood wasn't Edward's.'

'I know very little about things like this,' Maria said, 'but can they be certain? I mean, what if they mistook the samples or something . . . and the blood *was* Edward's?'

Langham shook his head. 'I'm sure they wouldn't make such a fundamental error, Maria.'

'Here it is,' Maria said, pointing to a patch of undergrowth in the shade of a hawthorn bush.

Langham could see where the police had shorn dock leaves and grasses to gather adequate samples, but splashes and spots of blood still remained on adjacent foliage.

Caroline grimaced and dragged Boardman to the besmirched flora. Nose to the ground, ears dragging, he sniffed. His snuffles increased and his tail wagged with enthusiasm.

'Now lead the way, pooch,' Caroline said, and allowed herself to be dragged further along the path into the shady woods.

Maria, Langham and Rasputin followed.

As they walked, Langham said, 'What's your opinion of his . . . "obsession", to use Alasdair's term, with Vivian Stafford? I must say that I was surprised that someone as level-headed and down to earth as Edward . . .'

'On the contrary,' she said. 'I think it's entirely understandable. Stafford is, after all, a fascinating subject.'

Maria was watching the American closely as she asked, 'And you really believe that Stafford is as old as he claims?'

Caroline hesitated, looking from Maria to Langham. 'I know that you must think me crazy . . . but, with respect, you haven't experienced what I have.'

Langham wondered how a woman as obviously intelligent as Caroline could bring herself to believe something so blatantly nonsensical as some charlatan claiming to be a hundred and twenty years old.

He said, trying to keep the mockery from his tone, 'And did Stafford tell you how he managed to live so long, by any chance?'

'No, Mr Sceptic, he didn't,' Caroline said with a smile.

Minutes later they emerged beside the river

without Boardman having located further evidence of blood. They faced the choice of turning either right or left, but the bloodhound made that decision for them. He dragged the actress along the path to the right, in the opposite direction to that which Rasputin had led Langham and Maria yesterday.

They hurried along the riverbank path, sunlight falling through the overhead canopy like great golden searchlights. The river tinkled to their left, as silver as a million new sixpenny pieces. Somewhere deeper in the forest came the regular, rhythmic knocking of a woodpecker hard at work.

'Well,' Caroline called out at one point, 'this is certainly one way to work off the effects of a hangover.'

'We should have dragged Alasdair along with us,' Langham laughed.

'He's not one to exert himself,' Caroline said. 'In that respect he's quite unlike his father. Edward alternates bouts of work with long walks. I remember back in LA, he'd often take off into the hills . . .' She fell silent suddenly, and Maria threw a glance across at Langham.

They had paused before the tiny humped bridge that crossed the river to the meadow where Endicott's Folly stood. Instead of continuing along the path, Boardman, tail wagging industriously, turned left with canine certitude and tugged the actress across the bridge.

They came to the well-ordered vegetable garden before the circular folly, cabbage-white butterflies and red admirals jinking along before them. A rough timber bench stood beside the door of the folly, and Langham imagined Edward Endicott taking time off from work to sit and admire his garden.

Boardman, nose to the ground, led them past the folly and across the meadow.

A hundred yards away an old stone wall, garbed in a mantle of ivy, bisected the field; a wooden stile allowed walkers access over the wall and beyond. As they walked a small figure came into view as he climbed over the stile and jumped down into the meadow.

'Reverend Denbigh,' Maria said.

He waved his straw hat when he saw them and hurried across. 'What a wonderful morning!'

'Taking inspiration from bounteous nature, vicar?' Caroline asked.

'Returning from another of a cleric's never-ending duties, rather,' Denbigh said, smiling at Langham. He seemed to be avoiding eye contact with Caroline, and Langham wondered why, in the actress's company, the vicar seemed so abashed.

'I take it you've heard about Dent?' Denbigh went on.

'No. What?' Caroline frowned and raised her sunglasses, jerking Boardman back to her side.

'Well, he was rather half-cut when he left your do yesterday, Caroline, clutching his prize.'

'Don't tell me he . . .?'

Denbigh nodded. 'On the way back to the hall he popped the cork and proceeded to swig the entire jeroboam.' He shook his head. 'That's the trouble with alcoholics,' he went on. 'They don't

121

know when to stop. Dent is fine when he's working, but when he's finished a piece it's as if he needs a release. And he drinks himself insensate.'

'What happened?' Langham asked.

'He fell over on the steps of the hall and cracked his head. Lay there all night, according to his housekeeper. She found him this morning and called Doctor Hartley. Upshot is, nothing broken, but he's got a nasty cut to his head and one heck of a hangover.'

'I did have second thoughts about letting him leave with the champagne,' Caroline said.

'Don't castigate yourself,' said the vicar. 'Dent's old enough to look after himself. Anyway, Doctor Hartley asked me to call round to have a chat with him – though heaven knows what he thought that would achieve. Dent doesn't much like me. But even black sheep are part of the flock.'

'How is he now?' Maria asked.

'Pretty ruddy sore, excuse my language, and not a little contrite. He's worried that he might not be fit to host his exhibition tomorrow. Apparently he has some important gallery owners coming up from London to look at his work. I told him he'd be fine.' He laughed. 'He was even civil to me and thanked me for calling in. Perhaps there is hope for him yet. Well, I'd better be on my way.' He smiled at Langham and Maria, waved his hat again and hurried off towards the bridge.

Langham looked at the actress. 'Are you and he . . .?'

'Oh, you've noticed how he can hardly bring

himself to look at me? He always was a little nervous in my company, but never this bad. Being one of nature's bachelors, of course, he finds the company of women . . . *exacting*, shall we say?'

Langham exchanged a glance with Maria, then followed Caroline along the path.

They came to the wall and, one at a time, climbed the stile, Rasputin almost dragging Langham over the contraption. 'Steady on, boy!' he called out, jumping down on the other side.

The land rose and, perhaps a mile away, the blocky outline of a big Georgian house stood on the horizon. 'Stafford Hall?' Langham asked.

Caroline nodded. 'Some pile, isn't it? But it's falling down around Dent's ears – he only lives in a part of it now. The rest is going to rack and ruin. A mighty shame.'

Boardman tugged her to the right, parallel with the wall and along a path that headed towards the woods.

'Do you really want to go through the woods, boy?' She looked at Langham. 'If we head left there's a shorter route back to the village.'

But Boardman, Langham saw, was not to be deterred. He dragged Caroline towards the trees and she had no option but to be tugged along after him.

She panted, 'I'm surprised . . . surprised Denbigh agreed to see Dent.'

'Dent doesn't like the vicar, does he?' Maria said. 'He wasn't very complimentary about him yesterday afternoon.'

Langham laughed. 'I suppose curates must develop a thick skin. Comes with the job.'

'That isn't why I was surprised he went up to the hall,' Caroline said. 'Young Denbigh is ever eager to please. No, it's because of what happened the last time he was there.'

'Ah,' Langham said. 'The occult evening. He walked out halfway through, didn't he?'

'Well, he left at some point. But not before confronting Stafford about what he was doing.'

Maria stared at Caroline. 'What did he say? To be honest, I cannot imagine the vicar confronting anyone.'

'Oh, he gave Stafford a piece of his mind, all right. He called the man evil, and said that God's wrath shall be visited upon the sinful and all that. He worked himself up into a fine old righteous lather.'

'And how did Stafford take it?'

'He just regarded young Denbigh with a rather superior, mocking expression. He let him say his piece, took him by the elbow and steered him from the room, whispering something as they went. I don't know what he said, but I wish I'd overheard it.'

'What happened?' Maria said.

'Exit our young vicar with his tail between his legs,' the actress said. 'And Stafford returned to the library looking rather smug and self-satisfied.'

Boardman gave a lurch and tugged the actress along the path to the woods. Caroline's upper body jolted forward, and she attempted to dig in her heels and slow the dog's mad rush towards

124

the trees. Boardman was not to be denied, however; he strained against the leash, nose questing diligently this way and that across the path.

'He's on to something,' Langham said.

'I must admit I've never seen him like this before. He's usually the most lethargic animal this side of a sloth.'

They entered the shade of the woods and hurried along a worn path through the under-growth. Rasputin trotted along at Langham's side, head in the air, as if disdainful of Boardman's eagerness to assist his mistress.

Seconds later Caroline gave a cry as Boardman sprang forward, tugging the lead from her grip. He gave three loud barks, shattering the sylvan quiet, and burrowed into the undergrowth at the foot of a tall elm tree. Only his back end showed, his tail wagging furiously.

'What have you found, boy?' Langham asked, trampling ferns and taking hold of the dog's collar. He dragged him out of the way and peered into the undergrowth.

Boardman barked again, as if demanding recognition of his conscientiousness. Langham stroked the dog's head. 'Well done, boy,' he said.

He took a step forward and stopped.

He saw the legs first, trouser-clad and ending in a pair of black brogues. The man lay on his back, his long, pale face staring, sightlessly, up at the treetops.

He heard an abbreviated scream, and when he looked back he saw the actress in Maria's arms, sobbing.

He returned his attention to the corpse, as there was no doubting that the man was quite dead. His face was as white as vellum, and the right side of his skull bore a deep, bloodied gash, the flesh parted to the bone.

Maria said, 'It's Edward, isn't it?'

Langham's pulse pounded in his ears. He recognized the face from the photograph. He turned to the women and shook his head.

'No,' he said. 'It's Vivian Stafford.'

ELEVEN

Maria and Caroline hurried back to Endicott's Chase to raise the alarm, accompanied by the dogs.

Langham examined the body from the vantage point of the path. He would have dearly liked to go through the man's pockets in search of identifying documents, but of course that was out of the question. He satisfied himself with making a minute inventory of what he could see of the man's outward appearance and attire. He appeared to be in his late sixties, was bald and gaunt-faced, with a thin-lipped mouth and pronounced Roman nose. He wore shabby tweeds and a faded maroon waistcoat; his right arm was thrown back above his head, while his left arm lay across his chest.

It was hard to tell how long he had lain like this, though by the evidence of the dried blood on the side of his head and face it had been a good number of hours. Rigor mortis had evidently been and gone, as in death the man appeared almost relaxed.

PC Thomson was the first figure of authority on the scene fifteen minutes later. He peered briefly at the corpse with evident distaste, informed Langham that he'd rung through to his superiors in Bury St Edmunds and proceeded to take a brief statement. Ten minutes later Langham returned to Endicott's Chase to await the

127

detective inspector who would conduct a more thorough questioning.

He found Maria and Caroline in the sitting room. Maria sprang up when he entered and they embraced.

'I told Alasdair about the . . .' Caroline said shakily. 'He's making a pot of tea. That seems to be your universal panacea: when in crisis, brew a cuppa.'

'And the stronger the better,' Langham said.

Maria said, 'I think I would prefer a brandy in the circumstances, Donald.'

Alasdair entered with a tray. He looked pale, still suffering the effects of the night before. He deposited the tray on the coffee table and crossed to a drinks cabinet. 'I'll join you, Maria. Hair of the dog. Anyone else?'

'I'll stick to tea,' Langham said, and the actress nodded her agreement.

'I find it hard to believe,' Alasdair murmured, passing Maria a balloon glass containing an inch of brandy.

She seated herself on the wide arm of Langham's chair and nursed her drink.

'Stafford was larger than life,' Alasdair said. 'Who would've . . .?' He looked at Langham. 'Are you certain he was murdered?'

'I'd say so. Bashed pretty severely around the head. Someone wanted him dead, and no mistake.'

'Do you think the blood . . .?' Maria began, gesturing towards the woods behind the Chase.

'It's a pretty safe guess that the blood was Stafford's,' Langham said.

'What do you think happened?'

He considered the options, then said, 'Either Stafford was attacked near the Chase and managed to stagger away from his assailant, until he was apprehended again in the woodland and finished off. Or he was assaulted and killed behind the Chase, then taken by the killer and dumped in the woods.'

'But who would do such a thing?' Alasdair said, more to himself.

Into the following silence Langham dropped, like a stone into a millpond, the thought that had just crossed his mind. 'I'm thinking aloud here. You must admit that it doesn't look good for your father, Alasdair. There's blood discovered behind his house, and then a body not too far away – and there's no sign of Edward. Also, he knew the victim.'

Caroline was shaking her head. 'But he wouldn't do such a thing to anyone, Donald. I know Edward. Violence isn't in his nature.'

'And anyway,' Alasdair said, 'why would my father want Stafford dead? It doesn't make sense. He's working on a book about the man. He wouldn't—'

Langham interrupted. 'On Sunday, Alasdair, when we came here, you wondered aloud if Stafford might be responsible for your father's disappearance. You said that he might have been angered that Edward was investigating his life.'

The young man coloured and stared at the rug.

Langham went on: 'So perhaps Stafford *did* kick up a rumpus. They argued, and maybe Stafford even attacked Edward. In self-defence

129

Edward fought back, killing Stafford in the process. And in panic, he flees . . .'

'I don't think,' Caroline said, 'that Stafford was the kind of man to . . . to assault anyone – physically, that is. He had . . . he had a greater armoury of . . . of powers, let's say, at his disposal.'

Langham stared at her. 'Meaning?'

Caroline shifted uncomfortably on the settee. 'I mean . . . I told you yesterday about what happened at the hall. What he could do, his powers . . . Alasdair will back me up. Stafford is . . . was . . . diabolical. The idea that he would resort to physical violence when he could summon the black arts . . .'

Langham smiled. 'If you don't mind my saying, Caroline, I think all that is hogwash. Stafford was flesh and blood, just like the next man.' He shook his head. 'And anyway, it speaks volumes for his reputed diabolical powers that he ended up dead in the woods, coshed on the head.' He looked questioningly across at Alasdair.

The young man murmured, 'I don't like to think that my father could have . . .'

'How about this,' Langham said. 'How about if Edward *believed* that Stafford was about to bring his occult powers to bear, and he attacked before Stafford could act?'

'But my father is a peaceable man!' Alasdair cried.

'I'm sorry, but even peaceable men, under extreme provocation, can crack – and attack in order to defend themselves.'

Maria said, 'And it does look bad that Edward has gone missing.'

130

'There must be some rational explanation for all this,' Alasdair said pitifully.

Langham opened his mouth to make the obvious comment: that hitherto Alasdair had invoked extreme irrationality to explain events. He held his tongue.

Maria stood up and, nursing her brandy glass, moved to the French windows. '*Attention*, the police . . .'

Two men in blue boiler suits were kneeling beside the path at the end of the garden, accompanied by a uniformed constable and a plain-clothes officer. A minute later the officer looked up and moved down the garden; he approached the French windows and tapped on the glass. Maria let him in.

He introduced himself as Detective Inspector Montgomery, a thin, balding man in a tight-fitting suit that looked a size too small for his slight frame. The effect was to make him appear even smaller, pinched and officious. He had a tiny clipped moustache and quick, suspicious eyes.

His manner was abrupt, bordering on the downright rude. 'Right, who found the body?'

Langham stood up. 'I did, Inspector. I was out walking with . . .' He began gesturing to Maria and Caroline, but the detective interrupted: 'I'll get the details when I question you.' He looked at Alasdair. 'If there's somewhere private where I might conduct the interviews?'

'Quite. Perhaps my father's study . . .'

Montgomery nodded to Langham. 'If you'd care to come this way, sir.'

Langham smiled at Maria and, as he followed the inspector, noticed a uniformed PC slip in through the French windows and station himself at the end of the room.

Alasdair escorted them down the passage and opened the study door. The detective gestured for Langham to enter first, followed him in and closed the door. Langham moved to the hearth and proceeded to light his pipe. Despite the fact that he'd written countless scenes involving police and murder interrogations, he always felt uncomfortable in the presence of on-duty officers.

'You don't mind if I . . .?'

He expected Montgomery to object, but the inspector said, 'Go ahead. I'll join you. Take a seat, Mr . . .?'

'Langham. Donald Langham.' He sat in an armchair beside the hearth.

Montgomery sat opposite and lit a Benson and Hedges, puffed on it while flipping through a notebook until he found a blank page, then wrote down Langham's name and asked for his address.

'Profession?'

'I write detective novels,' he said.

Montgomery looked up, making no attempt to hide his amused expression. 'I've yet to read one that got the procedures right,' he grunted. 'Perhaps you'll use this experience to good effect.'

Langham gestured with his pipe. 'I'll do my very best.'

For the next five minutes he described finding the body, the reason for his and Maria's staying at the Chase, and his acquaintance with its owner, Edward Endicott.

'But you didn't know the deceased?'

'I didn't know him personally; just through what others had said about him. And I'd seen photographs.'

Montgomery looked up. 'When I questioned Alasdair Endicott yesterday he said something about his father writing a book about this fellow. And Edward Endicott had gone AWOL. Still not turned up?'

'Not to my knowledge, no.'

Montgomery puffed on his cigarette, nipping it between thumb and forefinger and leafing through his notes. He read a page and looked up. 'Now according to Alasdair,' he said, 'he and his father believe the deceased to have been over a hundred and twenty years old.'

'So I understand, yes.'

'And I take it that you believe the same?'

'On the contrary. I think the claim ludicrous.'

The officer smiled and muttered, 'Thank Christ I'm not entirely surrounded by nutters. I never said that, OK?'

Langham smiled. He'd taken a liking to the dapper detective, despite his brusque manner. 'I didn't hear a thing.'

'Right. That'll do for now. You're staying here, you say?'

'That's right.'

'Well, don't go haring off anywhere in a hurry. Stick around for a few days. No doubt I'll need to question you again. Right, off you go. If you could send in the women one at a time, and then Alasdair.'

Langham returned to the sitting room and

relayed the inspector's instructions. The actress volunteered to go next. Langham sat on the sofa, finished his tea – cold by this time – and smoked his pipe. Maria sat beside him, from time to time taking sips of her brandy.

He was aware of the baleful presence of the uniformed constable at the end of the room, silhouetted against the sunlight. The dogs lay on the rug, chins resting on their forelegs, oblivious of the tension in the air.

One hour later they had all been questioned – Alasdair was with the inspector for over half an hour and returned looking pale and shaky – and the police took their leave.

'Well,' Alasdair said when they were alone. 'That was hellish. Montgomery was the one who grilled me yesterday. I thought he was pretty gruelling then.'

'That's his job, Alasdair, as I told you earlier. They've got to make you feel uncomfortable.'

The young man shook his head. 'He asked me where my father might be, then asked point blank if I thought it suspicious that he should have vanished.'

'What did you say?' Maria asked.

Alasdair shrugged. 'Muttered something in agreement, I think. I don't know. It's all a blur.' He sighed. 'I don't think he likes me. Went on about my "crackpot" idea that Stafford was a hundred and twenty . . .' He smiled sheepishly. 'I admit that it must sound a little strange to him.'

Langham smiled. 'More than a little, believe me.'

'Well,' Caroline said, 'that's that. I feel as if

134

I've been incarcerated against my will for hours. I just want to get out into the fresh air.'

Alasdair said, 'Look, I know I should be playing the host and offering lunch and all that, but to be perfectly honest I'm done in. Help yourself to whatever's in the kitchen, why don't you? I'm going back to my room.'

Langham looked across at Maria. 'How about we see if they'll rustle up a sandwich at the Three Horseshoes? I could murder a pint.'

'*Très bon*, Donald.' She looked across at Caroline. 'Would you care to join us?'

'Do you know, I think perhaps I would. I might have a drink, if not food. You'll be OK here on your own, Alasdair?' she asked solicitously.

'I'll be fine. See you later.'

Langham knocked the dottle from his pipe into the empty hearth, then followed the women out into the sunlight.

They sat at a table outside the public house. A couple of old men nursed tankards of ale, sitting on either side of the entrance like a pair of bookends. Langham took an experimental sip of his bitter, pronounced it satisfactory and watched the landlady carry a plate across to their table. It felt as if a long time had elapsed since breakfast back at the hotel and he was famished. Maria and Caroline had elected not to eat and had ordered, respectively, a tonic water and a double whisky.

The landlady delivered a plate of Stilton, pickled onions and a thick heel of white bread, and he tucked in.

'I don't know how you can possibly have an appetite, Donald,' Caroline said.

Maria laughed. 'I have never known anything to put Donald off his food, Caroline. He could wolf down roast beef while watching an autopsy.'

'I don't know about that. I didn't have that big a breakfast, and what with the walk . . .'

Boardman slurped water from a bowl beneath the table then settled himself at Caroline's feet.

The actress sipped her whisky. Langham noticed that her hands were shaking and wondered if she were suffering delayed shock. He was about to suggest that, after the drink, she take herself home for a lie down, when she said, 'It's strange, but for all I didn't like Stafford in the slightest, I find the fact of his death . . .' She trailed off, staring down at the grass.

Maria murmured, 'Death is always shocking.'

Caroline looked from Maria to Langham. 'I know what you think about my beliefs regarding Stafford and all this occult business. We approach the matter from completely different perspectives. But,' she stared into her glass, then continued, 'I know what I saw, Donald. I'm no fool. I believe the evidence of my own eyes; we have little more, after all, to go on. And in my experience Stafford was genuine, for want of a better expression.'

Langham sat back, nursed his pint and stared across the village green. Two small children were clambering over the timber stocks and a few ducks were splashing in the pond. He could tell that the actress was suffering from shock, and this time he thought it wise to bridle his scepticism.

She said, 'I don't mind telling you, I'm frightened.'

He lowered his pint. 'Frightened?'

'Of Stafford.'

He squinted at her. 'Stafford's dead,' he said. 'Stone cold. I saw him. *You* saw him.'

She held his gaze with her jade-green eyes and said with deliberation, 'I know he's dead, Donald, and that's why I'm frightened.'

He looked away, took a long swallow of ale in order to give himself time to think, and still couldn't summon an adequate response.

Maria filled the breach. 'Why are you frightened of a dead man, Caroline?'

Langham stared at the actress. He guessed what was coming.

'If you'd seen what he did at the hall, Maria – if you'd seen what he was capable of, then you – both of you – would be frightened too. He proved that there was life beyond death. That the dead are not dead, as we know it, but have merely entered upon another phase of existence.'

'And you think?' Langham prompted, pausing with a wedge of bread and cheese before his mouth.

'I think that Stafford was a dangerous man in life, and I think that he might be even more dangerous – evil – in death.'

Langham said, 'You'll excuse me when I say that I think that's nonsense?'

She smiled, bitter-sweetly. 'I would expect no other response from a rationalist, Donald.'

Maria said, 'But what do you think Stafford, dead, might be able to achieve?'

The actress drained her whisky, her hand trembling. 'That's the truly frightening thing, Maria. The uncertainty. I have no idea what he might be capable of. I simply don't know what to expect. And I find that terrifying. You see . . .' She paused, took a long breath, then continued, '. . . while alive he was, like all of us, constrained by certain laws, both social and judicial. My worry is that in death he will be liberated, free to wreak whatever diabolical revenge he likes upon . . .' She paused.

'Go on.'

'Upon his enemies.'

He exchanged a glance with Maria; she looked worried.

Caroline smiled, her lips trembling. 'I think he might already have . . . have done something to Edward.'

'I think that highly unlikely,' Langham said.

'Then where the hell is he?' Caroline almost shouted at him. 'Answer me that! Where is Edward?' She went on in an urgent whisper: 'It's all too coincidental. The blood in the garden. The body. Edward missing. Do you know what I think?'

Langham closed his eyes, opened them and shook his head. He wondered if he could take much more of this. 'What, Caroline? What do you think?'

'I think Stafford staged it all. Everything. The blood, his death. He'd come to the end of his corporeal usefulness and decided to move on to the next stage. And from there he will seek to get even with his enemies. He and Edward must have had an argument. Maybe Stafford was angered by something Edward had discovered.'

'You think Stafford staged his own death?' Langham said incredulously. 'But that's ridiculous!'

He saw Maria staring murderously at him. She mouthed, *She's fragile, don't you mock!*

Caroline's shoulders shook as she wept. Quickly Maria stood and moved around the table. 'Come, I'll take you home.' She helped the actress to her feet and murmured to Langham, 'Sometimes, Donald, you can be so rude!'

With that she picked up the dog's lead. 'Come on, Boardman. Good dog.'

Her free arm around Caroline's shoulder, Maria walked the woman away from the pub, the blood-hound climbing to his feet and trotting after them.

Langham stared after her, hurt by her words and wondering whether he'd deserved them.

TWELVE

Maria made a pot of tea in the kitchen and carried it out to the garden. Caroline was sitting on a bench surrounded by blooming roses, dabbing at her eyes with a lace handkerchief.

She looked up when Maria emerged. 'That's so kind of you,' she said. 'I'm sorry if I sounded dramatic back there. It's just, I don't know . . . what with Edward missing and all this Stafford business . . .'

Maria sipped her tea and smiled. 'I understand. And I'm sorry if Donald offended you. He can be so . . . intolerant at times.'

'Well, I must have sounded a little crazy to his rationalist way of looking at things.'

Maria sighed. 'Sometimes Donald can only see his own point of view. As I've told him in the past, there are no grey areas with him.'

Caroline lowered her cup to its saucer and smiled at Maria. 'You're very much in love with him, aren't you?'

'Is it so obvious?'

'My dear, you positively glow when you're with him.'

Maria sighed. 'Oh . . . it's sometimes so hard being in love, isn't it?'

'You're telling me, girl!' Caroline laughed. 'But why do you say that?'

Maria took a deep breath and shook her head.

'It's just . . . how to express how I feel? The thing is I love Donald so much it is painful. And . . . And although I'm sure that he loves me in return . . .' She stopped there, wondering whether she should be broaching the subject with someone with their own romantic travails, but at the same time feeling the need to talk. 'Sometimes I fear that it might be a passing thing with Donald, that . . . I don't know . . . that he will think I am taking him away from his work – which has been his life for years and years – and that he will just one day walk out on me.'

Caroline laid a soothing hand on her arm. 'Maria, listen to me. In my long life, with a little experience of men along the way, I recognize love when I see it. And believe me, Donald is smitten.'

Maria sighed. Suddenly, involuntarily, she felt herself on the verge of tears. 'It is just that . . .'

'Out with it, girl,' Caroline said.

'Oh . . . it is just that five years ago I had a . . . a bad experience. I was engaged to be married to a man I loved so very much. He was kind and thoughtful and intelligent, an artist – and I thought he loved me. We were all set to be married. I was planning the future . . . How can you not plan ahead like that? Oh, I saw us living in Paris, and I would have children, a boy and a girl, and . . .' She fell silent, a residue of pain resurfacing to blight the summer's day.

Caroline asked gently, 'What happened?'

'He walked out on me. His father did not approve of me. I was the daughter of a political rival, and he did not want his son marrying into

141

my family. He threatened Philippe that he would cut off his inheritance if he went through with the marriage . . .' She lifted her shoulders in a shrug, 'And he told me one morning . . . he said that he could not marry me, that he could not see me again.'

'Oh, Maria . . .'

She smiled at the actress, determined not to cry. 'But I think that he did not love me truly, yes? I mean, not as I loved him. I think he was getting . . . as the English say . . . cold feet, and he used his father's threat as an excuse to worm his way out of the relationship. But the hurt . . . Caroline, I was so unhappy for months and months. I had constructed a future, and with a few words he had torn it all away.'

Caroline gazed at Maria and said quietly, 'And you fear that Donald will do the same? That, at the last minute, he will get these English cold feet and leave you?'

'Oh, I don't know . . . Perhaps I am being silly and stupid. I love Donald so much, and I trust him, and I cannot see him doing such a thing . . . But there is a small voice at the back of my mind that is warning me not to take the future for granted.'

'Honey, you listen to me. Donald loves you. He's devoted. You should see the way he looks at you. It's so sweet. Mark my words, he wouldn't do anything as hurtful as leave you.'

'But . . .' Maria gestured. 'But why can he not commit himself?'

'You mean ask you to . . .?'

'I know he loves me, and I keep thinking that

one day soon he will ask me to marry him. But when I try to talk about the future . . . it is as if he's afraid of looking so far ahead.'

Caroline smiled. 'It sounds like a straightforward case of English reserve, Maria. Englishmen are prone to it. It's endemic. They find it hard to talk about things like emotion, commitment. My advice would be to give him time. Don't rush things. And he'll come round to it when he's good and ready.'

Maria nodded and sipped her tea. 'I'll do that.' She looked around the garden and changed the subject. 'Oh, all this is magnificent, Caroline.'

'Why, thank you,' Caroline said. 'I would never have thought that I'd get so absorbed in gardening. Ten years ago I would have laughed at the idea.'

'Were you still in Hollywood then?' Maria asked.

'I was just about to leave,' she said. 'I'd been there, working in the industry, for almost twenty years.'

'But you must have started when the movies were silent.'

'That's right. Makes me sound old, doesn't it?'

Maria leaned forward. 'How did you get into acting and Hollywood?'

'My, don't ask! I loved drama as a child. I was in all the plays at school. And then I met a young man – this was in my home town of Hoboken, New York – who was bitten by the acting bug too. So we hitchhiked to LA with stars in our eyes . . . and soon parted when things didn't work out. I think he went back to New York a year or so later, but I stuck it out.' Her eyes clouded as she thought back over the years. 'I was determined to succeed.' She smiled bitterly. 'Come hell or high water. And I did . . . For all the good that came of it.'

'But you were a big star, Caroline.'

'I was a mediocre actress in a string of poor B movies, with one or two good performances in among. But I came to hate the place as the years went by, and despise the people. I really couldn't take all the insincerity. That's what happens when a lot of ambitious people come together in one place, all competing for one thing: in this case, fame. It breeds dishonesty, insincerity. I saw it all around me – but do you know what shocked me most?'

'No,' Maria murmured.

'I recognized it in *myself*, in my everyday dealings with the people I met. It was as if I were playing a part. I found myself saying things that were contrary to what I really felt and thought, as if I were mouthing lines written by some Machiavellian scriptwriter. And the reason I was doing this was because everyone around me was doing the same – we all wanted to impress, to flatter, to ruffle no feathers, because we all wanted to get on, to succeed, to be the next big star.'

She sipped her tea and stared into the distance.

'I woke up one morning and was struck by a revelation. I realized the sham I was living. I'd just been awarded a part in an RKO thriller, a role I'd wanted for months. And do you know something? When I landed the part I realized that it really didn't matter. I wasn't cast because I was the most talented actress out there. I was cast because my face fit, because I'd been to a few parties thrown by the director and I knew the casting people. So the film would be made, and then I'd be looking around for the next role . . . and wanting *that* one more than I'd wanted any other. But all for what? It took a long time to dawn on me what a futile charade it all was, and that morning I achieved some kind of epiphany. Of course,' she smiled, 'it helped that I knew Edward.'

'How did you meet?' Maria said.

'At a party in 'thirty-five. I like to think there was a mutual attraction from the start. I know I found him fascinating, but the English,' she laughed, 'are so aloof. Edward was standoffish to begin with. He was probably suspicious of this gushing starlet coming on to him. I only stuck at the place so long because he was there.'

'Wasn't he married at the time?' Maria asked.

'He was,' Caroline said. 'To a mean-spirited, rather unattractive woman – but then I was biased. I don't think it was a happy marriage, and I guessed they were making a go of it because of Alasdair. Anyway, Edward and I became good friends over the years; he helped me see the sham that was Hollywood. He was level-headed, honest, and wouldn't kow-tow to anyone. This lost him work, of course, but he was good at his job and the studios knew it. He wrote about thirty movie scripts in the five or six years he was in Hollywood.'

She shook her head. 'And then his wife died. Cancer, over a period of three or four months.' She looked at Maria. 'And I'm not proud of what

145

I felt then, but a part of me rejoiced. I thought that, without Mary around, then we . . .' She shook her head. 'Not long after Mary died, perhaps a month, I told Edward what I felt for him – and realized that I'd badly misjudged the situation. He was horrified. He'd assumed that we shared a deep and abiding friendship – nothing more. He had this strange notion of faithfulness to his wife. It was as if he'd be sullying her memory if he were to start an affair so soon after her passing, almost as if it would be adultery. I couldn't understand this, of course. There I was, a liberal New York girl . . .' She waved, then laughed. 'Edward left America in 'thirty-nine and returned to England. I pined for years, hating LA more and more every day, but stuck it out until the war ended. Then I packed my few belongings, booked a flight and fled to Merry Olde England.'

'If you don't mind my asking,' Maria said, 'how did Edward take this?'

Caroline laughed. 'Listen to me, opening up like this. What is it about you? I feel as if I've known you for years. I hope you don't mind my babbling?'

Maria smiled. 'Of course not.'

'How did Edward react? Well, I contacted him from London, said I was over for a holiday and suggested we met up. We dined in the Savoy, of all places, and it was as if we'd never been separated, as if the war hadn't intervened. But Edward made it obvious, even when I told him that I intended to settle in Britain, that he couldn't see us being anything other than just good friends. He even couched his put-down in just such language: '"Can't see us being anything other than good friends, Carrie."'

'That old English reserve again.'

'Too true,' Caroline said. 'Anyway, I considered cutting my losses and fleeing back to the States, but I'm glad I didn't. I lived in London for a few years, and when Rosebud Cottage came on the market I bought it and moved up to the village, and Edward and I resumed our platonic friendship. And, all things considered, I'm happy with that. It's better to have Edward as a friend than not to have him at all, despite his reluctance.'

Maria sipped her tea, aware of the sadness in actress's words.

Caroline smiled. 'Nowadays he works like a demon and from time to time we meet for dinner and drinks.'

Maria shrugged, at a loss what to say. 'I'm sorry,' she managed at last.

'I suppose I should be thankful for what I've got.' Caroline smiled brightly. 'But don't let my story of romantic woe disillusion you, Maria. You've got a wonderful man in Donald. Just let him take his time is my advice.'

Maria smiled. 'Thank you, Caroline.'

They had a second cup of tea, chatted about Maria's work in London, and fifteen minutes later she hugged the actress and made her way from Rosebud Cottage.

THIRTEEN

Langham was on his second pint when Maria returned, sat down without looking at him and picked up the remains of her tonic water.

'I say, Maria, I'm sorry if I . . .'

She glanced at him. 'Donald, couldn't you have kept silent? You saw how upset she was.'

'But she was talking nonsense—'

Maria sighed. 'I agree, yes. But even so, she was in a delicate state, and you should have been aware of that. Why are men so insensitive sometimes?'

Langham shrugged. 'I'm sorry. You're right. I should have thought before putting my foot in it.'

She smiled at him. 'Well, I suppose I shouldn't have got angry with you either.'

He found her hand and squeezed. 'I say,' he said hesitantly. 'Are you all right? I mean, you've been quiet on and off lately. I know all this business hasn't helped, but . . .'

She stared at him as if calculating something. At last she said, 'You do love me, Donald, don't you?'

He stared at her, surprised. 'Of course I do! You know that. More than anything.'

'Only . . .'

He felt something turn to ice in his stomach and felt suddenly sick. 'What?' he said. 'What is it?'

She looked down at her empty glass. 'I've never told you this before, Donald.'

'Told me what?' he echoed, fearing the worst.

'Donald . . . five years ago I was engaged to be married.'

'You were?' He felt an odd, irrational stab of jealousy towards her erstwhile suitor. 'I didn't know.'

She smiled at him. 'How should you have known, Donald? I told no one, not even Charles. I kept it to myself.'

'What happened?' he asked, though he could guess. She had called off the marriage, walked out on the hapless man. Was this a precursor to telling him that she was doing the same now?

She said, avoiding his eyes, 'He called off our wedding, left me. I . . . naturally I was upset. However, I overcame the disappointment, but . . .'

He swallowed, feeling sick to his stomach. 'But you never got over your love for . . . for *him* . . . is that it? And now—'

She laughed. 'Oh, Donald! You silly man, of course I got over him! Only, you see . . .' She stared down at her entwined fingers, then looked up at him. 'I love you, Donald. But . . . how can I be sure that you feel the same for me? How can I be sure that one day you will not do the same as . . . as him, and walk out on me?'

He reached out impulsively and took her hand, his heart leaping with relief. 'Maria, my God . . . You had me worrying there for a minute, old girl. Of course I love you, more than anything in the world.'

'And you haven't had second thoughts?'

'Second thoughts? Of course not! If you think I'd walk out on the best thing that's ever happened to me . . . then you don't know Donald Langham.'

She stared at him and tears appeared in her eyes. 'Oh, thank you, Donald.'

'Well, now that we've got all that cleared up, I see your glass is empty.'

'I'll have another tonic water, please.'

'Coming up,' he said, and hurried to the bar.

As he returned with the drink, Langham noticed Marcus Denbigh step through the lychgate of St Andrew's and cross the green towards them.

The vicar tipped his straw hat. 'Donald, Maria. I've just heard the terrible news.' He sat down and leaned forward. 'Vivian Stafford. He was found dead just before lunch, in the woods south of the hall. Apparently he was beaten about the head.'

Maria said, 'It was Donald who discovered the body, vicar.'

'Well,' Langham said, 'technically speaking it was Boardman. But I wasn't that far behind.'

'Old Derek Thomson came to see me,' Denbigh said. 'He was the first bobby on the scene. Fair shook him up. I don't think he'd seen a body before this one.'

Langham sipped his pint. 'I wonder who disliked Stafford enough to . . .?'

The vicar fanned himself with his straw hat. 'I can't begin to imagine, Donald. He was a rather strange fellow, with very odd views, but why anyone would attack him like that . . .'

Langham drained his bitter. 'You know, of course, what the Endicotts, both Edward and Alasdair, believed about Stafford?'

The vicar blinked. 'I'm sorry?'

'They didn't tell you how old they thought he was?'

Enlightenment showed on the young man's face. 'Oh – oh, that? Alasdair did mention it. Piffle, of course.'

'You didn't believe him?'

'Of course not, Donald. What do you take me for?'

Langham smiled. 'So . . . who in your opinion was this Stafford character?'

Denbigh regarded his feet, looking uneasy. 'If you want to know what I think . . . Stafford was a relation of the Victorian. I don't know – maybe a grandson. Apparently there was a resemblance between the real Stafford and the man claiming to be him. I do know that he was dangerous, however.'

'Dangerous in his beliefs?'

'Quite,' Denbigh said, and rose to his feet as if reluctant to pursue that line of thought. 'I'll be saying a few words about Stafford during tomorrow's service at eleven, if you'd care to attend.'

Maria smiled up at him. 'That would be nice, Reverend.'

'We'll be there,' Langham added.

Denbigh waved. 'I'd better be pushing off, then. Sick parishioner in the next village,' he explained.

When Denbigh had departed, Maria said, 'You don't object to going to the service?' She sounded surprised.

'On the contrary. I'm interested in what Denbigh has to say about the satanist. It might be enlightening.'

'A busy day tomorrow, Donald. Church in the morning and Dent's show in the afternoon.'

'I'd forgotten all about the art show,' Langham said. 'I don't know if I can keep up with the social whirl.'

'It's more hectic than living in London,' she laughed.

He stared into his empty glass. 'That slipped down a treat. Would you mind awfully if I had a third?'

'Only if you buy me a G and T at the same time.'

'On top of the brandy? You're pushing the boat out, aren't you?'

They leaned forward and kissed.

He collected the empty glasses and stood up – then sat back down, quickly. 'Well, blow me down.'

'What is it?' Maria said, swivelling in her seat.

A tall, thick-set man in his sixties was striding down the lane towards the public house. He carried a backpack, swung a long staff and smiled beatifically as if all was well with the world.

'Donald?' Maria said. 'What's wrong? Who is it?'

He shook his head. 'Well, blow me down,' he said again. 'If it isn't Edward Endicott!'

FOURTEEN

Endicott approached their table and pointed his staff at Langham. 'Donald? Good God, it is! Donald Langham! What on earth brings you to this neck of the woods?'

Langham laughed. 'As a matter of fact, you do.'

'Hmm. I think this calls for a drink. What's yours?'

'Best bitter.'

'And for you, my dear?'

Maria stared up at the man, her eyes wide in surprise. 'Ah, I will have a gin and tonic, please.'

Endicott propped his staff against the table and strode into the pub. Langham shook his head. 'Well . . . I must admit that I was beginning to fear the worst.'

'What? That Edward . . .?'

'That he was responsible and scarpered.'

She gripped his arm. 'Just wait until Alasdair and Caroline find out he's safe and well!'

'I'm looking forward to seeing their expressions.'

Endicott emerged from the pub clutching two pints and a gin and tonic. He sat down and Langham introduced Maria.

'Delighted,' Endicott said.

He was a big man who carried excess pounds with the enthusiasm of an overweight schoolboy;

153

in fact, Endicott had always put Langham in mind of a boy scout, with his gung-ho vitality and his big open face. Only his greying thatch and liverish lips betrayed his advancing years.

He sat down at their table and accounted for half of his pint in a single swallow. 'By God, that's better. Been on the road since six. Now, what's all this about my bringing you here?'

'Where to begin? Well, I think there's been some mix-up between you and Alasdair. He came up on Sunday expecting you to be at home, and when he didn't find you I think he flapped rather. He found your study locked from the inside, you see.'

Endicott laughed. 'Silly young pup! He told me he'd be up on the *second* Sunday of the month. Last Sunday was the first. But that's Alasdair all over – gets confused then flies into a tizzy. As for the blasted study, I stepped outside on Saturday morning just as I was due to set off and the damned French window blew shut and the catch dropped, locking me out.'

'That's what I told Alasdair,' Langham said, rather pleased that his theory had been proven correct. A small victory for the forces of rationalism.

'Couldn't be bothered to break the catch so I went on my way. There's nothing like a few days under canvas to blow out the cobwebs.' He snorted. 'Pity Rasputin didn't think the same. Upped sticks and ran off on Sunday. Done it before. I expect he hightailed it back here.'

'Caroline found him,' Maria said. 'She was rather worried, too.'

'She was? Dash it, isn't a man allowed to take a few days off without telling the whole damned village?' He took another long draught of beer and eyed Langham. 'So how did you get involved?'

'I met Alasdair at a do in London on Saturday, and when he found you missing on Sunday he rang me.' He shrugged. 'I once worked for a detective agency, and Alasdair asked if I'd come up and take a look. The locked room rather spooked him.'

Endicott grunted. 'Hmm. Suppose it would.'

'Apparently he rang you on Friday, but there was no answer.'

'Of course there wasn't! I was working in the folly.' Endicott shook his head then drained his beer. 'Well, I suppose I should get back to the Chase and put Alasdair out of his misery.'

Langham hesitated, then said, 'There is one other thing . . .'

Endicott stood, shouldered his backpack, and looked down at Langham. 'Yes?'

'Ah . . . Well,' he said, watching Endicott's reaction closely, 'I'm afraid to say that Vivian Stafford was found dead this morning.'

The big man slumped back down on to the seat. He stared at Langham. 'Stafford? Dead?'

'I was with Maria and Caroline, and we came across the body in the woods. It appeared that he'd been hit over the head with something sharp.'

It was as if the blood had drained from Endicott's face. 'Stafford . . . *dead*?' he said. 'But . . .' He gestured ineffectually. 'But . . . he was

155

due to hold another "Evening of the Occult" up at the hall next week . . .'

'I'm sorry.'

Langham watched the man as he shook his head and stared across the green. Was Endicott experiencing the regular shock that was to be expected when you heard that the subject of your studies had passed away, or the disbelief at finding that someone who you had assumed immortal was nothing of the sort?

'But who would do such a thing?' Endicott murmured to himself.

'Perhaps we'd better be getting back to the Chase. Alasdair kindly invited us to stay . . .' Langham explained.

'Yes. Yes, of course,' Endicott said abstractedly.

They left the pub and crossed the green, the big man lost in thought. Langham was aware of the stares from two or three locals who'd no doubt heard – on the village telegraph – that Edward had gone missing.

They came to the Chase and Endicott crunched down the gravelled drive. Rasputin galloped from the house, barking, and romped up to his owner.

'Down, boy, you great idiot. Running off like that!'

Alasdair appeared at the door, his expression phasing from mild curiosity to disbelief, and finishing with delight as he beheld the larger-than-life figure of Edward Endicott.

'Father!'

He rushed from the house and paused, quite unsure, in the presence of Langham and Maria, how to greet his father.

Endicott acted for him – clapping Alasdair on the shoulder and leading him into the house. 'Bit of a mix-up, son. You said you were coming up on the second Sunday – next week. So I decided to go for a hike.'

Langham and Maria followed them into the sitting room and Endicott boomed, 'Look here, I'm famished. Rustle up a thick beef sandwich, would you, Alasdair? I'll be down when I've had a hot bath.'

Maria said, 'I wonder if I should phone Caroline with the news? She was worried . . .'

Endicott said, 'Go ahead. Tell her to come over. We'll have a spot of tea, hmm, and you can fill me in on everything that's been going on.' His face fell as he stared at Langham. 'Stafford . . . *Dead*?' He shook his head. 'I must admit, I find it hard to believe.'

Thirty minutes later Caroline Dequincy hammered at the front door and Langham let her in. She appeared radiant, breathless, and her first words were, 'I can't believe it! This is wonderful. I was beginning to think . . .' She peered down the gloomy hall. 'Where is he?'

'Taking a bath,' he said. 'He should be down in a few minutes.'

They moved to the sitting room where Alasdair was arranging a table with china cups and a big pot of tea. Boardman greeted Rasputin and they trotted off through the open French windows and rolled around on the lawn.

'And he'd taken himself off hiking without telling a soul?' Caroline asked.

Alasdair nodded. 'I got the weekend wrong. Told the old man I'd be up on the second Sunday and came last Sunday instead.'

Caroline laughed, gay with relief. 'Didn't I say he'd probably gone camping? And here he is,' she said, jumping to her feet as Endicott stepped through the door.

She crossed the room and hugged him. 'You silly man! You had us all worried. Why didn't you tell anyone!'

'Steady on, old girl. Can't a man abscond these days without telling all and sundry? Anyway, I'm back – and things've been happening in my absence, I've heard?'

Caroline resumed her seat, dabbing at her eyes with a small lace kerchief. 'You've heard about Stafford?'

'Donald broke the news. What I don't understand is who the bally hell would do him in?'

Langham said, 'Well, from what I hear he wasn't well liked.' He paused, and chose his next words with care. 'Those who didn't believe his claims to be the Victorian Stafford thought him an impostor.'

'That's no reason to want the man dead,' Endicott thundered.

'No,' Langham said, sipping his tea, 'but it begs the question – why the charade? Why was he claiming to be Stafford? If he had an ulterior motive then it's my guess that this had something to do with his death.'

Endicott gestured at Langham with his gargantuan beef and mustard sandwich. 'But there was no ulterior motive, Donald. Because there was no charade. He wasn't an impostor. He was the real McCoy. Listen here, I've read damn near everything there is to read about the man, I've done all the research and talked to him, and there's only one explanation . . . Confound it, I've seen him at work. We all have. Everyone who experienced one of Stafford's events will tell you the same. He was a bona fide occultist—'

'I don't think Haverford Dent would agree with you,' Langham said, resting his empty cup on its saucer and balancing them on the arm of the chair.

Endicott waved. 'Dent's a purblind rationalist,' he said. 'Can't see the wood for the trees.'

Langham looked from Endicott to Alasdair, and then to Caroline; he saw the light of conviction in their eyes and had the sudden, uneasy feeling that he was in the minority on the issue. He glanced at Maria for support, and was cheered by her quick grimace.

He stared at Endicott. 'So you're seriously trying to tell me that this man, this Vivian Stafford, born in . . . what was it? . . . 1835, was alive and kicking until just recently?'

Endicott held his gaze. 'That's exactly what I'm saying, Donald.'

Langham nodded, phrasing his next question. 'And . . . are you aware of how he achieved this miraculous feat of longevity?'

Endicott licked his liverish lips. He stared at Langham. 'I was working up to asking Stafford about his . . . his immortality,' he said. 'And now I'll never have the chance.'

'Perhaps he sold his soul to the Devil, Edward?

That's supposed to be one way to achieve immortality, isn't it?'

'You mock at your peril, Donald. You really shouldn't scoff at what you don't understand.' Endicott tried to make his voice light and bantering, but Langham detected an underlying tone of seriousness which made him uneasy.

Maria, bless her, weighed into the debate. 'And anyway, what I don't understand is how someone who is immortal . . .' she shrugged, '. . . how he could be killed like this, with a simple blow to the head?'

Endicott said, 'His enemies have ways and means, my dear, perhaps beyond our comprehension. It might appear that he died simply of a blow to the head, but the injury might disguise the real, more arcane method of despatch.'

It was all Langham could do to stop himself from snorting in derision.

Caroline said, 'I was worried, Edward. When you went missing . . . and then the blood was discovered at the end of the garden . . .'

'Blood? Stafford's?'

Alasdair shrugged. 'That's the assumption, anyway.'

'So he was attacked here and his body moved?' Endicott said.

'Or he was attacked,' Langham said, 'and managed to stagger away to where he eventually fell and died.'

'And when we found him dead, Edward,' the actress said, 'and you were still missing . . . well, I was worried that he, that he might have . . . from beyond the grave . . .'

Endicott crossed to her and gripped her hand. 'No need to worry now, Carrie, hmm? I'm home and safe.'

Langham looked at Caroline, who stared up at Endicott as he sat on the arm of her chair. 'And you don't know how good it is to have you back!' she said.

'I suppose the constabulary will want to ask me a few questions,' Endicott said. 'Alasdair, go and phone them, would you, and tell them that I've turned up.' He looked at Langham. 'Best to get this out of the way.'

Langham finished his tea and said to Maria, 'I don't know about you, but I wouldn't mind stretching my legs.'

They stepped through the French windows and strolled the length of the lawn. Langham sat down on a sturdy timber bench beneath a flowering cherry tree and looked back at the Chase. It appeared idyllic in the bright afternoon sunlight, mantled in wisteria and Virginia creeper.

She turned to him; he could tell from the sudden animation in her features that something had occurred to her. 'I know . . . why don't we get away this evening, Donald? Do you recall that nice hotel in Bury St Edmunds where we dined back in April? Why don't we go there for a meal tonight?'

'Capital idea. I'll ring through and book a table right away.'

He was in the hallway five minutes later, speaking to the local operator, when the police arrived and took Edward Endicott away for questioning.

161

FIFTEEN

Caroline sat in a comfortable armchair in Edward Endicott's study and gave up on reading her novel. She had helped herself to a small gin earlier, and now she drained the glass and poured another. The old house creaked and settled itself around her after the hot summer's day. Through the French windows she made out the flicker of bats in the light of the patio. Distantly she heard the high, sharp bark of a fox.

She laid her book aside and thought about Edward. She supposed that, from the point of view of the ferrety little inspector, Montgomery, it did look suspicious that Edward should have disappeared from the scene around the time that Stafford was murdered. But the police were in ignorance of Edward's relationship with the satanist: it was absurd even to contemplate for one second that Edward should kill off the man he had become interested in over the course of the past few weeks. No, they would release him when they realized they were barking up the wrong tree.

She wondered what Edward would do now that his muse was no longer around to occupy him. She smiled to herself when she realized that perhaps nothing much would change; Edward would continue with his book and research

162

Stafford's life, albeit without the man himself to aid in that research.

She was glad that Donald and Maria were around. They were the kind of people, she thought, who might, given time and the right circumstances, become good friends. Donald was humorous and down to earth, spoke plainly and without affectation, and concealed a practical intelligence behind his banter. And Maria was by turns droll and as sharp as a scalpel. It was clear that the couple were very much in love and, while Caroline found that refreshing to see, there was nevertheless a part of her that could not help but be jealous. It was hard to watch people who were in love, and whose love was reciprocated, without resenting the fact that this was denied her.

She sipped her gin, told herself to buck up her ideas, and resumed reading.

Fifteen minutes later the front door opened and she sat up in anticipation of Edward's arrival. The study door was open a fraction; he would see the light on and come to see who was burning the midnight oil. When the door did open, however, it was not Edward who appeared but Alasdair.

He blinked. 'Oh, Caroline.'

'I hope you don't mind? I couldn't go home with Edward being taken away for questioning like this . . . It is OK if I stay until he gets back?'

'By all means. I thought he'd be back by now.' He hesitated by the door. 'They'll release him tonight, won't they?' He moved to the overstuffed sofa on the opposite side of the hearth from her and sat down.

'Of course they will,' she said. 'They don't have a thing on him. He might have gone missing when Stafford was killed, but . . .' She gestured. 'They can't pin a motive on him and there were no witnesses.'

'But there were no witnesses, according to my father, to say that they saw him out hiking over the weekend.'

She smiled. 'The onus is on the police to prove his guilt, not for Edward to prove his innocence. Believe me, you have nothing to worry about. Edward wouldn't do anything like . . . like that, even in anger. Anyway,' she went on, changing the subject, 'where have you been till almost midnight?'

He coloured suddenly and stammered something about taking a constitutional.

'Alasdair, you can be honest with me. How's Marcus?'

He looked up quickly and said, 'What . . .? I mean, why do you ask?'

'Edward mentioned that you two were friends.'

He turned, if this were possible, an even deeper shade of scarlet and stared down at his fingers. 'We've known each other a long time,' he said. 'We are good friends.'

She took a sip of gin, regarding him. 'Despite the fact that you hold diametrically opposite views on the fundamentals of existence?'

A smile flickered on his thin face. 'That doesn't seem to get in the way,' he said.

She laughed. 'No, the idea that couples should

be philosophically compatible is vastly overrated, in my opinion. What matters is that there should be a meeting of the soul.'

Alasdair sat on the sofa, frozen, like a rabbit caught in the headlights of a car. 'You don't . . . don't disapprove of . . . of . . .'

'Of you and Marcus? Good God, Alasdair, life is short enough, and love and affection hard enough to find without worrying who might approve of it or disapprove. I've lived long enough to know that you should grasp the opportunity when it comes, and damn the naysayers to hell. But just listen to me! I sound like a maiden aunt dispensing second-hand wisdom!' Or a frustrated middle-aged woman wishing that she could take her own advice, she thought.

He smiled. 'I don't know . . . It's so damnably difficult, Caroline.'

'I can imagine.'

'Marcus is torn in two, mentally. That damned Church of his, its outmoded morality . . . It disgusts me!' He looked up from his knotted hands. 'Did you know that he's on drugs to help him get through the day?'

'Drugs?'

'Oh, prescription drugs. Some kind of antidepressant. He presents such a positive face to the world nobody would believe what he's going through. He comes over as so bright and alive when the reality is that he's tortured inside.'

'I don't know what to say, Alasdair. Stand by him. That's all you can do, really. Be there for him and don't give a damn what the world thinks

165

or says, which might be easy for me to say, but still . . .'

He smiled at her, then sighed and looked at the carriage clock on the mantelshelf. 'My word, is that the time? I'd better be turning in. I take it you'll be going to Dent's show?'

She laughed without humour. 'I expect I'll be there to see what travesties of so-called art he's foisting on the world now. Good night, Alasdair.'

She listened to the creak of floorboards as he walked back through the hallway and up the stairs. She glanced at the clock – it was almost midnight – and decided that another small gin would be permissible.

She would never, she thought as she sipped the drink, cease to be amazed at how small-minded people could be when it came to judging the relationships of others. She could only guess at the outraged reaction of villagers to the idea that their vicar might be conducting an illicit affair with another young man. She supposed that Edward himself was guilty of the same insular views, too; it was the one aspect of his character – his innate conservatism – that she found not to her liking.

The front door opened and slammed shut, and booted treads sounded down the hallway. There was no doubting, this time, that Edward had arrived home.

The study door swung open and Edward stared at her. 'Carrie? Didn't expect you to be here.'

And it's wonderful to see you, too, she thought.

He was such a big man in every sense: big physically, in his marine flannels like some

166

yachting captain just off the boat at Cowes, and big in that his presence seemed to fill the room no matter where he was. She recalled the first time she'd met him in Hollywood, at a small party thrown by a director to celebrate the start of a film shoot. Edward had entered the room and seemed immediately to dominate it with his genial English bonhomie. She had always thought that love at first sight was the retroactive illusion of incurable romantics, but she had been smitten from the second she'd set eyes on Edward Endicott.

She said, 'I couldn't stand the thought of going home with you still . . .'

He dropped into the sofa recently vacated by his son and said, 'Be Mum and pour me a bloody big double, would you?'

She picked up the crystal decanter and poured a stiff whisky into a shot glass. 'How did it go?'

He shrugged his big shoulders. 'I suppose they were only doing their duty. And looking at it from their point of view, I admit it must look pretty rum. Me skedaddling like that, and then the corpse turning up.'

She hesitated, then said, 'I must admit, I'm a little . . .'

He stared across at her. 'Out with it, woman.'

'Frightened,' she finished.

'Don't be. The police are only doing their duty. I'm as innocent as a new-born, so don't go crying on my account.'

She smiled. 'Actually, I was thinking more of . . . of what Stafford might do.' She looked up at him, then around her at the study, and shivered.

'I don't know . . . but don't you ever get the feeling that . . . that he's watching us?'

'I know what you mean, old girl. Watching us from the other side. Well, if anyone is, it'd be Stafford. But I shouldn't worry yourself on that score. He wouldn't have any gripes with us, would he?'

'Alasdair's worried that Stafford was upset about something you might write about him.'

Edward shook his head. 'Stafford never mentioned anything of the kind, and he thought you charming.'

This was news to her. 'He did?'

'Said as much once. "Charming and intelligent", his exact words.'

What a hypocritical old cad Stafford had been, she thought.

She hugged herself, staring across at Edward as he nursed his whisky and contemplated his outstretched legs. She wanted to confess everything to him: her past, her big mistake – which somehow Vivian Stafford had found out about – but there would be no way that someone like Edward, with his rather restricted views on moral probity, would accept her after learning of her past indiscretions.

Another thing she wanted to confess to Edward, but thought it wise not to, was her meeting with Stafford on Saturday evening . . . and her threat to kill him.

She tried to suppress the thought.

She said, surprising herself, 'I sometimes wonder where all this is leading, Edward.'

He blinked at her. 'Come again?'

She shrugged. 'This. Us. Me and you. Where is it leading?'

'Don't quite get your drift, Carrie.'

She sighed. He could be wilfully obtuse at times. 'I'm talking about feelings, Edward. *Our* feelings. Mine for you. Yours for me.' She wondered if it were the gin talking, prompting her to say things she had not said for years.

'Oh. I see.' He shifted uncomfortably.

She poured herself another drink, took a mouthful and went on: 'How long have we known each other?'

'Oh. Now let's see . . .' He seemed to perk up, now that she had stopped talking about awkward things like feelings and had moved on to more manageable, factual things like dates. 'We met in late 'thirty-four, wasn't it? Or was it 'thirty-five? So what'd that be? Twenty years. Almost twenty-one.'

'Over twenty years . . .' she murmured to herself in amazement. She'd been in her mid-thirties then, in her physical prime – and if she hadn't been able to attract him then, she thought, what chance did she have now? Twenty years spent pining after a man who thought little or nothing of her . . . No, she chastised herself, that was unfair; she was sure that Edward did, in his own limited way, care a little for her.

'Lot of water under the bridge,' he said maddeningly.

'And in all that time,' she said, before she could stop herself, 'all I've ever wanted is for us to be together like a normal, loving couple.'

He coloured suddenly, reminding her of his

169

son. 'Steady on, Carrie,' he said as if chastising a recalcitrant horse.

She slammed down her glass on the arm of the chair. 'I won't "steady on", dammit! I'll say what I have to say. And it isn't,' she went on, staring at him, 'as if I haven't said all this before . . . or have you conveniently forgotten?'

'Carrie . . .' He stared at his feet, uncomfortable.

'You know what I feel about you, Edward. Why can't you at least acknowledge that?'

He looked across at her. 'I've told you. After Mary. After what happened. I . . . I didn't want to go through all that again.'

'Edward, you can't let an experience like that blight your life, your relationships! Christ, no one would ever grow, emotionally, if they let bad experiences sour everything they did.'

'You don't know what it was like. It was hell being married to her – and hell when she died. The guilt. I . . . I thought in some odd way that it was my fault, her dying like that. I thought my taking her off to the States as I did, against her will, somehow contributed to her illness.'

'That's ridiculous, Edward, and you know it.'

He shrugged. 'Maybe, but it's a fact. Once bitten . . .'

She sighed. That was another thing that angered her about him, his refuge in silly clichés and platitudes.

She said, 'I've told you I was married briefly before I met you.'

'That's right. A cad. Beat you about, didn't he?'

'I thought I loved him. He was an actor. We

170

met at drama school. He was young, handsome, caring, or so I thought at the time. Only when I started getting parts, became successful, he couldn't handle it. He wasn't really very good, and he resented my little talent, and my luck. He started drinking and turned violent.'

He muttered, 'Must've been hellish, Carrie.'

'Oh, it was. It was hellish having all my love spurned, turned against me, and then hellish falling out of love and feeling guilty.'

'I'm sorry.'

She smiled. 'What I'm trying to say, Edward, is that I didn't let that bad experience make me bitter. I haven't let it blind me to the possibility of finding someone, and when you came along . . . I know I've said this before, and I know you'll just spurn me again . . . but I love you, and I wish you could find it in your heart to accept that and feel something for me in return.'

She stood up, and only when she did so did she realize how unsteady she was on her feet. She swayed a little, staring down at him. 'Think about what I've said, Edward. I'm not asking that we marry, or even live together. Just that you . . . you *respond*.'

She stopped there, before she became angry and spoiled things even further. 'I'll see myself out.'

She was at the study door when he looked up and said, 'Carrie, you know that I do care for you, in my own way.'

She smiled, tearfully, and slipped from the room.

She hurried from the Chase and down the

gravelled drive. A full moon was out, illuminating the silent countryside. *In your own way*, she thought as she strode down the lane. Which was exactly the problem.

Somewhere off to her right, in the elms, an owl gave its lonely call.

SIXTEEN

Langham woke at eight the following morning and blinked up at the stipple-plastered ceiling between the blackened oak beams. Sunlight streamed in through the window as he'd forgotten to draw the curtains late last night when they'd returned from the Midland. The dinner had been wonderful, bringing back fond memories of their first meal there three months ago. They had talked about everything except what had happened at Humble Barton, and it was a relief to clear their minds of recent events and consider other things: books, the plays they'd seen together recently and the forthcoming films they hoped to catch. At one point he'd even wondered, as the evening was going so well, whether he should pop the all-important question, but decided, what with the shadow of the murder hanging over them, that the time was not quite right.

The bathroom across the landing was vacant at eight thirty, so he drew himself a hot bath and stewed for twenty minutes. He dressed, tapped on the communicating door between his and Maria's bedroom, and on receiving no reply opened the door a fraction and peered in. Maria was still asleep, her hair mussed, her face child-like without make-up. He retreated and descended to the kitchen.

He found Alasdair attaching a lead to Rasputin's collar.

'Edward?' Langham asked.

'He didn't get back till a little after midnight. They gave him a thorough grilling, asked him to detail his movements since leaving here on Saturday.' Alasdair gestured to the table. 'Help yourself to toast. And there's a pot of tea on the Aga. I'm just going to take the hound for his constitutional.'

Langham poured himself a cup of black tea, buttered a round of toast and added a dollop of marmalade, then stepped out on to the patio. He sat at a small table in the sunlight, thinking that breakfast al fresco was something he was unable to enjoy back at his Notting Hill flat.

He was on his second slice of toast when Edward Endicott joined him, slapping a copy of the *Daily Express* down on the table and almost falling into the opposite chair.

'God, I'm tired. Didn't sleep a wink.'

'I heard the constabulary kept you up.'

'And how. Thought I'd never get away. Four bloody hours they kept at it, going over the same old ground. I swear I didn't know whether I was on this earth or Fuller's by the time they let me go.'

'Detective Inspector Montgomery?'

'That's the chap. Small, ferrety – in more ways than just his appearance. He sank his teeth in and wouldn't let go.'

'Well,' Langham ventured, 'you did mysteriously vanish rather coincidentally.'

He watched Endicott closely as he said this,

174

but the big man didn't bat an eyelid or demur. 'Oh, I know they're just doing their job, Donald. But I wish they'd left it until this morning. And when I did finally get to bed, dog tired as I was, I couldn't drop off. Couldn't help thinking of Stafford, dead. Hard to believe, poor man.'

Langham shrugged. 'As the Reverend Denbigh might phrase it, he's been called to his eternal reward.'

Endicott cocked an eye. 'Are you taking the Mickey, Donald?'

'Well, you believe in all that stuff Stafford espoused, don't you? Life beyond, ghosts, heaven and hell? Why, then, call him a "poor man"?'

Endicott sipped his tea reflectively. 'Instinctive human reaction, probably. When faced with the death of someone, naturally you're saddened. Or don't you feel that, Donald?'

'Of course I do. But then I have no belief in anything other than this life.'

Endicott shook his head. 'I would find your world view terrifying.'

Langham smiled. Terrifying it might be, from time to time, but that was no reason to go fleeing into the embrace of the irrational.

He finished his toast and gazed across the table at the big man. 'If you don't mind my asking, Edward . . .'

Endicott cocked an eye. 'Out with it.'

'I'll be frank. I always had you down as a level-headed sort of chap, not much given to belief in . . .'

'In anything other than the here and now?' Endicott finished for him.

'Exactly. I've read your books and they're all tough-guy no-nonsense stories with not a whiff of a spook in sight.'

Endicott laughed. 'That's right. But then I'm E.L. Endicott, not M.R. James. And I've kept my beliefs quiet, never went shouting about them.'

'How long have you believed in the occult?'

'I had a strange experience while I was in Hollywood. I suppose I was open-minded before then, if I thought about things like that at all.'

'What happened?'

Endicott stared into the distance, past the stand of elms that flanked his property. 'I threw a party for the director and cast of a movie we'd just finished. A horror movie, would you believe? Anyway, I thought it'd be fun to get a medium in, hold a séance . . .'

'Ah,' Langham said. 'And . . .'

'And I was convinced. The chap was amazing. Summoned the dead! And before you think I was conned, let me say that there was no way he could have done what he did. He was a bona fide medium and I was converted. Only chap who bettered him, in my opinion, was Stafford.' He lifted his hands and let them fall on his lap. 'Anyway, since then I've been a firm believer in the occult, in the idea that this life is not everything, that there is an afterlife, a continuation of life after death.'

'And then Vivian Stafford turns up . . .' Langham said. 'How long after your first meeting was it before you decided you were going to write about him?'

Endicott smiled. 'Would you believe about two hours? I was still talking to him when I thought, by Jove, we have a character here, and decided that he was worth a book or two. Met him at the Three Horseshoes. He'd turned up at the hall wanting to take a gander at his old stomping ground, and Dent – sensible man – dragged him down to the pub. Anyway, the day after that I started doing a bit of research on the man, read up about his exploits way back. I came across references to him in the papers and books by the contemporaries of Crowley and earlier Victorian diabolists. He was a shady figure, hovering on the edge of society – unlike Crowley and the other egotists, he didn't seek the limelight. Anyway, at our next meeting I invited him to the Chase. I told him that I was contemplating writing a book about him . . .'

'And how did he take it?'

'D'you know something? I think there *was* a streak of ego in his make up. He'd lived a secret life for so long, lived the last fifty years as a recluse with no one knowing his secret – and he was delighted that someone was taking him seriously after so long keeping mum.'

'And you were that someone.'

Endicott shrugged. 'I was on his side, you might say. I *wanted* to believe his claims, and pretty quickly came to do so.'

Langham hesitated, then said, 'Alasdair thought that Stafford might be against your writing about him. He even wondered if it was Stafford who'd spirited you away and taken your papers.'

Endicott shook his head. 'Well, he was wrong.

Stafford never tried to prevent my work. And I locked my papers in the safe.'

'And your relationship with Stafford? Did you consider him a friend?'

'I wouldn't go that far. He was a . . . a very reserved man. He was wise – as you'd expect someone of his great age to be – and certainly cynical in the ways of the human race. I don't think he allowed himself to get too close to his fellow man.'

'Not even to you,' Langham asked, 'someone who knew his life story so well?'

'Not even me. And as far as I was concerned . . . How to explain this? I suppose I was a little in awe of the man, of his powers. I treated him with . . . cautious respect, let's say. I have no doubt that he was a great man, which is why I find his passing hard to comprehend.'

'Especially as it was so *mundane* an end?'

Endicott smiled, not to be caught out. 'If, Donald, it turns out to be a "mundane" end, as you call it.'

Endicott pulled the *Express* towards him, effectively signifying that the interrogation was at an end. He leafed through the pages then asked, 'What've you and that rather wonderful woman of yours got planned today?'

Langham smiled. 'Church this morning, and then Haverford Dent's having an open exhibition up at the hall. We thought we might pop along to that.'

Endicott lowered his paper. 'Church? Had you down as a dyed-in-the-wool atheist.'

'I am. But I thought it might be rather

interesting to hear what the Reverend Denbigh has to say about Stafford.'

'Denbigh! Don't get me started! Denbigh took against me at the occult evening up at the hall the other month. Accused me of being in league with Satan.'

'Apparently he confronted Stafford at the same time?'

'And how. Not that Stafford was one to take it lying down. Rather put the whippersnapper in his place, I can tell you. Ah, here's your girl. I'll leave you two to it.'

He exchanged a greeting with Maria as he entered the house. Maria strolled on to the patio nursing a big mug of coffee. 'Good morning, Donald.'

'Sleep well?'

'Like a log, as you say.' She sat down beside him and asked, 'Did you have an interesting conversation with Edward?'

'Quite. I'll tell you all about it while we dress for church.' He laughed at the idea.

'What?'

'Dressing for church – my father would disown me.'

'Ah, the man who read the *Daily Star* every day at breakfast and Marx before bed.'

'Any wonder I've turned out as I have?' He stroked a strand of hair from her face and kissed her cheek.

'I wouldn't have you any other way, you strange man.'

While Langham had no time for religion and detested its often hypocritical morality, he

179

appreciated church architecture and the sense of peace and serenity that prevailed within the buildings. St Andrew's was a small, twelfth-century Norman church which had largely managed to survive the depredations of the Reformation. Sunlight streamed in through the stained-glass windows and laid prismatic patterns across the aisle.

The service was well attended; whether that was a reflection of the piety of the villagers or the need for reassurance with murder in their midst, Langham was unable to say. Perhaps fifty locals filled the pews, dressed in their finest. Caroline Dequincy was present, *sans* Boardman. She smiled brightly and waved when she saw Langham and Maria shuffle into a pew halfway down the nave.

He fell to wondering, as they waited for the service to begin, if Maria might want a church wedding – always assuming, of course, that she agreed to his proposal. He rather thought she would like a church do, if only to satisfy her father. Personally, he would rather get it over and done with in a registry office and have a quiet reception later for family and friends. Not that he would press the issue. Had Maria demanded a druidic wedding at Stonehenge on the winter solstice, he would have gladly agreed.

'You are miles away, Donald. What are you thinking about?'

'Druidic rites and Stonehenge,' he said.

She gave him an odd look.

He had to smile, a minute later, when Reverend Denbigh took the pulpit. He was such a slight figure, and the oak pulpit so heavy and ornate, that he looked like a child peering over the edge of a cot.

Maria heard his quiet chuckle and whispered, 'What?'

He leaned towards her. 'Denbigh. He looks about ten.'

'Shhh!' she admonished, elbowing him.

Denbigh opened with a few words of thanks to those attending, both locals and visitors, and said something about the grace of God being ever present even in times of trouble. Langham's attention wandered, as it was wont to do during the few services he'd attended, which had always seemed interminable and platitudinous. He scanned the congregation and was surprised to see the dapper, moustached figure of Detective Inspective Montgomery in the second row. He wondered if he were on duty.

A hymn was sung, 'Cast away the works of darkness', and Langham found himself mouthing the words without issuing any sound. Perhaps best, he thought, for those nearby. To compensate for his lack in the vocal department, Maria had a high, sweet singing voice.

The verger then read a psalm, two more hymns were sung, and Denbigh took the pulpit once again to give his sermon.

Its subject was the weakness of the flesh and the temptation to give in to evil, and how only by following the path of Christ might one lead a virtuous existence. Denbigh was not that accomplished a public speaker, which surprised Langham. The vicar seem to lose track of his sermon from time to time, repeat himself and cast about for the right word or phrase. He wondered if the young vicar was feeling ill.

'Which brings me,' Denbigh said, 'to the tragic affair that has, ah . . . visited our quiet village. None of you can be unaware . . . be unaware of what I refer to, and I know that many of you have been distressed by the incident and its consequences. On a practical level, be assured that the authorities are working hard to bring the matter to a satisfactory resolution. As for the victim . . .' He paused, stared down at his notes and continued hesitantly, 'He was, I know, an occasional visitor to the village, and was known by one or two of you. And while Vivian Stafford was . . . was not without his faults, he was a child of Christ and I would commend you now to remember the man and say a silent prayer for his eternal soul. If you could be upstanding . . .'

Langham climbed reluctantly to his feet and, while heads were bowed in prayer, glanced up at the hymn board; he was relieved to see that only two hymns remained.

Fifteen minutes later, after renditions of 'To me a sinner, chief of all' and 'Time by moments steals away', the Reverend Denbigh finished by reminding parishioners of two forthcoming meetings. The service over, Langham shuffled into the aisle after Maria and waited as the congregation moved towards the exit.

'What did you think of that, Donald?'

He mouthed, 'Not much. You?'

She frowned. 'I did wonder if Denbigh might be drunk.'

'Well, he did lose the thread here and there.' As they approached the exit, he said, 'What say we repair to the Three Horseshoes for a pint and a sandwich?'

'After I've gone back to the Chase and changed, *oui*?'

They filed through the stone archway and approached Denbigh, who was thanking the last of his parishioners with forced spontaneity and limp handshakes.

As Langham offered his hand, Denbigh said, 'Ah, Donald, Maria, how awfully nice of you to turn up. I do hope it wasn't too excruciatingly dull.'

'Not at all,' Langham smiled.

The vicar turned pale and leaned against the pitted stone of the arch. Maria rushed forward and Langham took the man's shoulder.

'Are you all right?' Maria asked.

'A little faint, that's all. I'll be fine. I wonder . . .'

'Come on,' Langham said. 'We'll get you home.'

'It's only . . .' Denbigh began, gesturing vaguely across the churchyard to an ivy-clad vicarage.

Langham took the vicar's elbow and assisted him from the church and along the path between the tilted gravestones, heading towards the iron gate in the stone wall dividing the church from the vicarage.

They passed down an overgrown path to the front door.

'It's open,' Denbigh said, and Maria dashed to the door and pushed it wide. Langham eased

Denbigh along the hallway towards a small front room crammed with chintz-covered furniture.

The vicar collapsed on a small sofa and Maria said, 'Is there anything I can get you?'

'Perhaps a glass of water. And on the table in the kitchen . . .' he pointed towards a door that stood ajar. 'If you could bring me the bottle of pills?'

Maria dashed off and Denbigh smiled weakly. 'I'm sorry. I get these turns from time to time. Nothing serious.'

Langham perched himself on the arm of a chair and cast about for something to say. 'I thought your sermon . . .'

'Frightfully dull?'

Langham smiled. 'I was about to say that I thought you struck the right note of reassurance.'

The young vicar looked pathetically grateful. 'Do you think so? I don't know. These are terrible times in the village, Donald. And . . . and I must admit I've felt rather stressed of late, and somewhat out of my depth. You see, this is my first real posting. I was a year in London a few years ago, and . . . and . . .'

He seemed to lose the thread of his words, and Langham helped him out with, 'I assume one's first parish is something of an ordeal, and then this comes along . . .'

A shadow passed across the vicar's face; he appeared pained, as if recollecting a particularly unpleasant memory.

Maria returned with a glass of water and a small bottle. She passed it to the vicar and he

184

tipped half-a-dozen tiny pills into his shaking palm and downed them with a mouthful of water.

'Thank you. You're most kind . . . both of you.' He sat back, looking exhausted.

Maria said, 'If you're sure you'll be all right?'

Langham stood in preparation to leave.

Denbigh looked up at them, something almost like an appeal in his eyes. 'I was wondering, now that you're here . . .'

'Yes?' Langham said.

'You see, I . . . I find myself caught on the horns of a dilemma.'

'A dilemma?' Maria echoed.

'I find that I can't make a decision on a certain matter until I have some information which . . .' He trailed off.

'Go on,' Langham said, resuming his seat.

Denbigh licked his lips, nodded and looked from Maria to Langham. He said, 'You mentioned yesterday, Donald, that it was you – or rather Boardman – who discovered the body.'

'That's right,' Langham said, surprised. 'What of it?'

'When PC Thomson saw me the other day, I didn't ask him *exactly* where the body was discovered.'

'And you'd like to know?' Langham said. 'Do you mind my asking why?'

'Well,' Denbigh began hesitantly, 'on Sunday morning before the service I saw someone in the woods. I was taking a stroll before the service. The path through the woods is one of my favourite walks.'

Maria said, 'Ah. You saw someone on the path?'

185

The vicar nodded. 'You see, they were acting a little strangely – bending down on the edge of the path, reaching towards something in the undergrowth. In retrospect I wonder if they were ensuring that something was covered, concealed.'

'And did the person see you?' Langham asked.

'I'm not sure. I think not. My path took me in another direction. And to be honest, it didn't strike me as all that odd at the time . . . Only later, when I heard that the body was discovered near the path.'

'I see, and you want to know exactly where the body was, and if perhaps that person *was* in the process of concealing it?'

Denbigh nodded, looking relieved. 'That's about the top and bottom of it, yes.'

Langham glanced at Maria, who inclined her head minimally. 'We came across the body approximately twenty yards into the woods from the meadow,' he said. 'In fact, it was just beside a rather tall elm.'

The vicar opened his mouth as if in silent exclamation. He said, 'And that is where I saw . . .'

'In that case,' Langham said, 'you really must tell the authorities. I noticed Inspector Montgomery at the service this morning. He might still be around the village. I'd tell him straight away.'

'Of course. Yes, I'll do that. I feel a little better already. I'll give it five minutes and seek him out.'

Maria asked, 'Do you mind telling us, vicar, who you saw in the woods on Sunday morning?'

186

Denbigh bit his lip, considering, and then said, 'No, not at all. It was Caroline Dequincy.'

Langham looked across at Maria; she was wide-eyed with surprise.

As they took their leave – after ensuring that there was nothing else they could do for Denbigh – Maria said, 'But what would Caroline be doing there, with the body, on Sunday?' She shook her head. 'So . . . when we went for that walk – she knew all about the body.'

'It certainly looks like it,' Langham said.

'And her reaction, her sobs. I had to comfort her . . . she was so convincing.'

Langham opened the gate to the churchyard and allowed Maria to pass through before him. 'Well, she is an actress, after all,' he said, removing his jacket and tie.

She shook her head. 'I can't believe . . .' she began.

They came to the village green and Maria said, 'I won't be five minutes. I really need to change into something less formal.'

'You looked stunning in the dress you were wearing the other day – the white one with big red flowers,' he said. 'Be a sweet and take these, would you? I'll see you at the Three Horseshoes.' He passed her his jacket and tie, kissed her cheek and watched her as she hurried across the village green.

He crossed to the Three Horseshoes. Detective Inspector Montgomery sat at one of the outside tables, leafing through his notebook. An empty glass stood beside a second, half full. Langham thought he must have raced here straight from the church. 'Mind if I join you?'

Montgomery looked up. 'Ah, Langham. No, pull up a pew.'

'Drink up and I'll stand you one.'

'You're a gent and a scholar. Fuller's.'

When Langham returned from the bar with two pints of bitter, Montgomery tucked away his note-book and finished off his second beer.

'Cheers!' He raised his replenished pint. 'I owe you an apology, Langham.'

'You do?' He sat down opposite the detective.

'For intimating yesterday that your police procedure wouldn't be up to much.'

'And?'

'Found one of your books at the library in Bury and read a few pages. Forget the title. Decent stuff. And you got the nitty-gritty right.'

'Well, I have inside help, you see. Jeff Mallory at Scotland Yard.'

Montgomery lowered his glass. 'You know Jeff?'

'We're good friends. I've known him since he stepped off the boat from South Africa before the war. He was a fellow scribbler back then. Now he's too busy investigating real crimes. But he still has time to read everything I write and underline the howlers.'

'It's a small world. I worked with Jeff at Shoreditch just after the war.' Montgomery smiled. 'Did most of our work at the Butler's Arms, mind. We're still in contact from time to time.'

'It's a small world indeed. I'll tell him I bumped into you.' Langham took a mouthful of bitter. 'How's the investigation going?'

Montgomery grunted and took refuge in his pint. When he emerged, wiping foam from his toothbrush moustache, he said, 'Between you and me, nowhere fast.'

'Careful. You're talking to a suspect, remember.'

Montgomery lit up a Benson and Hedges, blew out a billow of smoke and jabbed a finger at Langham. 'That's where you're wrong. We've discounted you and that rather fetching filly of yours.'

'You have? That's good to know.'

'You were at some literary do in Pimlico on Saturday afternoon and early evening, and from eight till almost eleven you and Miss Dupré were dining at the . . .' He fished out his notebook, found the page and read: 'At the *Moulin Bleu* in Highgate.'

Langham tried not to smile at the detective's accent: *Mewlin Bloo*.

'And on Sunday you were taking a constitutional on Hampstead Heath.'

'Good work. How on earth . . .?'

'Simple. Alasdair Endicott said he'd met you at the do, and I corroborated that you were there with your agent' – he glanced at his notebook again – 'one Charles Elder. He also said you'd gone on to this French place. All I had to do then was contact the maître d' there, and Bob's your uncle. Then I had a local bobby trace your movements on the Sunday. You were seen that morning by one Dame Amelia Hampstead.'

189

Langham sat back and sipped his beer. 'So . . .
I take it that Stafford was murdered between
Saturday evening and some time on Sunday?'

Montgomery nodded. 'Any sharper and you'd
cut yourself, Langham. We believe between about
ten on Saturday night and noon Sunday. He
arrived at the Three Horseshoes around eight and
according to the landlord went straight up to his
room. No one saw him leave, either later that
night or in the morning.'

'Had the bed been slept in?'

Montgomery shrugged. 'Hard to tell. If he'd
spent the night there then he'd made the bed in
the morning before he left.'

'I wonder if he met his end where he was found,
or in the woods behind the Chase?'

'Forensics are still out on that one. My guess
is that he was attacked in the copse behind the
Chase and ran from his attacker, only to succumb
to his wounds in the woods, where his attacker
concealed him.'

'Murder weapon?'

'Not found. But not your proverbial blunt
instrument. Something sharp, going by the
damage to the skull.'

'So . . . premeditated?' Langham mused. 'I
mean, it wasn't as if the killer just picked up a
rock and coshed him with it on the spur of the
moment. He – or she – used some kind of . . .
what?'

'Axe or meat cleaver, more than likely.'

'Lovely.'

'But you're right. More than likely this was
murder aforethought. Unless, of course, there

was a handily placed axe to hand, which is unlikely.' Montgomery regarded the burning end of his cigarette, funnelled smoke through his nose and shook his head. 'Trouble is we haven't been able to establish the victim's true identity. He certainly wasn't Vivian Stafford, who vanished without a trace over fifty years ago. And unlike some people around here, I don't buy the idea that the deceased was a hundred and twenty years old.'

'No clues on the body?'

'Not one. Just a few pound notes and a bit of change. We've issued a description and gone through the missing persons files, but nothing doing. It's as if the man passing himself off as Stafford appeared out of the blue. I'm working on the assumption that he came from London, perhaps, but there's no evidence of an abandoned vehicle in the area. He didn't have a return train ticket on him, and we didn't find one in his room at the pub. And there's nothing to identify him in his luggage.'

Langham regarded his pint. 'The killer could always have gone through his pockets and removed any identity documents for whatever reasons.'

'I haven't discounted that.' He pointed to Langham's almost empty pint. 'Another?'

'You've twisted my arm.'

Montgomery regarded the three empty glasses before him and laughed. 'Another thing you writer chappies always get wrong. You always have your coppers refusing a drink with, "not while I'm on duty, thank you", when the truth is that we drink like the proverbial fish, on duty or off.' He gathered up the dead soldiers.

Langham shook his head. 'Read more of my stuff and you'll see that I get that right, too. I know Jeff Mallory, remember?'

Langham watched the dapper little copper hurry into the public bar, then sat back in the sunlight and considered what the Reverend Denbigh had said.

The idea that Caroline might have had something to do with the victim's demise was more than a little disturbing. He liked the actress – there was something open, friendly and forthright about her.

But why the hell, if she were innocent, hadn't she reported the body at the time?

His thoughts were interrupted by Montgomery's return. ''Fraid this'll have to be the one for the road, Langham, much as I could sit here all afternoon. Back to Bury St Edmunds for a team briefing.'

'Ah. Look here, I saw the Reverend Denbigh earlier and . . .'

Montgomery sipped his pint. 'Go on.'

'Well, he was in a bit of a state about something he saw on Sunday morning.' Langham proceeded to recount what Denbigh had told Maria and himself not fifteen minutes ago.

Montgomery raised his eyebrows. 'Dequincy? Is he certain?'

'I'd say so, yes.'

'Right, I'll pop into the vicarage before I head back.' He lit up another cigarette, took a mouthful of beer and cocked an eye at Langham. 'This

Dequincy woman. She's involved with Edward Endicott, by all accounts.'

'Well, they're friends.'

The inspector nodded. 'How well do you know Edward Endicott?'

'Not that well. I met him after the war. He'd just got back from Hollywood and was making ends meet writing thrillers. I've seen him perhaps once a year since then.'

'Made his packet in Hollywood?'

'I'm not too sure about that. I always assumed he had. But then . . . why was he writing mysteries for forty quid a throw? Always puzzled me.'

'And recently he started writing a book about a Victorian satanist.' Montgomery hesitated, then said, 'I wanted to ask you: do you think Endicott's all there?'

Langham squinted at the detective. 'Do you mean, do I think he's compos mentis?' He shrugged. 'Well, he strikes me as sane – but misguided, let's say.'

'And his son?'

'I'm no shrink, but I'd say the same.'

'I had my deputy do a bit of digging. Turns out that the Vivian Stafford who owned the hall from 1855 to 1901 did dabble in the dark arts, then vanished without a trace in 1902. Last seen near Eastbourne . . .'

'Wonder if he threw himself off Beachy Head?'

'No reports of his body washing up.'

'So . . . I wonder who the impostor was?' Langham asked. 'Did Stafford have children?'

'To the best of my knowledge, no. But that

doesn't mean to say that the dead man wasn't some offspring who came up here on the make.'

'In what way?'

'Dunno, old chap. That we've yet to find out. Why did he return to the village five weeks ago?' He sighed. 'It'd all be a damn sight easier if we knew who the bloody man was.'

'Was Edward able to account for his movements on Saturday and Sunday?'

Montgomery wiped foam from his moustache. 'He says he set off from the Chase around ten on Saturday morning. Spent the whole day walking and said he didn't meet a soul. He pitched his tent twelve miles south of here, just outside a village called Little Deering. I'm having the local bobbies check to see if anyone saw him or noticed a tent.'

'If he were spotted, then that'd pretty much rule him out.'

Montgomery nodded. 'As for his son, Alasdair . . . He was seen leaving the literary bash on Saturday just before six, and says he went straight to his flat in Hackney. He claims he left London the following morning on the nine o'clock train, though we've only his word for that.'

'I can't see young Alasdair bashing anyone over the head.'

Montgomery grunted in agreement. 'He'd have difficulty lifting a serving spoon, by the look of him.' The detective looked up. 'Ah, here's your charming . . . wife?'

'To be, if all goes well,' Langham said.

'Good luck on that score, old chum. Me, I've been married thirty years. You get less for manslaughter.' He sighed and stood up. 'Right, I'd better go and quiz the vicar.'

He saluted Langham, tipped his trilby at Maria as she passed and crossed the green towards the vicarage.

Maria smiled down at Langham. She was radiant in the white dress splashed with magenta flowers. 'You look,' he said, 'more than beautiful, my girl.'

'And you look, Donald, more than a little drunk. What did that funny little man have to say?'

'I'm as sober as a judge,' he protested. 'Sit down and I'll tell you everything over lunch.'

SEVENTEEN

Haverford Dent's art show was an annual event to which all the villagers of Humble Barton and beyond were invited. The artist threw open the gates of Stafford Hall and staged an exhibition that combined a show of his art work – his paintings, sculptures and mechanical 'reinventions' – with the more traditional aspects of a country fair: stalls selling home-made produce, tombolas, a flower and vegetable show, pet parades and cream teas. Dent himself might not have been well liked among the villagers, but their disdain of his morality did not prevent their availing themselves of his hospitality.

Langham and Maria strolled up the winding lane that climbed the hill to the hall accompanied by a procession of locals. There was a carnival atmosphere in the air, and Langham was curious to discover what Dent's art was actually like. Apparently some bigwig gallery owners from London were up for the day, which suggested that in some circles his work was taken seriously – even if, locally, their creator was not.

'What a beautiful day for it!'

They turned to see a smiling Caroline Dequincy hurrying to catch up, Boardman trotting at her side. The actress wore a low-cut summer frock which revealed an immodest depth of cleavage.

'Isn't it wonderful that Edward is back among us!' she went on, and Langham caught the unmistakable scent of gin on her breath. 'Have you ever been to one of Dent's shows before? No, of course you haven't. You're in for a treat. I'll show you round.'

'Are they always this well attended?' Maria asked.

'Not usually, but this year we're blessed with exceptional weather.'

Langham glanced at the actress as she chatted to Maria about the various stalls to be found in the grounds, and considered what the Reverend Denbigh had said that morning. He recalled Caroline's shock when Boardman discovered the body, and her petrified question, '*It's Edward, isn't it?*'

She had known about the corpse all along, according to Denbigh – but why, he asked himself not for the first time, would she fail to report her discovery . . . if 'discovery' it had been?

'Strange that although Dent isn't liked, this event should be so popular,' he observed.

Caroline smiled. 'People can dissociate their prejudice about the man from the good time to be had, Donald. It's called pragmatism.'

'Ah, just as while some people might not have approved of the satanist Vivian Stafford, they attended his occult events?'

'Or,' Maria said, elbowing him playfully in the ribs, 'just as atheists attend church services.'

'Touché,' he said.

They approached the imposing gateway of Stafford Hall, where members of the Women's

Institute were selling tickets for the raffle and for entry. Langham bought a raffle ticket and paid the entrance fee for the three of them. They strolled up the long drive towards the hall.

'Stafford must have made many enemies in the village,' he said.

The sun in her face, Caroline squinted at him. 'What makes you say that?'

He shrugged. 'A satanist in a sleepy Suffolk village . . . A man who wasn't averse to airing his views, if Dent's story of their first meeting in the Three Horseshoes is to be believed. I would have thought that he'd rub a few backs up.'

'To my knowledge, Donald, only Denbigh really took against him.'

'What about Dent?'

'Well . . . Dent opposed everything Stafford stood for. Yet I'll give Dent this, he didn't take against the man himself. He regarded Stafford with a rather wry, detached amusement. Even let him into the hall to conduct his occult event, of course.'

Langham asked, watching the actress closely, 'And you?'

'Me?'

'What did you think of Stafford?'

She hesitated. 'Why, I only met him a few times. I found him strange, but . . . civil enough.'

She sounded, Langham thought, as if she were being economical with her true feelings about the man.

'I wonder why anyone would want him dead?'

She shook her head and smiled openly at him. 'I can't begin to imagine,' she said.

The drive climbed and turned, and revealed to their left was the four-square magnificence of Stafford Hall, the decrepitude of its east wing concealed behind a wall of ivy. The extensive lawns before the building were pitched with tents and marquees, stalls and kiosks.

Caroline said, 'This is what most of the villagers come for – the stalls and all. Once you've paid your sixpence, you see, everything is free within the grounds. Look, Dent has even hired a troupe of morris dancers. You don't know how strange they appear to American eyes.'

Langham smiled. 'And not only to American eyes,' he said. 'Metropolitan eyes find them pretty creepy too.'

'Creepy?'

'Don't you think so? Those gargoyle papier-mâché heads, the sudden cries. The tradition harks back to an earlier, pagan age.'

Maria shivered. 'I think Donald is right. I find them bizarre. Oh, I don't like those big heads!'

Langham laughed and slipped an arm around her waist.

Caroline pointed beyond the busy lawns to a stretch of rolling parkland. 'And in among the trees over there,' she said, 'Dent has his mechanical inventions. His more conventional work is in the hall, the paintings and sculptures.'

Langham peered over the treetops and made out the occasional brass and copper prominence, like miniature cities made from metal. Vanes windmilled and spires turned in the wind. From the little he could make out, Dent's inventions looked like something Heath Robinson might have concocted after having had a particularly bad Dali-esque nightmare.

'What do you think of his art?' he asked.

Caroline considered the question. 'His paintings and sculptures are technically accomplished, though their subject matter doesn't appeal to me. His apprehension of the female form is . . . well, what you might expect from a man like Haverford Dent.'

'And his mechanical inventions?'

'Completely different, Donald. It's almost as if they were created by another person. Where his canvases display a certain warped humanism – though not to my taste – the inventions are . . . inhuman, mechanistic. I find them unsettling.'

'I'm intrigued,' Maria said.

'Edward hates them,' Caroline said. 'He's forever railing about their materialism. In fact,' she went on, pointing, 'there he is. Shall we join him?'

Edward Endicott was striding away from the beer tent, clutching a foaming pint and heading towards the vales beyond. Langham paused before the line of kegs, asked for a half despite Maria's critical gaze, and was told that they only served pints. He came away with a full tankard, smiling.

'I think I will have to carry you home, Donald Langham. That must be your fourth today.'

'Well, we are on holiday. And it is free. Must cost Dent a fortune.'

'He does nothing by half measures,' Caroline said. 'I don't think he understands the meaning of the word restraint.' She shivered. 'I don't know

. . . but I always feel that there's an air of . . . of the bacchanalia about these events.'

They passed the whirling morris dancers, hopping and cavorting and yelling out loud; a giant, leering head dipped towards them and whirled away. A male dancer equipped with great pink papier-mâché breasts swung by, yodelling. Maria shrank towards Langham and they hurried on.

'Edward!' Caroline called out.

Endicott turned and lifted his staff in greeting. 'Just on my way to look at Dent's latest abominations, Caroline. Hullo there Donald, Maria. Come on, let's see what the silly old goat's been up to in the scrap metal department.'

They rounded a box hedge and paused on the embankment of a natural amphitheatre.

'What on earth,' Langham said, 'is that?'

'It's . . .' Maria began. 'I don't know what it is, Donald.'

It combined the tawdriness of a fairground calliope with the antique craftsmanship of a Victorian orrery. Looking down on the vast clockwork mechanism, Langham realized that it was indeed a great metal representation of the solar system. At its centre was the golden ball of the sun with a hundred stylized petals to signify flames, while around the sun, on circular rails of increasing diameter, swung the spinning orbs that were the planets. The faces of the planets, however, were not decorated with their respective geographical features – in so far as any of them were known – but painted with abstruse mathematical formulae, and they were rotating not in the sedate and stately manner of the spheres in the heavens but in a reckless, headlong, maniacal gyre. At the foot of the incline the keg-sized orb of Pluto whipped by, clunking and rattling, with the speed of an automobile.

'It's . . . fantastic,' Langham said.

'But also a little dangerous.' Caroline laughed uneasily.

Maria gripped his hand as she stared at the whirling, madcap machine.

A line of observers ringed the amphitheatre, staring down at the orrery with varying degrees of fascination. One or two brave souls had descended to within feet of the mechanism, smiling and waving back at their more circumspect friends like children at the beach braving the waves.

On the far side of the orrery the tall, bent, uncoordinated figure of Haverford Dent shambled widdershins around the outer track, indicating the finer points of his invention with his meerschaum pipe. He was accompanied by a man and a woman – the gallery owners from London, Langham surmised. He wondered what they would make of the crazed exhibit.

'What I don't like about Dent's work,' Endicott was shouting above the din, 'is that it does not in any way take account of the human heart. This is a mechanistic abomination, a mechanical reduction of the universe; in essence, he's stating that God's creation is no more than a reductionist nightmare, a . . . what's that French, faddish word, m'dear?'

'Existential?' Maria supplied, smiling.

'That's it! An existentialist nightmare without an ounce of meaning.'

Langham clutched his pint and glanced at Endicott; sober and willing to debate the point, he might have taken issue with Endicott's interpretation. He thought the orrery could be seen as a celebration of the wonder of the solar system. He was feeling mellow, however, and wanted nothing more than to enjoy the summer's day and the sheer bizarre bravado of Dent's creation.

'And his paintings are no less reductionist, as you'll see, Langham. How he represents the human figure is appalling.'

Langham indicated Dent, who had seen them and was climbing the incline, the smartly dressed man and woman in his wake. He sported a scabbed gash on his forehead, the result of his inebriation following Caroline's 'at home'.

'Does he know what you think of his work?' Langham asked.

'Of course! We've spent many an hour in the pub arguing the toss back and forth. Isn't that right, Dent?'

'What's that, Endicott?'

'I was telling young Langham here about our opposed world views. I detest everything you do, but you know that!'

Dent clapped Endicott's meaty shoulder. 'And the vitriol is returned, with interest. Edward's acceptance of spiritual claptrap appals me!' He bellowed a laugh. 'We agree to disagree.'

The artist introduced the man and woman, who were indeed West End gallery owners, and

Endicott invited their opinion of the giant orrery.

The woman was the epitome of diplomacy. 'We think the . . .' She consulted a mimeographed leaflet in her hand. 'We are of the opinion that "Dervish Mechanique", while novel and industrious, is not what our patrons might appreciate.' She smiled at Dent. 'Your paintings, however, are another matter.'

'Before we go inside and take a shufti at the daubs,' Dent said, 'I really must show you exhibit number two on the itinerary.'

He took her by the arm, murmuring into her ear, and led the way from the vale.

Intrigued, Langham took Maria's hand and followed.

They moved from the amphitheatre and ambled up a gently rising greensward, on top of which stood what looked like a guillotine. The metal structure rose against the sunlight – two parallel tubular spars like great pistons with, at the summit, something that resembled a car's bonnet poised like a blade.

'What the hell is it?' Endicott cried.

'My latest creation,' Dent said. 'I call it "The End of Civilization".'

'That's all very well, Dent,' Caroline said, 'but what is it?'

Dent flung back his head and laughed. 'Stand well back and watch,' he said, and approached the base of the exhibit.

He pressed a stud on a control panel set into the base and retreated.

They stared up as one and watched the car bonnet descend at speed and smash into the anvil of the base with a resounding crash. Severely dented, the bonnet was hauled back up to the summit where it stopped.

'I think the meaning is self-evident,' Dent said, staring around at the little group. 'Mechanization will spell the end of civilized society.'

Endicott shook his head. 'Poppycock,' he said, and this time Langham did not disagree with him.

'But to the paintings!' Dent declared, and led the gallery owners off towards the hall.

Endicott sighed and raised his bushy eyebrows at Caroline, but they nevertheless followed the artist.

Maria stuck out her lower lip and blew upwards in an attempt to cool her face. 'I'm so thirsty I could even drink some of your awful beer, Donald.'

He proffered the tankard and watched her raise it to her lips with both hands. She swallowed, pulled a face and handed it back. '*Ugh!* How can you drink that poison! I'll have a lemonade, thank you.'

'Come on, I'll get you one.'

'And perhaps then we should take "a shufti at the daubs", Donald?'

They moved towards the refreshment kiosk and Langham secured a glass of lemonade for Maria. Beside the kiosk the Reverend Denbigh was locked in debate with Alasdair Endicott. The vicar glanced up as they passed, but resumed what sounded like an argument with Alasdair without so much as a nod their way.

'I wonder what was exciting the vicar?' Maria murmured.

'Arguing the toss as regards Alasdair's occult beliefs, I shouldn't wonder,' Langham replied.

They climbed the broad sweep of stairs to the doors of the hall and passed into the welcome shade of the panelled hallway.

Several corridors led off from the hall, and all but one were rendered out of bounds by maroon braided cords hanging from brass stands. Arrows drawn on pieces of foolscap directed visitors along a passage to what had once been the ball-room, now given over to the hanging of Haverford Dent's paintings. The four walls provided insuf-ficient space for all his work, however, and more of it was hung on screens which divided the room. The hallowed hush of a gallery prevailed as viewers moved from oil to oil with the gravitas and solemn expressions of fish in an aquarium.

The exception was Edward Endicott. He stood at the far end of the room, in a shaft of sunlight falling through the full-length windows, and bellowed, 'But just look at it! I mean, what the hell is it supposed to be? Women don't look like this! It's a travesty!'

Langham and Maria joined the small group standing before a painting which showed a reclining nude with a small head and a dispro-portionately bloated body. It was rendered in pastel shades which gave the subject an ethereal, spectral aspect.

'It's not supposed to be figurative,' Dent was explaining. 'Christ, man. I've gone over this with you a hundred times before! It's a bloody impres-sion, not a photograph!'

'So you're trying to tell me that this is how

you see the fairer sex?' Endicott asked, becoming red in the face.

'It's my imaginative interpretation, yes. This single image stands as a kind of universal paradigm, let's say, of a certain type of woman I have . . . experienced.'

Endicott harrumphed and moved on to the next painting, this one showing a standing nude, a young girl with nascent breasts, a hand demurely positioned between her legs. 'And this?' Endicott asked.

'This one stands as a symbol of the vulnerability of womanhood.'

'But it's a bally young gal, for Christ's sake!'

Dent smiled. 'As I said, Edward, it's a symbol.'

The woman from the London gallery laid her head on one side and ventured, 'I detect in your visions a concomitant pagan primitivism evident in many of your . . . ah . . . mechanical sculptures, Mr Dent. Your talent goes to the heart of your wrestling with the dilemma of humankind in relation to its addressing the issues of the modern, post-World War Two era. I would even go so far as to say that, while your techniques are intentionally primitivist in nature, the intellection behind the work is ultimately sophisticated – and this sets up an interesting tension, not to say paradox.'

'Exactly,' said Dent, scratching the scab on his forehead and cocking a goatish smile in the direction of an apoplectic Endicott.

Maria nudged Langham and suggested with a glance that they move on. They left the artist, his champions and detractor, and strolled around the room. As far as Langham was concerned, and he professed no great knowledge of paintings, he found the constant subject of women in various modes of undress less indicative of the human condition in the mid-twentieth century than of Dent's unbridled lust. And whether this made for good art, or not, he had no idea.

'What do you think?' he murmured to Maria at one point.

She pursed her lips in consideration. 'In a word, Donald: amateurish.'

'Wouldn't argue with that.'

They left the room and moved along the corridor. The next room, a library bearing the morocco and buckram bindings of a thousand old volumes, was given over to Dent's sculptures. Thankfully these did not represent the female form but showed leaping stoats and callisthenic weasels, and Langham thought them the most accomplished of Dent's work he'd seen so far.

'I'll give the old goat this,' he said, 'he's versatile.'

'I much prefer these animals to the other things.'

He looked at her. 'But would you have them in your front room?'

She gave a little shiver. 'Do you know? I would not. They are . . . weird, Donald. All deformed, elongated. I don't like them. Come on, there's a tea room along the corridor and you could do with sobering up.'

'But I'm not drunk!' he protested as Maria dragged him from the library and along the corridor.

They found Caroline Dequincy seated at a table

with a china cup of tea. Boardman was lying at her feet, his dewlaps splayed across the parquet. Langham finished his pint, queued up at the trestle counter before the window, and was duly served with two cups of Earl Grey. He carried them across to the table.

'I couldn't take another second of Dent's egomaniacal posturing,' Caroline said. 'I'm sure he does it just to bait Edward, and Edward, like a fool, falls for it every time.' She laid a perfectly manicured hand on Maria's forearm. 'Not that I'm for one minute defending Edward's philistinism! Though, to be honest, I often think that *that's* just a stance he takes to rile Dent in turn.' She rolled her eyes at Maria and exclaimed, 'Men!'

Langham took a sip of tea, set his cup and saucer on the table and said, 'Do excuse me. Must dash!'

As he hurried from the table, Maria leaned towards the actress and explained, 'Four pints at least!'

He returned to the hallway and looked for a sign to a loo along the various closed-off corridors. He found none, but did see a familiar figure, shrunken in perspective, at the far end of a passageway.

Ensuring that he wasn't observed – though he'd seen no one on hand to enforce the stricture of the cordons – he stepped over the braided rope and hurried along the corridor.

'Oh, hello there,' Alasdair said and returned his gaze to the ceiling. 'Rather singular mouldings. I do think they're original – eighteenth century.'

Langham said, 'I noticed you with Marcus. How was he?'

Alasdair looked at him oddly. 'How do you mean?'

'Well, Maria and I saw him earlier today, after the service, and he wasn't that chipper.'

'Oh, he's OK now. A little overworked, perhaps.'

Langham gestured around him. 'It's a magnificent old pile. Pity it hasn't been kept up. Perhaps if Dent did make a sale to those London bigwigs . . .'

Alasdair snorted. 'Believe me, he wouldn't sink his ill-gotten gains into the house.'

He glanced at the young man. 'No?'

'Fat chance. It'd all go on booze and loose women.'

'So the stories they tell of wild parties up at the hall . . .?'

Alasdair blushed. 'Not so much parties, but he does have women driven up from London.'

Langham examined the patched plaster-work. 'It really is a shame that someone couldn't take this place in hand.'

'Same up and down the country. Landed gentry falling on hard times. Places falling to pieces.'

'I didn't have Dent down as the scion of some aristocratic line.'

'Oh, he is. Last of the Dents from Cornwall. Inherited the family pile after the Great War, sold it before it started crumbling and bought this place at a snip in the thirties. According to my father it was in decent shape back then, but Dent's let it rot.'

'Crying shame.' Langham stared around at the

peeling wallpaper and crumbling mouldings. 'I say, I wouldn't mind a quick recce. Wasn't the occult event held in the old east wing?'

Alasdair pointed. 'Just along here, according to my father. I'll show you.'

They moved along the dusty, darkened corridor and turned left, along another even dustier and gloomier passage. 'We are now entering,' Alasdair said, affecting an uncharacteristic but suitably sepulchral tone, 'the area of the hall which is haunted.'

'*Reputedly* haunted,' Langham amended.

'Haunted,' said the young man with authority.

Langham glanced at him. 'You've been here before?'

'When I was fourteen, just after we returned from America. Dent invited my father up for a few drinks. He dragged me along and put me to bed upstairs. I imagined every creak the footfall of a spook, and the hoot of an owl a ghoul.'

'But you didn't see anything?'

Alasdair slowed down and frowned. 'Do you know something? I did, actually. A cavalier walked through the wall, approached my bed, stared down at me then walked on through the far wall. You don't forget something like that in a hurry.'

Langham laughed. 'No, I expect you don't.'

They came to a staircase and climbed, then turned right along a wide corridor. Faint sunlight illuminated the passage from distant windows. Alasdair came to a halt and looked around. 'According to what Caroline and my father told me, this is where Stafford manifested the ghost of the servant girl.' He shook his head. 'Can you feel it? The chill?'

Langham whispered, 'We're in an old unheated house, well away from the sunlight. What do you expect?'

'Oh, ye of little faith.'

'Oh, ye of much credulity.'

They stood very still for a minute. Langham said, 'The spirits are keeping shtum this time, Alasdair.'

The young man smiled. 'I rather think it needs someone with Stafford's abilities to summon them forth.'

'Quite,' Langham said. 'Must admit, though, it would make a capital place to shoot a horror film.'

Alasdair pointed at a closed door. 'That's where the ghost of the girl disappeared.'

Langham approached the door and pulled it open. He made out piles of boxes and dust-sheeted furniture in a small, dark room.

'Are all the rooms like this, unused?' He moved to the next room and opened the door, to be met with the miasma of mothballs and damp plaster. The room was empty.

'Well,' Alasdair said, 'not all the rooms are derelict.' He pointed to a closed door along the corridor.

Langham moved to the door and pulled it open. Inside were shelves stacked with what he thought at first were books. 'A library?' he said.

'Don't ask,' Alasdair said.

Langham glanced at the young man, then back at the shelves. They were filled not with books,

212

he realized on closer inspection, but with canisters of film – hundreds of them. 'Didn't know Dent was into the cinematic arts, too.'

Alasdair looked along the corridor as if nervous of being seen. He stepped forward so that he was hidden by the half-open door. 'I overheard my father telling Mr Jones, the verger, all about it.'

He peered at the young man in the gloom. '"It"?'

'This room. The films. They're his pornography collection.'

'Why am I not surprised?' Langham gazed around the room. 'Heavens, there are hundreds of 'em!'

'Something of an expert on the history of the blue film, old Dent.'

Langham made out an old projector on a central table. Next to it was a reel-to-reel tape recorder with the tape reels missing. He moved to the wall, slipped a cold steel canister from its cradle and attempted to read the handwritten label on its circumference. The light was bad, and anyway it appeared to be in French. '*Le Petit* . . . something or other,' he read.

Alasdair hissed from his station by the door, 'I say, let's be getting a move on. If Dent caught us in here . . .'

Langham slipped from the room and closed the door. 'Well, that explains something,' he told Alasdair as they made their way along the corridor.

'Dent's constant leching?'

'Maybe that, too, but I was thinking of

213

something else. How Stafford pulled the wool over the eyes of so many people last Halloween.'

Alasdair turned to him. 'How?'

'The projector. The tape recorder. He simply projected the spooks, accompanied by a few ghostly hootings.'

Alasdair gave a sceptical laugh. 'I don't think so, Langham. So many people wouldn't be fooled by a simple projection.'

Langham shrugged and dropped the subject as they retraced their steps along the passage and back down the creaking stairway.

They came to the entrance hall and a sudden and intense ache made its presence known in the region of his bladder. He asked Alasdair if he knew where the closest loo was situated.

The young man pointed along another cordoned corridor. 'Second on the right,' he said. 'I'll be outside. I think the raffle's about to be drawn.'

Two minutes later, feeling vastly relieved, Langham recrossed the hall and made his way to the tea room. He passed the ballroom and peered in, but there was no sign of Dent and the others, and nor were they in the library.

When he returned to the tea room and approached the table where Maria sat, alone now, she looked up and tapped her tiny wristwatch. 'I know you had pints and pints to drink, Donald, but why did you take so long?'

'Sorry. I was waylaid.' He recounted his meeting with Alasdair and their exploration of the east wing.

'And you found no spooks?'

'No, just Haverford Dent's collection of pornographic films.'

'*Mon dieu!*'

'Exactly. And the one I looked at was in French, too.'

Her eyes were wide. 'You *looked* at one?'

He laughed. 'Just at the outer case,' he assured her. 'Come on, I need some fresh air.'

They left the tea room and emerged into the blazing afternoon sunlight. The crowds on the main lawn had swelled, drawn by an announcement that the raffle – first prize a ten-pound Fortnum and Mason's voucher – was to be drawn in five minutes.

They entered a red and white striped marquee and strolled down the aisle between trestle tables bearing prize examples of flowers, fruit and vegetables. Maria bought a jar of strawberry jam from a stall and Langham a bottle of homemade elderflower wine.

They stepped from the marquee and crossed to a makeshift stage where Haverford Dent stood clutching a loudhailer in one hand and a tankard of beer in the other. He called out, 'And the third prize . . .' He peered at the ticket in his hand and said, 'Blue, forty-five!'

Langham glanced at his ticket: green, 313. 'Well, two more chances.'

Maria hung on his arm and laughed. 'But you once told me that you *never* win raffles, Donald.'

'That's right. Never won a prize in my life.'

They strolled around the stalls, passing the morris dancers who, their performances over for the time being, were relaxing on the lawn with well-earned pints of ale. A dozen giant heads, redundant now, reposed beside them on the lawn

215

like some macabre exhibition of mass decapitation.

'And the second prize . . . .' Dent's voice boomed out, 'is pink ticket ninety-seven!'

'Bad luck again, Donald.'

He squeezed her hand. 'I feel far from unlucky,' he told her. Whether due to the effect of the beer, or being with Maria, or a combination of the two, he felt a curious sense of elation.

He glanced at his watch: it was just after three o'clock. He might even suggest that they motor into Bury St Edmunds again this evening and find a cosy little restaurant.

'And the winning ticket,' Dent announced, 'is green, 313!'

'Donald!' Maria cried. 'You've won!'

He felt a sudden surge of excitement, soon quashed when he saw a young couple running from the parkland where Haverford Dent's inventions were installed. The woman had her hands pressed to her face and the man was ghost white. He called out something and indicated the dell at his back.

Langham left the crowd and moved towards the wooded area; he was aware of the pulse in his ears and Maria hurrying along at his side. They passed the man and woman, holding each other; the woman was sobbing uncontrollably.

Langham ran up the slight rise then slowed as his chest wound gave a twinge. He grimaced, panting, and came to a halt. He looked down into the natural amphitheatre where Dent's giant orrery held pride of place.

'Oh!' Maria sobbed, covering her eyes and turning away.

Others had joined them by now, and the air rang with exclamations of horror and revulsion.

Langham stared down at the orrery.

A body lay beside the outer rail, its head stove in by the passage of Pluto which, along with all the other planets, continued its ceaseless rotation. Langham moved down the incline, repulsed but at the same time drawn by the need to confirm the identity of the corpse.

He stopped a matter of yards from the body, overcome by a wave of nausea. He stared at the halved skull as if hypnotized by the sight of the mutilation.

Two items of clothing – a straw hat and a clerical dog collar – told him that the body was indeed that of the Reverend Marcus Denbigh.

EIGHTEEN

The public bar of the Three Horseshoes, equipped with traditional horse brasses, low oak beams and worn leather button-studded seats, was uncommonly quiet despite being full of customers. A stunned sense of shock prevailed, and it was as if the patrons, initially gathered to dose themselves with the anaesthetic of alcohol, now wondered at the propriety of such conduct in light of the tragic death of their vicar.

Oddly enough, Langham had come across just such an atmosphere once before. In 1942 on the island of Madagascar, the unit to which he was attached as a field security officer had come up against Vichy French troops at Diego-Suárez. During the conflict their commanding officer, a fearsome Scot well liked by his men, had been fatally wounded, the unit's first casualty of the war. Langham recalled the sense of shocked disbelief among many of the men in the aftermath, and how some of the unit, himself included, had 'liberated' a sea-front bar and drunk it dry. At one point, hours into the binge, several of his colleagues had wondered aloud if Macgregor, a teetotaller, would have approved – and the drinking had continued under this guilty shadow.

'Donald, did you hear me?'

He smiled at Maria and gripped her hand on the seat next to him. 'Sorry. Miles away. What did you say?'

She replaced her brandy glass on the table. 'I just don't believe it, Donald. Even though I . . . even though I saw it with my own eyes.' She stopped, her big eyes staring into space. 'Poor, poor Marcus.'

He murmured something in agreement.

She looked at him. 'But it was just a terrible accident, wasn't it? I mean, surely no one would . . .?'

'I'm sure it was an accident,' he said to reassure her. 'He got too close to the thing and slipped.'

'I'm amazed that no one saw what happened, Donald.'

'Me too.' The police had been called and PC Thomson had been first on the scene; he'd used Dent's loudhailer to call for witnesses, but no one had stepped forward to say they had seen what had occurred. Langham had tracked down the couple he'd seen running away from the scene, but they said that the vicar was already dead when they noticed the body from the crest of the rise. Furthermore, they claimed to have seen no one in the vicinity of the orrery.

'I suppose almost everyone was on the lawn, attending the drawing of the raffle,' he said, swallowing a mouthful of whisky.

He'd seen a white-faced Dent, accompanied by the village odd-job man, rush down to the orrery and stop its irreverent whirling. By then some enterprising local had had the gumption to dismantle a kiosk and use the canvas to shroud the body. An ambulance had arrived thirty minutes later, shortly followed by a police car from Bury St Edmunds.

'But . . .' Maria shook her head again, as if with incomprehension. 'I don't understand how he cannot have been aware of the orrery and got so close, Donald! It was obvious it was dangerous. It was *frightening*, wasn't it? Clanking and swirling around like that! One's instinct was to stand well back.'

He gripped her hand. 'I know.'

He noticed a slight figure at the bar clutching a double Scotch. Alasdair saw him and smiled unsurely, then crossed the room. 'I say, you wouldn't mind if I joined you?'

Maria smiled. 'Of course not.'

The young man sat down. He looked pale and his hands trembled on his lap. He smiled from Maria to Langham. 'Poor Marcus,' he murmured, close to tears.

'I'm sorry,' Langham said, aware that his response was wholly inadequate.

Alasdair looked up and smiled bleakly. 'And on top of Marcus's death . . . I've just learned that the police have taken my father in again for questioning. You see, they found the murder weapon this morning.'

Langham looked at Maria, who was staring at the young man. She laid a hand on Alasdair's arm and said, 'The murder weapon?'

'A lawn-edger.'

'Where did they find it?' Langham asked.

'In the river. The killer must have thrown it there just after the attack.'

'But why did they take Edward in again?' Maria asked.

'Because the lawn-edger belonged to him, you see. He'd been trimming the lawn on the Saturday morning before he set off.' He looked up and groaned. 'Dash it – here's Montgomery. He's coming over. I don't think I really want to share the same table . . . Do excuse me.'

He shot off before either Langham or Maria could say a word.

Clutching his pint, Detective Inspector Montgomery stood over their table and stared at the retreating young man. 'What's wrong with him?'

'I think he's a little upset at your taking his father in for questioning again.'

Montgomery shrugged and sat down in the vacated seat. He removed his trilby, ran a hand across his balding head and dropped the grease-stained hat on the table. 'Well, I was quite prepared to quiz Endicott at the Chase, but he got a bit bolshy so I had no choice but to take him down to the station for questioning.'

Langham said, 'About the murder weapon?'

'Ah,' Montgomery said, 'young Alasdair told you?'

'He said it belonged to his father,' Langham said.

'A lawn-edger, blade like a razor. We're sure it was what accounted for Stafford's death. Killer obviously wiped his prints off it and tossed it into the river. Bloody stupid thing for Endicott to do, if it were him. And if it were someone else, then perhaps they threw it into the river in the hope of implicating him.'

'Or then again, whoever did it might have panicked . . .'

Montgomery shrugged. 'That's also a possibility.'

Langham sipped his whisky and felt its smooth burn slide down his throat. He said, 'What we were talking about yesterday . . . We said the murder was likely to have been premeditated.'

Maria looked at him. 'Why is that?'

'It was done with a sharp weapon – people aren't in the habit of carrying something like that around with them.'

'Ah,' she said. 'I see. But now . . .?'

'Well, if the lawn-edger were standing there,' Langham said, 'and the killer snatched it up in rage, a spur of the moment thing . . .'

Montgomery nodded. 'It certainly helps, finding the weapon. As you say, it isn't as if the killing was necessarily premeditated. Might've been an act of sudden rage.'

Maria stared into her brandy. 'But I cannot see why Edward would have killed the very man he was writing about. It doesn't make sense.'

'I agree.' Langham looked at the detective. 'And you're no nearer to discovering the real identity of "Stafford"?'

'I have people in London working on that, but until we find out who the hell he was . . .' He shook his head and finished his pint. 'And now this business with that bloody machine up at the hall . . . excuse my French.'

'It was a terrible accident surely, Inspector?' Maria said.

Montgomery shrugged. 'We're keeping an open mind on that, miss.'

Langham looked at Maria, then said to Montgomery, 'Did you manage to catch Denbigh before . . .?'

Montgomery shook his head. 'By the time I got to the vicarage he wasn't there.'

'He might have gone off in search of you,' Langham said.

Montgomery grunted. 'I went back to Bury and apparently Denbigh rang the station when I was briefing my team. He spoke to a secretary who said he sounded pretty flustered. And the next I heard . . . Well, he was dead.' He sighed. 'I'll have a word with this Dequincy woman later today. If she *is* implicated in Stafford's death . . .'

Maria said, 'Perhaps she innocently found the body on Sunday but panicked and fled?'

Montgomery looked up from his empty glass and said to Langham, 'I thought you said Denbigh didn't know whether Caroline saw him?'

Langham traced the scar at his temple. 'That's right.'

'So if Dequincy *thought* that Denbigh had seen her . . .' Montgomery said.

Maria said, almost desperately, 'But surely Caroline cannot be responsible? I mean, why would she kill Stafford? She was close to Edward – she wouldn't kill the subject of his studies.'

Montgomery shrugged. 'Who knows what motivates people in these situations?'

'And the idea that she would then silence Denbigh in such a terrible way . . . No, I don't believe it.'

Below the level of the table, so that Montgomery wouldn't see, Langham squeezed Maria's hand.

'Right.' Montgomery glanced at his watch. 'That slipped down a treat. I could murder another one, but duty calls.' He picked up his trilby, lodged it on his narrow skull and nodded to Maria and Langham.

'I feel a little sick,' Maria murmured when Montgomery had departed. 'I know you had to tell the inspector about what Denbigh said, but even so . . .'

'I'm sure everything will be satisfactorily explained when he's questioned Caroline.'

She stared at him. 'You don't think that she . . .?'

'No, of course not. I think what you said is right: Caroline found the body and panicked . . . and I also think that Denbigh's death was a tragic accident.'

'Oh, Donald, I hope so.'

He suggested they go for a long walk to clear their heads, so they left the Three Horseshoes and strolled along the lane past the Chase and into open country.

The sun was westering and the evening was still warm; a hazy glow hung over the countryside. They climbed a hillock a mile from the village, sat on its tussocky summit and stared across at Humble Barton. The scene was idyllic, and peaceful in its stillness; it might have been a canvas by Constable, aside from the police car parked beside the village green. Amid the thatched roofs and swelling oaks, the spire of St Andrew's caught the light of the setting sun. Langham slid an arm around Maria's waist. She leaned her head on his shoulder and quietly wept.

That night, back at the Chase, Langham was visited again by nightmares. He was in Madagascar, firing at the silhouette of the French soldier in order to save his friend's life. This time, instead of falling back out of sight, the soldier staggered forward and approached Langham accusingly, and with the surreal logic of dreams Langham saw that his machine-gun fire had removed half of the soldier's skull.

He came awake and cried out loud, and was aware of an angelic figure sitting beside him. She pressed him back on to the bed and mopped his brow with a cool, wet cloth.

'Sleep, Donald. Go to sleep,' she said. 'It was only a dream, a very bad dream.'

NINETEEN

Langham woke early next morning and lay in bed until he heard stirrings from the adjacent room. He and Maria descended together and had tea and toast under the cherry tree at the far end of the lawn. It was another brilliant summer's day and Langham was glad he was away from London; the capital would be stifling in the heat and humidity, its populace fractious and bad-tempered. Here, birdsong filled the air and a warm breeze soughed through the cherry blossom.

'I had a dream in the night, Maria. An angel sat on my bed and mopped my brow.'

'That is strange. I had a dream, too. I was an angel, and I was mopping the brow of a wounded soldier.'

'And you don't know how wonderful that felt.'

Maria hugged herself and shivered, despite the warmth. 'This angel would like to leave Humble Barton and get back to London.'

'I'll have a word with Montgomery if I see him today. If you'd really like to get back, I'm sure we'll be able to go if I give him our contact details.'

The French windows of Edward Endicott's study swung open, glinting in the sunlight, and Endicott strode across the lawn. 'There you are,' he called out. 'There's a phone call for you, Maria. Caroline would like a quick word.'

226

Maria looked at Langham. 'I wonder what she wants?' she said as she stood and strode towards the house.

Endicott dropped into the seat beside Langham and sighed. 'Ghastly business yesterday. Village is in shock. Fortunately I was still in the hall. Didn't see . . .'

'You were lucky. I saw the couple who were first on the scene and wondered what the heck was going on. I wish I hadn't gone for a look-see.' He paused, then said, 'Like something from the war.'

Endicott glanced at him. 'Where'd you serve?'

'Madagascar, then India. Field security.'

'See much action?'

'A few skirmishes, mopping up the Vichy French in Madagascar. In India it was mainly routine security work, keeping an eye on the nationalists and praying the Japs wouldn't push south. You?'

'North Africa. Tanks. Hellish. Bit of a contrast to Hollywood.'

'I can imagine.' Langham stretched his legs in the sunlight and nursed a china cup of Earl Grey.

'It's poor Denbigh's funeral next week. Never had much time for the fellow, to be honest. Too wishy-washy C of E for my liking, but he didn't deserve that. Expert bods are calling it a freak accident.' He grunted. 'Some sick wag in the Three Horseshoes last night called it "the hand of God".'

Langham glanced at Endicott. 'Come again?'

'Hoist by his own ecclesiastical petard,' Endicott went on cryptically. 'You see, Denbigh had a secret.'

Langham sat up. 'A secret?'

Endicott raised a hand. 'I don't sit in judgement, Donald. Saw plenty of it during the war – men cooped up together, without women.'

'Ah . . .' Langham said. 'How did you find out?'

Endicott looked uncomfortable. 'Overheard Denbigh and Alasdair in the library one evening. Denbigh was pouring his heart out, the poor sod. Thought it best to beat a rapid retreat.' He glanced at Langham. 'Anyway, word in the village is that it wasn't an accident.'

'It wasn't . . .?'

The other man nodded. 'All became a bit too much . . . keeping it secret, living a double life. Upshot, he topped himself.' He shook his head. 'Odd chap. He put on a good front, a show of joviality and bonhomie. But underneath he was a nervous wreck . . . Alasdair was rather chummy with him, despite their differences. Said the chap sustained himself on booze. No wonder the poor blighter did himself in.'

'That's speculation, of course.'

'Of course.' Endicott shrugged. 'We'll probably never know. Anyway, he was well enough liked in the village. Expect there'll be a fair turnout next week.'

'We should come up from London for it . . .' Langham said. 'Maria and I were talking about pushing off, probably tomorrow. It's been awfully decent you putting us up like this.'

'Don't mention it, Donald. Been nice having you around. And your girl is easy on the eye. Plan to get hitched?'

'Well, that's the idea, Edward. When I screw up the courage to ask.'

Endicott laughed. 'Ah, marriage . . . I remember it well. I was hitched for ten years, then Mary fell ill in Hollywood and passed away. Hell of a shock, despite the fact we were daggers drawn most of the ruddy time. Alasdair was still a nipper. Came back here and an aunt in Cheltenham helped out, took him in during the war.' He slapped his thigh. 'Anyway, no use crying over spilt milk. And here's your girl, to save you a longer sob story.' He smiled at Maria as she approached.

'Oh,' he said. 'Almost forgot. How about dinner here tonight, seeing as how you'll soon be skeddadling? Caroline's coming over to cook something. She's a genius in the kitchen.'

Maria shielded her eyes from the sunlight. 'That will be lovely, thank you.' She turned to Langham and said, 'Caroline would like to see us. She said we could come over for morning tea at ten thirty.'

Langham consulted his watch. 'It's ten past now. We could set off and stroll through the village.'

Endicott stood up and called Rasputin, who came bounding from the study with his lead clutched in his slavering jaws. 'Duty calls. I'll see you tonight.'

Maria watched Endicott lead the setter across the lawn and then turned to Langham, her expression worried.

He stared at her. 'Something's wrong? Is Caroline . . .?'

'She was very upset, Donald. She wanted to see

us both. You don't think she suspects that we . . .?'

'What, that we told Montgomery about Denbigh seeing her?' He shook his head. 'I wouldn't think so. I don't think Montgomery would disclose his sources like that.' He smiled up at her. 'She was probably dragged in for a grilling last night and wants to talk about it with a friendly face. Mark my words.'

They left the Chase and strolled down the lane, passing into and out of the shadow of the elms that lined the way. 'Oh, and I heard something about Denbigh from Endicott.'

He told her the story, and the speculation that his death had not been an accident.

Maria held a knuckle to her lips. 'Oh, but that's terrible, Donald! The poor man!'

'*If* he did take his own life, Maria. My money's still on a freak accident.'

They passed the village green. Montgomery's unmarked car was parked up outside St Andrew's and a uniformed bobby stood to attention at the gate of the vicarage.

'You don't think . . .?' Maria began.

'What?'

'That it was neither an accident nor suicide? That it was Caroline who . . .'

He stared down at the patched macadam as they turned on to the lane where Caroline Dequincy lived. 'I just can't see her doing something like that.'

'Is that just because she's a woman?'

'Of course not!' he protested. 'She strikes me as a decent person. I'm sure she wouldn't . . .'

Maria nodded. 'Yes, that's how I think of her, too. I only hope we are right.'

They came to Rosebud Cottage and pushed through the white gate. Boardman was on hand to greet them with his dolorous stare; he climbed stiffly to his feet and led the way across the lawn.

Caroline waved at them. 'Over here,' she called.

She sat at a table in the shade of an apple tree, a glass of clear liquid before her. She wore a yellow dress with a matching chiffon bow in her hair, and appeared to have spent a lot of time on her make-up. Despite this, Langham could see that her mascara had run, and the evidence of a balled tissue in the grass at her feet suggested that she had been crying.

She was animated and gay – perhaps overly so – as she called for her maid to fetch the tea things. 'Or perhaps you'd care for something a little stronger?' she went on, indicating a jug. 'Gin punch. I know it's early, but I find it's a wonderful pick-me-up.'

'Tea for me, thanks, Caroline,' Langham said, and Maria agreed.

'I hope you didn't mind my calling like that, Maria?' Caroline said. 'I just needed . . .' She beamed at them. 'Well, I just needed to talk to someone.'

The maid came out with a tray and poured two Earl Grey teas. Langham helped himself to a Rich Tea biscuit and repositioned his chair in the shade. He looked at Caroline Dequincy, her green eyes and handsome face. Despite the fact that she was clearly troubled by something, she maintained an enviable poise, even elegance.

Try as he might, he just could not envisage her taking a lawn-edger to Stafford's head, nor pushing the Reverend Denbigh to his death.

She took a sip of gin punch, her hand hardly trembling. 'I was visited by the constabulary last night,' she said. 'That strange little inspector, Montgomery, and his sidekick – I forget the man's name. They questioned me for what seemed like hours and worked the old softening-up routine – Montgomery taking the role of the tough-guy and his sidekick coming on all smiles and sympathy when Montgomery was through.'

'I didn't like it when Inspector Montgomery questioned me,' Maria said. 'I thought him rather rude.'

Caroline smiled. 'He was downright nasty, Maria. You see, they more or less accused me of killing first Vivian Stafford and then Marcus Denbigh.'

Langham said, 'On what evidence?'

The actress took a longer drink this time, set the glass down with deliberation and smiled at them. 'Well, you see,' she said, a slight catch in her voice, 'despite what I led you to believe, I actually discovered Stafford's body on Sunday morning.'

Langham feigned surprise. 'Sunday?' he said, relieved at her admission.

Her smiled faltered. 'You have every right to be annoyed at me for not telling you the truth,' she said. 'I'm not proud of pulling the wool over your eyes.'

Maria leaned forward. 'What happened, Caroline?'

The actress sighed. 'Quite simply, and honestly – though I doubt whether Montgomery believed me – I was taking Boardman for a walk on Sunday morning. I often go through the village, take the river path past the Chase and over the bridge to the grounds of Stafford Hall. We were passing the woods when Boardman tugged on the lead and dragged me along the path. He dived into the undergrowth, rooting for something, and when I took a closer look . . . Well, you know what was there. I recognized Stafford immediately, of course.'

Langham shook his head. 'But why didn't you simply report what you found?'

Caroline raised a hand. 'I'll get to that in a minute,' she said. 'Anyway, while I was staring at the body I saw someone on the path a couple of hundred yards further into the woods . . . I couldn't be certain if they'd seen me or not, nor who the person was. I half-guessed it was Denbigh, but I couldn't be sure.' She shook her head. 'I panicked, just fled and ran to the Chase. But of course, Edward wasn't there . . .' She raised her glass and gave an ironic smile. 'And I'm afraid when I got home I hit the gin.'

She took another sip of her drink. 'And then yesterday evening . . . Montgomery told me that someone had seen me in the woods on Sunday morning, where the body was later found. He said that killers often returned to the scene of their crimes. I protested my innocence, of course. I admitted being there, and finding the body . . . I said I panicked and fled, having seen someone watching me and not wanting to be suspected of having anything to do with the . . .' She took a deep breath and went on: 'Then Montgomery's sidekick, who'd been as nice as pie until that point, dropped the bombshell and accused me of killing the Reverend Denbigh. He said that it was Denbigh who'd seen me in the woods near the corpse and he claimed that I must have recognized him . . .' She looked from Langham to Maria, her poise beginning to fracture as she said, 'And the damned thing was . . . yesterday, before the . . . before the accident, I was the last person seen with Denbigh. We were near that infernal contraption of Dent's.'

'You spoke with him?' Maria asked.

Caroline nodded. 'He came up to me, said he wanted a private word. I must say he seemed in a bit of a state.'

'What did he want?' Langham asked.

Caroline hesitated, then said, 'He told me he'd seen me near the body on Sunday, said that he'd "made the information public" – those were his exact words. And then he apologized. He seemed truly sorry . . .' She smiled. 'The odd thing was, I felt sorry for the dilemma I'd caused him. Anyway, I admitted to Montgomery that I'd spoken to Denbigh, but told him what I've just told you. I said that the last time I saw Denbigh he was walking towards the orrery, lost in thought. I heard the announcement that the raffle was about to be drawn and hurried back to the lawn.'

Langham said, 'And how did Denbigh seem when you left him?'

She shrugged. 'He was upset.'

234

'He didn't appear . . . depressed, suicidal?'

She shook her head. 'No . . . I wouldn't say so. I'm sure he wouldn't have taken his own life. He was too God-fearing for that.'

Langham asked, 'What do you think happened?'

She held his gaze. 'I think it was a terrible, terrible accident, Donald. I think he slipped or stumbled . . .'

He nodded, taking a sip of tea and glancing at Maria. She leaned forward, staring at the actress, and asked, 'But Donald's earlier question – why didn't you report finding Stafford's body in the woods?'

The actress's smile faltered again; she took a breath and nodded. 'I . . . I was telling the truth when I said that I panicked when I found the body, but the reason that I panicked was because, you see, I had a very good reason to want Stafford dead.'

Langham lowered his cup to its saucer with a surprised crash. 'What?'

'You see, I . . . I am pretty sure that Stafford was blackmailing me.'

Maria exclaimed under her breath and Langham said, 'Blackmailing . . .?'

'I received a letter shortly after we first met, over a month ago now. We'd been talking about my early career in Hollywood. He proved to be very knowledgeable on the subject of the movie industry. A few days later I received an anonymous, typewritten letter through the post: it stated simply that the writer was sure that I would like certain information regarding my past – and he went into detail – to be kept from public

235

knowledge. To ensure this, the writer demanded that I send him fifty pounds in used notes.'

'And you think that this person, this black-mailer, was Vivian Stafford?' Maria asked.

'I do.'

'On what evidence?' Langham asked.

Caroline hesitated. 'During our conversation regarding my early career, he seemed . . . and I don't know how exactly to describe this . . . but I received the distinct impression – from a certain archness of expression, the way he looked at me – that he knew something about me. Also, the address to which I had to send the money—'

'Surely he didn't give his own address?' Langham said.

'No, a PO Box number in Holborn. I happened to know, from what Edward had told me, that Stafford stayed in the area.'

Langham pursed his lips. 'And from this you assumed that it was Stafford blackmailing you?'

'There was another thing, the clincher. Edward showed me some correspondence he'd had from the man – I forget what the content was – and the font he'd used matched exactly that in the letter I'd received.'

Maria shook her head. 'But many typewriters have the same font,' she pointed out.

Caroline smiled. 'And do many of them have a letter "d" with a broken upstroke?' she asked. 'That's what convinced me, you see. When I first received the demand, I *suspected* Stafford but later, when I saw Edward's letter – that's when I knew for sure.'

'And you paid up?' Langham asked.

Caroline inclined her head with, in the circumstances, uncommon grace. 'I did.'

'And were there other demands after the first?'

'I've received two further demands,' she said.

'And you paid the money both times?' Maria asked.

Caroline held Maria's gaze and said, 'Yes, I did. You see, I didn't want . . . I didn't want what I did to become known. Moreover, I didn't want Edward to find out. You might think me foolish to run after a man who clearly doesn't love me, but I harbour the hope that one day that might change. And if he ever found out . . . if he discovered my secret, then . . .' She took a breath. 'I'm not proud of what I did back then – this was in the twenties, you see. I was young and naïve and foolish, and I wanted to get on in Hollywood. I was a little idiot . . . and my actions came back to haunt me.'

'Do you have any idea how Stafford found out about what you did?' Langham asked.

She gave a thin smile and took another drink of gin. 'Oh, I know, but I doubt whether you, Donald, being of a rationalist persuasion, will be convinced.'

He smiled. 'I think I can guess . . .'

She said, 'Stafford, for all his veniality, his evilness, was a brilliant man. There were no secrets anyone could keep from him. Ask Edward if you don't believe me. I don't know how *exactly* he knew, but I believe that the occult must have been involved.'

Langham considered it neither the time nor place to mock her beliefs. He said, 'I take it that

237

Montgomery isn't aware that Stafford was blackmailing you?'

'I certainly hope not,' she said. 'But I live in fear that he'll find out.'

She stopped there, her gaze dropping. She took a long breath, gathered herself and looked up with a bright smile. 'Anyway, that's why I asked to see you. You see, Alasdair mentioned that you had certain . . . contacts – a private investigator. If the police do discover that Stafford was blackmailing me then they won't look any further for the killer.'

'And you want me to get my contact on the case?'

She smiled. 'I suddenly find myself fifty pounds a week better off,' she said, 'and I think the money might be better spent hiring the services of a private detective, don't you?'

He smiled. 'I think it might. His name's Ralph Ryland and he's good. I served with him during the war.'

'He won't be too busy with other cases?'

'I'm sure he'll make time for a friend,' Langham said. 'If I could use your phone, I'll contact him right away.'

'By all means.' She looked relieved.

Langham left the table and moved into the cottage, the small hallway refreshingly cool after the heat of the sun. He picked up the phone, sat on the lowest step of the staircase and dialled the number of Ryland and Hope. Back in 'forty-six, after a few weeks at the agency without seeing Ryland's business partner, he'd asked Ralph just who the mysterious Mr Hope might be. It turned out that Hope was fictitious; Ralph said that 'Ryland and Hope' sounded better than just plain Ryland – and anyway 'Hope' was an optimistic name to have in the business's title.

''Ello? Ryland and Hope, private investigators.'

'Ralph. Donald here.'

'Don! Good to hear from you.'

'How's business, Ralph?'

'What? You're kidding, right?' Ryland's cockney tones sounded put out. 'July, remember? Every beggar in London's off enjoying hisself and here I am, kicking me bleedin' heels.'

'Excellent. Glad you're quiet.'

'Thanks a bunch, mate.'

'Because I can put some work your way, if you're interested.'

'Now you're talking, Cap'n. What's the gen?'

'Oh, just the usual . . . blackmail, murder.'

Ryland sounded disappointed. 'I geddit! You want to pick me brain again for one of your bleedin' novels, right?'

Langham laughed. 'No, I'm serious. This isn't fiction. Would you believe that I have a Hollywood actress here who's been blackmailed, and that there's been a murder?'

'You've been reading too much Raymond Chandler, Don. This for real?'

'Well, the actress thinks she knows who's blackmailing her, but he's just turned up dead and she's the main suspect.'

'Sounds interesting. Where are you?'

'Humble Barton, Suffolk. If you're doing nothing, could you drive up? I'll fill you in on what's been going on.'

239

'Humble what? Never heard of it. Hold on a sec while I get the map-book. Right-o. Say again. Humble . . .?'

'Barton,' Langham said. He gave Ryland the directions and the details of where he could be contacted.

'Got it,' Ryland said. 'Right, I'll be with you in . . . say a bit over two hours. And tell the actress I'll be charging a tenner a day.' He laughed, then said, 'Never met a real, live, livin' and breathin' Hollywood actress before, Don. This broad a looker?'

'Knocking on, but way out of your league, Ralph.'

'Catch you later,' Ryland said, and rang off.

Langham returned to the table beneath the apple tree and smiled as Caroline looked up expectantly. 'All set. Ralph will be here later this afternoon and his rates are ten pounds a day.'

Caroline smiled. 'Reasonable, by LA standards,' she said. 'I was about to say that this calls for a celebratory drink, but I think I've had enough. Say, would you care to stay for lunch? I have some smoked salmon, and Molly has just baked one of her divine blackberry and apple pies.'

TWENTY

Ralph Ryland arrived just after one o'clock. Langham heard the grumble of a car engine in the lane and drew aside the lace curtain as Ralph's battered Morris Minor pulled up outside the cottage.

'I'll take a turn in the garden with Ralph, bring him up to speed with what's been going on. Then, if it's all right with you, Caroline, I'll bring him in here for a chat.'

He left the cottage and met Ryland in the lane.

'Why do I always feel uncomfortable in the countryside?' Ryland asked as he rounded the car and took Langham's hand in a loose grip.

'Unfamiliarity, Ralph. You're a city boy born and bred. Come on, the girls are in the cottage, but I thought I'd tell you what's been happening before the introductions. Care for a tea?' he asked as he led Ryland into the garden.

'Could kill for a cuppa, Don. Strong and white, three sugars.'

Langham popped inside, relayed Ryland's order to Molly, then returned to find Ryland sitting under the cherry tree, staring up at the blossom. 'It fair pongs, Don.'

'That's the countryside for you, though we do have cherry trees in parks in London.'

'Parks? Never been to one in my life.'

Molly arrived bearing a tray and Langham poured two teas.

Everything about Ralph Ryland was thin. He had thin feet, thin hands, a thin face with thin lips and a stringy ginger moustache. He had no shoulders to speak of and looked like a weasel in human form, right down to his tiny, dark eyes. Langham's friendship with the cockney was easy and uncomplicated, the result of serving with the man for three years in Madagascar and India.

'So what've you been getting yourself into this time?' Ryland asked as he held his cup in both hands and blew on it to cool the beverage.

'Blackmail, murder and associated evils,' Langham said. 'It's a long story, so I'll start at the beginning.'

Ryland listened attentively, staring into his tea, as Langham outlined the events of the last few days.

'Did she say why she was being blackmailed?' the detective asked when Langham had finished.

Langham shook his head. 'She was understandably cagey on the subject.'

Ryland sucked up his tea and shook his head. 'I've got no time for this occult malarkey. Show me a spook and I'll show you someone trying to pull a con trick. The thing is who the hell was this Stafford bloke? If we can work that out, we're halfway there. Don't suppose you have a snapshot of the geezer?'

'No sooner said . . .' Langham fished the photos from his jacket pocket and passed them to Ryland, one showing the Victorian Stafford, the other outside the pub.

'Same bloke, no doubt about that, Don.' Ryland held the Victorian photograph close to his eyes and frowned. 'This one's a mock-up. Look at it closely.' He passed Langham the photograph.

'I've stared at the damned thing till I'm blue in the face,' Langham said. He shook his head. 'I don't see . . .'

'When's it supposed to have been taken?'

'Around the turn of the century.'

Ryland lit a Woodbine, slipped it into the corner of his mouth and smiled. 'It was taken relatively recently and doctored to look old. Not hard to do, if you know how.'

'Go on. Put me out of my misery.'

'When I drove through the village I saw the First World War memorial on the village green. Look at the photo, Don.'

Langham peered. 'So . . .?'

Ryland said, 'The snap's taken on the green, and see that thin dark line in the top left of the photo?'

'My word.'

'It's the very edge of the crossbar of the crucifix on top of the war memorial. It's almost not there, no more than a sliver.'

'Damn it, you're right.'

'So the photo *can't* have been taken in Victorian times.'

'Good work.'

'Confirmation, if we needed it, that our Mr Stafford was some kind of impostor.'

'This'll ruffle a few feathers among the believers,' Langham said.

'Mind if I keep these, Don? I'll check on missing persons when I get back to London.'

'They're all yours.'

Ryland drained his tea. 'Now, I'd like a few words with the movie star, and then perhaps have a gander at where you found the body and a quick look at the damned contraption that did for the vicar. Then I'll be making tracks.'

They moved into the cottage and Langham introduced Ryland to Caroline and Maria.

'Lovely to meet you,' Ryland said. 'I must have seen every film you've made over the years. Annie – that's my better half – won't half be suited when I say I've shaken your hand.'

'Why, that's very kind of you.'

Maria said, 'Lovely to meet you at last, Ralph. Donald's told me so much about you.'

'All good, I hope,' Ryland said. As they took their seats around the coffee table, Ryland turned to Caroline and asked, 'Don't suppose I could have your autograph – for Annie, like.'

Caroline gave her most dazzling smile. 'I can do better than that, Mr Ryland.' She moved to a bureau, took out a sheaf of glossy photographs and passed one to Ryland. It showed the movie star in a characteristic Hollywood pose, reclining on a chesterfield with a hand to her permed auburn tresses. She looked around twenty years old.

Ryland passed it back. 'I don't suppose you could sign it and add a few words for Annie?'

'By all means.' She found a fountain pen in the bureau and added her autograph and an inscription.

Ryland beamed down at the photo like a schoolboy and tucked it into his jacket pocket.

'Now, I hope you don't mind if I ask a few questions, Mrs Dequincy?'

'Not at all, and please do call me Caroline.'

Langham and Maria made themselves scarce while the interview proceeded, slipping from the cottage and strolling the length of the garden. He told her that Ryland had started earning his fee already by spotting the faked 'Victorian' photograph.

'You're always saying he's one of the best, Donald.'

'If a little unconventional.'

'I must say he isn't at all my idea of a private detective. He's a little shabby and down at heel, no?'

'Goes with the territory. He's more likely to be hobnobbing with bent bookies and East End spivs than solving village murder mysteries.'

Maria smiled. 'He was obviously delighted to meet a movie star. His eyes nearly popped from his head.'

'He was tickled pink. Funny, I never had him down as a movie buff.'

He told Maria that Ryland was going to check on missing persons in London in an attempt to trace the true identity of Stafford. 'If he can find out exactly who the man was, then that might help us work out *why* he was killed.'

'I wonder how Edward Endicott might react when he finds out that Stafford was an impostor?'

Langham shook his head. 'I dread to think.'

'Poor Edward.'

The back door of the cottage opened and Ralph Ryland stepped out, pocketing a notebook and clicking the top of his biro pen. 'All done. Now, you promised a guided tour.'

Caroline followed Ryland from the cottage. 'And I do hope you can get to the bottom of all this, Mr Ryland.'

The detective doffed an imaginary hat. 'Ask Don. I'm like a terrier when I get me teeth into a case. In't that right, Cap'n?'

'You'd better believe it,' Langham said. 'Right, we're going for a tour of the place. I could meet you back at the Chase in an hour or so, Maria.'

Langham and Ryland left the garden and stepped out into the lane. Instead of turning right into the village, Langham ushered the detective left towards the river and the woodland footpath.

Ryland pulled an envelope from his breast pocket and showed it to Langham. 'One of the blackmail demands. Typed, and no doubt wiped of any dabs if the blackmailer had half a brain. Caroline pointed out the fault with the letter d, which might be useful.' He returned the envelope to his pocket. 'I'll check out the PO Box number she sent the money to, but I don't expect that to lead me anywhere. Stafford would have covered his tracks pretty well.'

Langham removed his jacket and slung it over his shoulder. 'You never told me you were a film buff.'

'I'm not. Never heard of Caroline Dequincy in me life.'

'You old rogue! So all the autograph business . . .'

Ryland tapped the side of his nose. 'Met a very wily old dame a few weeks ago. Graphologist – ever heard of one of those?'

'A handwriting expert?'

'Must admit, Don, she amazed me with what she could tell from a few squiggles.'

'Which is why you asked Caroline to add an inscription?'

'You got it.'

'Very clever.'

'I'll show the pic to my new friend and see if she agrees with what I think.'

Langham glanced at the detective. 'Which is?'

'That Caroline is on the level. I get these gut feelings about people. I have a hunch when they're telling the truth, or not. And Caroline's no murderer.'

'Did you get any inkling of why she's been blackmailed?'

They came to the river and strolled along the bank; to their left the water smoothed its way over browned stones and twinkled silver in the sunlight. Swallows skimmed the surface, catching insects on the wing.

Ryland shook his head. 'I didn't pry. Got the impression, though, that it was something risqué. Maybe an affair she wanted to keep mum – an illegitimate child?' He shrugged. 'Anyway, I like her. One classy dame. And she was a stunner in her younger days.'

'It's sad, Ralph. She has the hots for Edward Endicott, who doesn't seem all that interested.'

'Man's a fool.' A hornet buzzed Ryland and he batted at it, startled, before continuing: 'And the blood you mentioned – it was found on his land?'

'That's right. And the murder weapon, discovered in the river, was his. The police have hauled Endicott in a couple of times for grillings, but what I can't work out is if he did do for Stafford – then why? Why kill the man you're writing about?'

Ryland shrugged his milk-bottle shoulders. 'How about he found out that this guy pretending to be Stafford was an impostor, and he flew into a rage and bashed his head with the lawn-edger?'

'I don't know. I just can't see Edward as a murderer. I know, I know . . . that doesn't mean he isn't. But . . .'

They passed the end of the path that led to the Chase and came to the timber bridge. They crossed it, loose boards rattling underfoot, and took the path past the folly. 'Who lives there?' Ryland asked.

'It's not a house, as such. Think of it as a rich landowner's garden hut. It belongs to the Chase. Endicott comes here to write from time to time.'

'Some hut,' Ryland sniffed. He stumbled on the uneven path and Langham grabbed his elbow.

'Bloody countryside,' Ryland muttered. 'Give me the Old Kent Road any day. And these pesky flying things . . .' He batted away another airborne nuisance – a bee this time – and mopped his balding head with a handkerchief.

They climbed the stile and crossed the meadow to where the woods continued. It was a relief to step from the unremitting heat of the sun into the cool shade of the trees. Langham led the way along the path for twenty yards until they came to the elm tree. He stopped and indicated the trampled undergrowth.

'And this is where the body was discovered.'

Ryland knelt and cast an eye over the area. He looked up. 'Right. Where did you say the vicar was killed?'

Langham led the way from the woods and up the rise towards Stafford Hall. Ryland panted up the grassy knoll beside him, and Langham reflected that the decade since they'd both served in the army had taken its toll on the detective. He recalled Ryland being super-fit, a bit of an amateur boxer; now he'd developed a paunch that hung on his thin frame like an orange in a Christmas stocking. He liked his pint and whisky chaser, and didn't delay his consumption until the end of the working day.

'Run it by me again, Don. How was the vicar killed?'

'It was bizarre, to say the least. You know what an orrery is?'

'Go on.'

'It's a model of the solar system, usually made of brass, about this big.' He held his hands about a yard apart, like a fisherman. 'Only this particular orrery was as big as a fairground roundabout, and instead of horses and whatever there were planets.'

'Planets?'

'Jupiter, Saturn, Pluto . . . made from brass or something and moving on tracks about this high off the ground.' He held his hand at waist height.

'And you say that one of the balls bashed the vicar on the head?'

'It's a sight I'll never forget, unfortunately.'

'Know what you mean. The things I saw at Dunkirk . . .'

'It's one thing in wartime,' Langham said, 'but you don't expect to see it at a village fair.'

They arrived at the crest of the rise and looked down over the sedate lawns of Stafford Hall, presided over by the ivy-clad stately home. 'This way.'

They descended and crossed the main lawn; the tents and marquees had been taken away. All that remained to show that the fair had taken place was gouged earth where tent pegs had been removed, and trampled grass like the ruffled nap of velvet where the crowds had trooped.

'But you don't think the vicar's death was linked to Stafford's?'

Langham shook his head. 'I think it was simply an awful accident.'

Ryland sniffed. 'Want my opinion? Two deaths don't happen like this without being connected. It's just too coincidental.'

'Well, I hope you're wrong . . .' He paused. 'I don't know. If his death was an accident, that would be tragic enough. But the thought that he might have been murdered . . .'

They climbed the knoll that overlooked the dell where Haverford Dent had erected his industrial works of art. Langham came to the crest and stopped in his tracks, surprised at what he saw.

'Blimey, Don. What the hell is it?'

'That,' he said, 'is the orrery. Or was.'

The orrery lay in a state of disrepair, the tracks dismantled and the great orbs of the planets no longer on their tracks but scattered across the grass – as if some angry god had backhanded his creation in a fit of petulance.

Then Langham saw Haverford Dent and realized that his fanciful metaphor might not have been that far off the mark. The artist stood amid the brass wreckage of the orrery, resting from his labours on the shaft of a sledgehammer.

Dent saw them and called out, 'Something you don't often witness, Langham! The artist *destroying* his work!'

Ryland glanced at Langham. 'He sounds . . .' He frowned, searching for the right word.

'Deranged, I'd say.' Langham hesitated. 'Should we . . .?' He gestured towards the amphitheatre.

'After you, sir,' Ryland said.

He led the way into the dell, avoiding the sawdust-covered grass where the vicar had met his end, and moved through the remains of the orrery towards Dent.

The artist appeared to be as broken as his creation; he was grey, and shaking from exertion or rage.

'I hope we're not interrupting,' Langham began lamely.

Dent clutched the shaft of the sledgehammer and gazed about him at the twisted rails and broken orbs. Planet Earth lay beside him, a crack fissuring the sphere from pole to pole.

'I was a fool, Langham! A bloody fool! I should have thought – the danger! Anyone might've . . .' He cast a haggard glance around him, then stared at Langham. 'It was an accident waiting to happen, Langham. The poor, poor man . . .'

Langham shook his head. 'You weren't to know . . .' he began.

'Of course I wasn't to know! But I should have *thought*. I should've erected some kind of safety barrier. If only I'd done that then poor bloody Denbigh would still be alive.' He took up his hammer like some enraged and superannuated Thor and swung at the nearest object. Venus cracked asunder with a sound like a bell struck by a piledriver, and fell into two halves.

Dent panted, rage in his eyes. 'And do you know something, Langham? I used to think that art was everything! Everything! That art was even more important than an individual's life. Mine, anyone's! What's that old saw – what's more important, the life of an anonymous Chinaman on the other side of the world, or the existence of the Mona Lisa? Would you, if you could, flick a switch to kill this unknown Chink in order to save the work of art?' He shook his head, his face etched with grief. 'I thought long and hard on that one over the years, and I came to the conclusion that the life of one Chinaman was worth it, because a work of art stands as testament to the humanity of our race and gives untold pleasure and insight to generations . . . But do you know something? I was wrong! Art is worth nothing, *nothing* beside the life of a single soul, not even some tortured, disease-ridden beggar wherever the hell he is! Each man is the world unto himself!'

Dent swung the sledgehammer again, shattering

a previously intact section of track. He moved away, anticlockwise, visiting destruction on his creation as he went.

Langham gestured to Ryland and they quietly made their way from the amphitheatre. At the top of the rise he paused and looked back. Dent cursed and crashed like a demented dervish, and Langham hoped that the destruction might, at least, serve the tortured artist as some kind of catharsis.

They left the grounds of the hall and retraced their steps through the meadow.

Ryland said, 'And you said that no one witnessed the vicar's death?'

'Not a soul, apparently.'

'Don't you think that odd?'

'Well . . . the announcement to say that the raffle was about to be drawn had just been made. I suppose everyone was heading to the lawn.'

Ryland pursed his thin lips, lost in thought. 'Doesn't the fact that his death wasn't seen suggest either suicide or murder?'

Langham looked at the weaselly detective. 'How so?'

Ryland held up a pale hand. 'I'm thinking aloud here. Look, if it were an accident, then it was just that – an accident, unplanned, unpremeditated . . . So, statistically, wouldn't it be more likely to have been seen by someone if it were an accident? You get my drift?'

'Go on,' Langham said.

'But, you see, Don, if it were murder . . . then the killer would *ensure* that everyone had left the area, wouldn't they? And the same if the vicar had topped himself. He would make sure there was no one about to see him and then do the business.'

Langham sighed. 'I see what you mean. And I can't deny that it is a logical assumption, yes.'

'I sense a "but" coming, Cap'n.'

Langham shook his head. 'I don't know . . . As I said earlier, it's even more appalling if it were murder, or suicide. I know – that doesn't mean to say that it wasn't.'

He fell into a troubled silence as they passed the folly and approached the wooden bridge.

Ryland said, 'What we've got to work out is who might want the vicar dead.'

'And you're ruling out the obvious suspect – Caroline Dequincy?'

Ryland twisted his lips to one side. 'For the time being, yes.'

Langham sighed. 'I don't know. I can't begin to guess who might have borne a grudge against Denbigh. He seemed such a bland, harmless soul.'

They took the riverside path past the Chase and came to the lane where Ryland's old Morris – which he'd nicknamed 'the Camel' for its khaki hue and dependability – was parked.

'Right,' Ryland said, 'I'll be getting back to the city – and not a second too soon. The countryside might be pretty, but you can keep it. I'll be in touch if anything crops up. How long are you planning to stay up here?'

'We thought we'd push off tomorrow or maybe the day after. I'll give you the phone number of the Chase.'

He tore a page from his notebook, scribbled down the number and passed it to Ryland.

The detective saluted and slipped in behind the wheel. 'Be seeing you, Cap'n.'

Langham watched the Morris putter off down the lane and then, lost in thought, made his way slowly back to the Chase.

Edward Endicott's claim that Caroline was a marvel in the kitchen turned out to be an understatement. Caroline, with a little help from Maria, served up a dinner that evening as continental as it was excellent. The first course was gazpacho – a cold cucumber and tomato soup Langham had never sampled before – which was surprisingly good and startlingly refreshing. This was followed by chicken paillard with steamed vegetables, done with a lightness of touch that would have been the envy of many a top restaurant. Dessert was crème brûlée followed by Irish coffee. As if the culinary delights were not sufficient, Endicott insisted on plying his guests with the appropriate alcoholic drink to accompany each course, starting with a martini aperitif, then a light French white wine followed by a burgundy. By ten o'clock, Langham was more than a little tipsy.

Alasdair was absent from the table. 'Rather cut up about what happened to young Denbigh,' Endicott explained, 'which is understandable, I suppose. They were rather chummy.'

The conversation flowed. At one point Endicott mentioned that Inspector Montgomery had been around again that day. 'Man's like a terrier with a rat – not that I'm casting myself in the role of the rodent. He never lets go, went over my movements at the weekend again and again.'

'But you must have told him a hundred times what you were doing,' Caroline said. They were seated side by side, and Langham could not help but notice the adoring glances she shot Endicott's way throughout the meal.

'Seems like a thousand, m'dear. He kept banging on about people I might have seen while I was hiking – or rather who might've seen me, and could corroborate my story. Fact is I didn't clap eyes on a single soul, as far as I recall. He seemed to think it strange that I didn't turn back as soon as Rasputin deserted me on Sunday. I told him that the old devil knows his way home and I wasn't worried in the least. Certainly wasn't going to curtail my hike for some blasted hound.' He helped himself to more wine. 'Montgomery more or less said that the investigation was coming along and that he was confident of pressing charges by the end of the week.'

'Sounds highly unlikely to me,' Langham said. 'A friend of mine's looking into the case. And in my experience he'll do a better job than the local coppers.'

'Let's hope so, then we can all get back to a normal routine.'

Langham recalled the photograph of Vivian Stafford – in Victorian guise, taken on the village green – and Ralph Ryland's exposure of it as a fake. He wondered whether to mention it to Endicott.

Caroline made the rounds with the burgundy

and insisted on lightening the tone. 'All this talk of the *unpleasantness*,' she said. 'Maria, I want to know how you came across this charming young man?'

Maria smiled archly across at Langham. 'You mean Donald?' she said. 'But Donald isn't young!'

He raised his glass in drunken acknowledgment.

She leaned forward, rested her chin on her clasped fingers and stared at him. 'Oh, I think I've admired Donald for years and years! You see, I work at the agency which represents Donald, and every few months this tall, dark, handsome man would wander in with his latest manuscript, hardly say hello to me and then go out to dinner with the boss.'

'That's unfair, Maria! I often brought you flowers . . .'

'To brighten up the office, you always said.' She smiled at him. 'But Englishmen are so constitutionally reserved, as my father says. I more or less had to throw myself at him before he even acknowledged me!'

Langham grumbled into his wine. 'Well . . . I suppose I was a bit reserved. I mean, what would a beautiful woman like Maria see in an ageing hack like me?' He winked at her.

'What broke the ice?' Caroline asked.

Langham gave Maria a should-you-tell-them-or-me look.

She said, 'As a matter of fact, Donald came to the rescue of my boss, Charles Elder – chased the scoundrel who was blackmailing Charles and got coshed on the head for his pains. I think I knew then that Mr Langham was the man for me. He staggered back to the agency, bleeding from a head wound, and collapsed at my feet.'

Langham smiled at the recollection. 'I recall coming around in Charles's flat and seeing this angelic vision staring down at me . . . It was almost worth getting hit for.'

Caroline was staring at him. 'My word, and I thought writers were supposed to lead boring lives!'

Conversation moved on, and Endicott plied Langham and Maria with snifters of French brandy.

'And all this talk of leaving tomorrow,' Endicott said. 'Nonsense, of course. It's been a breath of fresh air having you around. You'll stay until the weekend, and that's an order. Isn't that right, Caroline?'

The actress smiled. 'Of course, and I'll cook another meal if I survive this bout of alcohol poisoning. That's the trouble with Edward's dinners – he thinks everyone is as bibulous as he is.'

'Rubbish, woman,' Endicott muttered, though with affection.

Langham looked across at Maria. 'You all right with that?'

She smiled. 'Only if you take me out on long country walks, Donald.'

'That's a deal, then. We'll stay.'

The faint trilling of the telephone sounded from the hallway. Endicott swore. 'Dammit! Can't a man have any peace these days?'

Caroline sprang to her feet. 'I'll get it.'

Langham reached out for the brandy, thought better of it and diverted his hand towards the cheese board. He was about to help himself to a wedge of Stilton and a Jacob's cream cracker when Caroline returned.

'It's for you, Donald. Mr Ryland.'

Langham pulled a surprised face at Maria, excused himself and hurried into the hall.

He picked up the receiver. 'Ralph?'

'Job done, Don.'

'What?'

'Found out the true identity of Mr so-called Vivian Stafford.'

'Good God, Ralph. That was quick.'

'Told you I don't hang about. I checked at the Missing Persons Bureau at the Sally Army HQ on Old Brompton Road. Yesterday an old queen called in with a snap of his lover – been missing since Saturday. The picture they had on file and the ones you gave me are an exact match.'

'So . . . who was "Vivian Stafford"?'

'Old gent by the name of Cedric Hartwell – an actor. I got his address from the Salvationists and popped round. Only the law'd been to the Sally Army before me, then visited his lover and broke the news to him – one Vincent Bennett, another thespian. Bennett was pretty cut up, of course. I explained I was working on the case, trying to find Cedric's killer. Bennett said he couldn't possibly talk now, but if I came round in the morning . . . So I made an appointment for eleven. I thought you might want to come along as my sidekick, like.'

'Excellent. I'll do that.'

'Tell you what, Don. Meet me at the office at ten tomorrow and we'll motor up to Belsize Park.'

'See you then, Ralph, and well done.'

'All in the line of duty, Cap'n. Nighty-night.'

Langham replaced the receiver and, in a daze, made his way back along the hall.

A trio of faces stared at him as he entered the dining room. Caroline leaned forward. 'Any news?'

'Yes,' he said, and took his seat. He looked at Edward Endicott. 'That was the detective I hired today. I'm sorry, but he's found out the true identity of Vivian Stafford.'

Caroline clutched Endicott's hand and asked Langham, 'Who was he?'

'It appears,' Langham said, 'that Vivian Stafford was an actor whose real name was Cedric Hartwell.'

Endicott's lantern jaw dropped, but no words were forthcoming. He resembled, as he sat in stunned silence, a fairground clown whose gaping mouth was set to receive a ping-pong ball.

Langham reached across the table and helped himself to a brandy after all.

TWENTY-ONE

Caroline spent the following morning in the garden.

She busied herself with weeding the herbaceous border and considering the events of the previous day. She had been surprised by the appearance of Donald's friend, the detective Ralph Ryland. She had expected a stereotypical private investigator, a tough guy with a five o'clock shadow and a way with laconic one-liners – not someone who resembled an undernourished rat-catcher. His cockney whine and shifty glances had not impressed her, either, but it appeared that she might have underestimated the little detective. The last thing she'd expected yesterday evening was the phone call from him saying that he'd discovered the identity of the man claiming to be Vivian Stafford.

But why might an actor called Cedric Hartwell have deceived Edward like that?

Perhaps, when Donald returned from London later today, he might have learned more about the motives of the dead man.

She considered her reaction to discovering that Stafford was not who he'd claimed to be . . . Did this mean that he was not a satanist, either? But she had experienced what had happened at the hall: the apparitions, the ghostly moaning, the Beast of Brampton . . . though, to be fair, she had not seen the creature, merely heard its growls in the woods.

When Donald and Maria had retired last night, she had stayed behind at the Chase for a while and talked with Edward about Ryland's discovery.

She had expected Edward to be devastated, but had misjudged his reaction.

'Of course,' he'd blustered, helping himself to a stiff whisky, 'there's no knowing whether this detective chappie has got his facts right. Might be way off the mark as far as we know. I mean, why would an actor want to impersonate Stafford? What had he to gain by doing so? Sounds rum to me.'

The pain in his eyes, like a dog that had been kicked by its owner, was heart-rending to behold. He was facing the prospect that all his recent work might come to nothing. She had tried to buck up his spirits. 'Let's not assume too much until Donald gets back tomorrow with the facts.'

'That's the ticket, girl. No good jumping the gun, eh?'

At midnight she had left Edward in his study, nursing his third glass of whisky. As she had passed down the hallway she'd considered going upstairs to see how Alasdair was, but dismissed the idea. She had knocked on his bedroom door earlier in the evening, only to be met with a sullen, 'What do you want?'

'It's only me, Caroline. I just wondered if you might want to talk . . .?'

'No . . . No, thank you.'

'I could bring you something to eat.'

'To be honest, I couldn't face a thing right now.'

262

'No, of course not. But if you do need someone to talk to over the next few days, you know where to find me.'

As she'd walked home last night, she'd considered the pain the young man must be experiencing; to grieve after someone was bad enough, but to grieve without being able to acknowledge, to anyone, that you were doing so must be a torture almost beyond endurance.

Now, as the sunlight fell through the boughs of the apple tree and she knelt in the dappled shade, tugging at the more recalcitrant weeds in the border, she resolved that she would go to the Chase after lunch and talk to both Alasdair and Edward.

Beside her, Boardman lifted a lethargic ear, then climbed laboriously to his feet and gave a single, *basso profundo* bark. His call was returned instantly, and she recognized Rasputin's high-pitched yelp. Ten seconds later she heard the sound of Edward's hobnails on the lane and the regular rap of his staff as he marched along.

She climbed to her feet and hurried into the kitchen to wash her hands and arrange her hair. A minute later Rasputin galloped into the house, found Boardman, and both dogs trotted off into the garden.

She dabbed at her hair and turned, smiling, to greet Edward.

'Carrie . . . Glad you're at home.' He appeared in the open doorway, banging his staff on the threshold like a self-conscious schoolboy. She could count on one hand the number of times he'd called on her during the past few years.

'Edward . . . are you all right?'

'Could be better, all things considered.'

Her heart jumped, and her first thought was that something had happened to Alasdair. 'Is Alasdair . . .?' she began.

'Oh, he's cut up something rotten about Denbigh. Blasted business. I've tried talking to him, but what can I say that'd make much difference? He won't come out of his room.'

She gestured outside. 'Look, shall we go into the garden? I made some fruit punch earlier.'

'Just the ticket.'

She fetched a tray, the jug of punch and two glasses, and carried them out to the table beneath the apple tree.

He took a long drink and shook his head. 'Been thinking about the whole rotten business,' he said. 'Stafford, or whoever the hell he was. Why someone would do something like that . . . Thing is, Carrie, I believed him. He was so damned convincing.'

'I know, Edward. You're not the only one to be taken in.'

'But what I can't work out is his motivation in deceiving me like that. What was he up to, dammit – what was he after?' He shook his head again, exasperated. 'I mean, I can't work out what the man hoped to gain. Certainly nothing in terms of money. He never asked for a red cent, or anything else from me for that matter.' He was silent for a time, then said, 'My fear is . . .' and stopped.

'Go on.'

He sighed, thumped his staff on the lawn and

shook his head. 'My fear is that his deception didn't end at playing the part of Stafford.'

'You mean . . .?'

He nodded. 'I mean, what if everything about him, *everything*, was a lie? Not just the story about his being Vivian Stafford, and a hundred and twenty years old. But his . . . his powers.'

'But you saw what he could do. I mean, we both witnessed what happened at the hall.'

'Carrie,' he said with earnestness, 'what if everything about him was a charade? What if he had no occult powers at all, no arcane knowledge, no *talent* . . .? What if he were an impostor in every respect?'

'But the séance, the manifestations . . .' she said in a small voice.

He barked a grim laugh. 'What did Dent call it all? "Smoke and mirrors"? What if he were right? What if it were all smoke and mirrors? A massive confidence trick?'

She stared at the man she loved. A part of her wanted to console him, assure him that he was wrong in doubting the powers of the impostor. And yet, at the same time, she felt the first faint stirrings of relief deep within her. If the man had not been the harbinger of evil, the possessor of arcane knowledge and terrible powers . . . then perhaps she had no need to fear his reaching out from beyond the grave.

'Dammit, Carrie. I sat up all night, mulling things over.' He looked up and smiled ruefully at her. 'I had plenty of time to think things through, consider my life.'

'Oh, Edward.' She wanted to reach across, take

265

his hand. She wanted to take him in her arms and tell him not to worry, that she would care for him.

Instead she just sat, frozen, shaking her head and pitying this big, sad, defeated man.

'Makes you think about things, something like this,' he said. 'Makes you question yourself, look at things in a different light. I don't quite know how to phrase this . . . It makes you reassess your life and the people in it.'

He fell silent, gazing down at the grass between his boots.

He roused himself and said, 'I've been a bloody fool, Carrie.'

'Edward, you weren't to know,' she began.

'I don't mean about Stafford, or Hartwell, or whoever the hell he was.' He looked up at her. 'I mean I've been a bloody fool in how I've treated people. All I was bothered about was my writing, first the thrillers and then this Stafford nonsense . . . Ego, Carrie. That's all it was, when all's said and done, bloody self-centred ego. I couldn't look any further than my work and what I wanted from it. I could see no further than myself. And in consequence I neglected the people close to me. Alasdair.' He hesitated, then murmured, 'You . . .'

Her heart seemed to miss a beat. 'Edward?'

'Christ, Carrie, I've been a fool. There I was, sitting on my tod in the study at three o'clock on my fifth whisky and thinking about you. You, coming all the way over here, buying this place so you could be near me . . . Being on hand whenever I needed you, being like a mother to

Alasdair. And the thanks you get? I treat you like some kind of scullery maid. Not a bloody word of thanks. Thing is . . .'

He hesitated again, for longer this time, then said, 'Recall back in Hollywood, 'thirty-eight? Mary died. Hell of a time . . .'

She shook her head, confused by the change of subject. 'What about it?'

He stared at his blunt fingers wrapped around the staff. 'For a time after that, y'know . . . I mean, you and me. What I felt for you . . .'

'Edward, what are you trying to say?'

He banged his staff on the ground as if in frustration at his inarticulacy. 'I mean, dammit, I was this far, *this far*, from telling you how much I felt for you, Carrie.'

'Well, why didn't you?' she said, with a catch in her voice.

He looked up into her eyes. 'A couple of months after Mary passed away I met this medium chappie at some party or other. Convincing cove. I opened up a bit about Mary . . .' He shrugged. 'Upshot was I threw a party, invited the medium. You were out in Arizona, filming that terrible western.'

She laughed. 'My first and last, Edward! Anyway, the party . . . What happened?'

'Good God . . .' He shook his head at the recollection. 'Mary appeared. Clear as daylight. Gave me a hell of a shock. I saw her, Carrie. I tell you I saw her as plain as the nose on my face. She was there, staring at me. Others saw her, too. So it wasn't just me, hallucinating. And she said . . .' He stopped suddenly.

Caroline was aware that she was holding her breath. 'What did she say?' she asked in barely a whisper.

He shook his head and said, almost inaudibly, 'She said that she was waiting for me. That she loved me. That she was sorry . . .' He looked up. 'She never said what for. Just that she was sorry. And I . . . Well, it rocked me, I must say. Rather hit the old bottle in the weeks after that.'

'I remember. I thought it was . . . well, grief . . . losing Mary.'

'It was fear, Carrie. Guilt. I mean, dammit, I was head over heels in love with you, for God's sake, and what could I do about it? What with Mary watching over me like that? Call me a bloody fool but I just couldn't do anything about what I felt for you. So I shut you out of my life. Self-protective instinct kicking in, I s'pose. The séance scared me half to death. I'm not trying to make excuses . . . or perhaps I am.' He looked at her. 'Does that make any kind of bally sense at all, Carrie, or am I talking complete rot?'

She smiled, holding back her tears. 'It . . . it makes complete sense, Edward.'

'Thing is you're a good woman. You're beautiful and pretty damned smart too. And the séance was so many years ago, and Mary has been dead for so long . . . And last night there I was, slumped on the old sofa wondering why the hell I was all alone when a man of my age should be . . .'

He banged his staff on the ground, colouring to the roots of his greying hair and looking everywhere but at her.

'Oh, Edward,' she said to herself.

He shook his head and murmured, 'What I can't understand, Carrie, is what the hell you see in me? A fifth-rate scribbler, someone taken in by a fraudster. A father who doesn't even understand his own son . . . Good God, it isn't even as if I've got my looks any more.'

'And I'm not exactly twenty-five and ravishing, Edward.'

He looked at her and smiled. 'You know what, Carrie? I think you're the most beautiful woman in the world.'

She shook her head and smiled, euphoria welling in her chest. 'I'll tell you what I see in you, Edward. I see someone who is honest, and who is big enough to accept what's happened to him and admit his failings.' She smiled. 'And I don't just mean what's happened now. When you were in Hollywood and you worked like a Trojan on those scripts, and then you were kicked off projects, or they got some talentless hack in to do a rewrite . . . and you accepted it and buckled down and set to work on the next one. And then later, when the studio dumped you . . . That could have driven a lesser man to the booze. But what did you do? You came back here and did what you'd wanted to do for years – wrote some pretty decent mystery novels.'

'They're no good, Carrie,' he said.

'They are, too. You worked hard on them. And you didn't give in, fold after the first rejection. You kept at it. And you know what? I admired you like crazy for that. And now . . .'

'Now?'

She smiled. 'Now you won't let all this Stafford business get you down. You'll fight back, even if you . . . if you might need help from me to do so.'

He smiled at her. 'Hell's bells, Carrie, you deserve someone better than me.'

'I think I should be the judge of that, don't you?'

He gave a heartfelt sigh. 'By Christ, I can't wait until all this is over. I just want them to find the blighter's killer, find out why the hell he was deceiving me like that . . . I just want a simple life, Carrie. Is that too much to ask?'

She smiled. 'Of course not, Edward. It's what most of us want, if we're honest with ourselves.'

A simple life, accompanied by someone one loves and respects.

He thumped his staff on the lawn as if he'd just come to a decision. 'Tell you what, why not come over to the Chase for lunch? There's some cold ham in the refrigerator, and some dashed good tomatoes and lettuce growing in the veg patch.'

She beamed at him. 'Give me five minutes to get ready,' she said, 'and we'll walk back together with the dogs.'

'Capital.'

She hurried into the house, elation swelling somewhere in the region of her heart. She paused at the door and looked back at the big, somewhat overweight old man, slumped in the garden seat and staring at his blunt hands clutching the staff, but all she saw was the honest, misguided man she had loved for years and years.

TWENTY-TWO

Ralph Ryland hunched over the wheel of his Morris Minor as they accelerated over Putney Bridge, heading north towards Belsize Park.

Langham sat in the passenger seat and filled his pipe. After Suffolk, the residential streets of London, even in the sunlight, seemed dark and oppressive. Rows of mean houses crowded in on either side, and the occasional tree or patch of parkland looked less like something natural than an artificial exhibit of what the city had supplanted. Even the bustling crowds reminded him of film extras hired to play the parts of pedestrians and shopkeepers.

He grunted to himself. It was an observation he would have to include in his next book.

'What?' Ryland said, a Woodbine glued to his lower lip.

'Just thinking what an ugly city London is,' Langham said.

His tobacco smoke and that of Ryland's Woodbine filled the car with a dense fug. He wound down the window to clear the air, but only succeeded in adding petrol fumes to the mix.

'Know something, Don? You don't notice the ugliness after a while. You just see the beauty.'

'The beauty?'

'The decrepit houses, the fog on the river, the grumbling cars and buses. They're all beautiful

271

in their own way. Take the actress, Caroline Dequincy.'

Langham cocked an eye at his friend. 'Caroline?'

'Some people wouldn't consider her beautiful, but I don't know . . . It all depends on how you look at things.'

Langham smiled. He'd never really considered Caroline and the city of London as analogous. 'You're a philosopher on the quiet, Ralph.'

'Plenty of time to mull things over between cases.' He glanced at Langham. 'Oh, I consulted my old graphologist friend last night.'

'And?'

'Interesting. She said that Dequincy was highly strung, of a very nervous disposition – but she doubted she'd be capable of murder.'

'That's good to know.'

They drove on for a while in silence. Langham stretched his legs as much as the cramped foot-well of the Morris would allow. 'It'll be interesting to see what light Hartwell's lover can shed on the business. You said you saw him last night?'

'Briefly, on the doorstep. He was in a state, make-up all over the place, mascara running . . .'

'Make-up?'

'Like I said, he's an old queen. What do they call themselves? Drag queens. Dress up as women. All the rage with these theatrical types.'

'Is it? I must lead a sheltered life.'

'Takes all sorts,' Ryland said, sticking his right arm through the open side window to indicate he was turning. They left the main road and drove down a leafy side street. Ryland leaned forward, his chest pressed against the steering wheel, and squinted at the passing row of shabby Victorian houses. 'Here we go. Number twenty.' He pulled in to the curb and braked.

Langham peered out at number twenty, the black paintwork of its door and window frames peeling, dirty curtains drawn. 'For some reason, this isn't quite the place I thought Vivian Stafford might live.'

Ryland laughed. 'Wait till you see inside, Don.'

They pushed their way along a short path overhung with untended hydrangeas. The glass panes in the front door were broken and backed by mouldering newspaper pages. A decade-old headline announced the Allied push across Europe.

Ryland knocked, dislodging flakes of blistered paint, and a minute later Langham heard several bolts being shot.

The door opened and a tall, gaunt man in a navy blue dressing gown smiled sadly at Ryland. His face appeared pale in the gloom of the hallway, and Langham saw that the application of powder was what accounted for the cadaverous pallor.

'Mr Bennett,' Ryland said. 'This is Donald Langham, my assistant. Donald, Mr Vincent Bennett.'

'Only too glad to be of assistance,' Bennett said in Shakespearian tones, taking Langham's hand in a limp grip and murmuring, 'Delighted.'

The hallway provided a stark contrast to the decrepit exterior of the house: the walls were lined with maroon and cream flock wallpaper and hung with theatrical posters, photographs of old music hall acts and framed vaudeville programmes.

Bennett led the way into a front room more like a Victorian museum, with a velveteen chaise longue, what looked like a Persian rug, and a collection of china figurines in glass-fronted cabinets. The overall effect was fussy and maiden-auntish.

'Please, take a seat,' Bennett gestured with a languid hand. 'Would you care for tea? We have Earl Grey, Lapsang Souchong, Darjeeling.'

'Earl Grey for me, please,' Langham said.

Ryland said, 'Make that two.'

'Milk or lemon?'

'Just black for me,' Langham said.

'White, three sugars,' Ryland said, and glanced at Langham as Bennett left the room. 'Like a bleedin' palace in here, Don.'

'Not quite what I was expecting.'

A brass carriage clock sat on the mantelshelf beside photographs of theatrical troupes and individual performers. Langham made out three pictures of someone who was obviously a younger Vivian Stafford – or rather, Cedric Hartwell. In one he had an arm around the gangling, gaunt figure of a youthful Bennett.

He rose to examine the photographs, and Bennett returned with a silver tea tray. 'Ah, you're admiring my little collection. The earliest photograph goes all the way back to 1901, would you believe? The Sydenham Players. You see Cedric in the back row? He would be just eighteen then. That's me, second from the right in the front row.'

Langham smiled. The young Cedric Hartwell had one hand resting on Bennett's shoulder.

'We'd met just the previous week. It was our first professional engagement.' His thin lips were pulled into a sad smile. 'We would never have believed we were destined to spend almost fifty-five years together . . . nor that it would end like this.'

His smile became animated as he set the tea things on a japanned occasional table. 'I'll be Mum,' he said, and proceeded to pour three china cups of Earl Grey.

Langham resumed his seat on the chaise longue as Bennett went on: 'Cedric was a character actor of the old school. He could turn his talents to anything. Shakespeare one week, vaudeville the next. I was useless – yes, absolutely wooden – but I could ham it up with the best of them. Did you know that Cedric played alongside Granville Barker in a run of Shaw's *Saint Joan* at the New Theatre? He was a sensation. I was so proud. Cedric glowed, positively glowed.'

Langham pointed to a yellowing movie poster beside the hearth. 'I see he was also in films.'

'Well, of course, the talkies came knocking. This would be in the late twenties. Cedric was a star of the West End, so it was natural that the film companies should seek to use his talent. And then there was the time . . .' He sipped his tea, pressed his fingers to his chest and whispered conspiratorially, 'of the Hollywood offer.'

'Did he go?' Ryland asked.

'We considered the possibility. He was to play the part of an English earl, alongside Fairbanks. But we came to the decision, having met several studio representatives, that the whole business

275

was rather too vulgar. The money would have been nice – there were positively oodles of it on offer, my dears – but the promise of filthy lucre at the expense of one's art is a temptation best refused. And do you know, we never looked back and regretted the decision for one second.'

Langham smiled. 'Good for you.'

'Cedric starred in several rather good British films of the thirties and forties. You might have seen him in *Fair Winds* in 'thirty-five, or *East to Tobruk* in 'forty-six – he played a rather dashing tank commander, if I say so myself.' His smile faltered. 'And while Cedric was landing these plum parts, I made do with scraps of rep in the provinces, walk-on work in the West End, the occasional bit part in minor films – parts entirely commensurate with my limited talent. I, for my part, was not in the slightest jealous of Cedric's success, and Cedric did not succumb to the expectations, from some quarters, to ditch me for some up-and-coming young buck. Oh, he liked his little affairs on a regular basis – his flings, as we called them, but he always returned to me.'

Langham smiled to himself and sipped his tea.

Bennett went on: 'I suppose it's not the done thing to admit that we had a rather good time during the war. Oh, it's a terrible admission to make, I know. But the fact was that it was a hoot. We signed up for ENSA and were always flying off on exotic tours: Africa one month, Asia the next . . .'

His grey eyes flickered from Ryland to Langham. He looked suddenly tragic, his powdered face that of a third-rate Hamlet back in the dressing room after a badly received performance. He said, sotto voce, 'It was in the late forties that things began to go, as they say, pear shaped. The parts dried up, for both Cedric and myself. I could take the slings and arrows, but it was heartbreaking to see poor Cedric rejected again and again. One's public can be so fickle, I find. Cedric's face no longer fitted. He was no longer young and dashing, which was what the casting directors wanted – and when he tried for older parts he was knocked back again and again by spotty secretaries who claimed that the public didn't want to be reminded that their erstwhile idols are prey to the depredations of the flesh . . . not that the hussies phrased their rejections quite like that. Oh, we survived. We tightened our belts, got by with a little radio work, the odd part with touring companies. We didn't go short. Cedric had the happy knack of coming up with the goods when we were on our uppers . . .'

He fell silent, staring into his bone china cup, his grey fingers folded around the saucer like broken twigs.

Langham cleared his throat and asked, 'Do you know how he came to be playing the . . . the role of Vivian Stafford?'

Bennett frowned. In a low voice he said, 'Oh, it was all very hush-hush. Cedric was loath to tell me much about it. You see, I think he was . . . ashamed of what he was doing. Is ashamed the right word? Perhaps it would be better to state that he was not proud of the part he was playing.'

Ryland said, 'That of a Victorian satanist?'

Bennett pursed his lips. 'Precisely.'

'Do you know how the part came about?' Langham asked. 'Who hired him?'

Bennett shook his head. 'I'm afraid that this was one of the provisos of Cedric's employment for . . . whoever it might be. As I said, it was all very hush-hush. As far as I know, he never actually met the man . . . or woman . . . who was employing him. He received all his instructions by post, along with the money. And I don't mind telling you that it was well paid, *very* well paid, especially when one takes into consideration that he was called upon to play the part on just four or five occasions. Fifty pounds a time and all expenses included. Fees like that, my dears, cannot be sniffed at. It was an equine endowment, as the saying goes, whose dentistry could not be examined too closely.' He faltered, then went on: 'If only we had known where it was all destined to lead.'

'Did Cedric talk to you about what he was called on to do, exactly?' Ryland asked.

'Oh, he let the odd thing drop, especially when we shared a bottle of Vermouth – our secret little vice, you know.'

Langham smiled at this. 'What did he say?'

'He did tell me something about the role.' Bennett smiled, perhaps at the recollection of speaking with his deceased lover. 'He said it was both an easy part to play, and in certain respects difficult.'

'Why was that?' Ryland asked.

'It was easy in that he could play the part of a Victorian satanist in his sleep; in terms of acting, it was undemanding.' He smiled. 'He had the peculiar ability to assume roles as if they were made for him; he could adapt himself to any part, any character. It was quite uncanny to watch. And the fact that he bore an uncanny resemblance to Stafford helped no end. A little powder here and there and he was the spit.'

'And the difficulty?' Langham prompted.

'He was called upon to learn the life story of the person he was impersonating,' Bennett said, 'the real Vivian Stafford, who did indeed exist back in the Victorian era, and who apparently vanished in mysterious circumstances at the turn of the century. It was not what he had to *learn* that was the difficulty, so much as what he had to invent – he had to fill in the gaps, as it were, in order to convincingly play the part of this man.'

Langham shook his head. 'And he never told you *why* he was playing the part, for what reason?'

Bennett frowned. 'I received the impression that he was doing it to convince a group of people. He went down to Suffolk perhaps four or five times in as many weeks.'

'Did he say anything about these people?' Langham asked.

Bennett leaned forward and pinched the bridge of his nose with his pale fingertips. After a while he looked up and said, 'I recall one occasion, about two weeks ago. He'd held an "occult evening" and was exhausted. We opened a bottle of something and got rather blotto . . . He mentioned something, I seem to recall, about someone he was principally trying to convince – a writer or historian.'

Edward Endicott.

Bennett went on: 'He didn't go into detail except to say that he didn't care for this man; he said he was one of those hail-fellow-well-met types, a macho bore of the bar room. And yet this man's attitude towards him was almost . . . deferential, perhaps awestruck. He really did believe that "Stafford" was a centenarian.'

'Did Cedric mention anything else about the role?' Langham asked.

'He told me it was sheer hell having to learn the tricks he was required to perform, the various sleights of hand and legerdemain. Of course, like the old trooper he was, he put his back into the job. The evening was held in a tumbledown country pile owned by an eccentric artist – it was where this fellow Stafford lived in the Victorian era. The artist was another character Cedric took a dislike to. The man was reluctant to allow his hall to be used, but apparently he received a generous remuneration – again from whoever was behind the charade – to open his house up to "Stafford" for an occult event, and he relented. He was a prickly individual, by all accounts. But apparently the evening went swimmingly. He positively scared the pants off those present.'

Langham set his cup and saucer aside. 'And it was all trickery, set up by whoever hired Cedric?'

Bennett nodded. 'He told me that the "stunts" were set up beforehand – I presume by the person who was hiring him. And quite sophisticated they were too, employing projectors and tape recorders and what-have-you. Cedric was impressed.'

'Odd business,' Langham said. 'He never speculated about what might be going on?'

'Only, as I said, that he thought he was being hired to pull the wool over the eyes of this writer fellow.'

Bennett paused, then looked from Ryland to Langham as he said, 'I have no doubt at all that the part he was playing was directly responsible for Cedric's demise, as I told the police when they . . . when they broke the news last night.' He looked, almost pleadingly, from Langham to Ryland. 'They didn't actually tell me whether Cedric . . . whether his death was quick and painless, or protracted. They merely said that he had been beaten to death.'

Langham hesitated, but Ryland said, 'We're certain, Mr Bennett, that Cedric died instantly.'

Langham watched Ryland as he said this, and he respected his friend for the lie.

Bennett lowered his eyes. 'That is one small grain of comfort to be gained from this sorry affair,' he murmured.

He looked up and, with a change of behavioural gear – from the grieving lover to the perfect host, a theatrical leap from pathos to bathos – he trilled, 'But your cups are empty! How remiss! Here, allow me to replenish . . .'

Langham sat back with his refilled cup. 'Did Cedric mention any animosity shown towards him – any resentment, let's say?'

Bennett thought about it. 'There were certain parties, I think, who rather took against "Stafford"

– that is, against the persona Cedric was playing. But he didn't go into details.' He smiled thinly. 'It was rather like receiving a bad notice from a vindictive theatre critic, I rather think: H_2O from a mallard's rear, as they say.'

Ryland sat forward in the armchair. 'And in his personal, everyday life, apart from the role he was playing, he didn't have any enemies?'

Bennett hesitated, which Langham thought significant. 'Please . . . it could be important in our investigations.'

Bennett drew a long sigh and gave a thin-lipped smile. 'Isn't it odd how we perceive the ones we love, gentlemen? Human relations never cease to amaze me. I mean . . . we invest our love in someone for reasons, we think, wholly to do with the qualities we perceive in the subject of our adoration . . . but it has often more to do with satisfying our own selfish *needs*.'

Beside Langham, Ryland moved impatiently. 'I don't see,' he began, but Langham raised a hand to quell his objections. 'Please, go on,' he said to Bennett.

'I suppose I am trying to say that I . . . I was always insecure, gentlemen. I needed someone. And when Cedric came along, his dashing good looks – in his early days, that is – his wit and charm . . . Well, I was quite smitten.'

'But?' Ryland said.

Bennett sighed. 'But Cedric had his dark side. He could be quite . . . vindictive, I suppose, to those who crossed him. He had the most appalling upbringing, I will say in his defence. His father was a positive beast, an alcoholic bully. He never

282

accepted Cedric for who . . . or what . . . he was. And I suppose this had an effect on the person Cedric became.'

'Which was?' Langham asked.

'Cedric was a cold person who allowed a few, a very few, people into his life. He was constantly suspicious, and made enemies at the drop of a hat. To be perfectly frank, he was not very well liked in theatrical circles. But . . . I could see past all his foibles. I could apprehend the reason he was the person he was, and love him despite his faults.'

Ryland glanced at Langham, then said, 'Do you know if he made enemies who might have had reason to—?'

Bennett interrupted, 'To kill Cedric?' He shook his head with vehemence. 'I can't imagine that Cedric would drive anyone, anyone at all, to such extreme . . . measures.' He drew a long breath and went on: 'What is all the more tragic, gentlemen, is that Cedric was due to give one last performance at a second "occult evening" in about a week from now. However, he had decided that the strain of the first event had proved trying enough. He fully intended to contact the person who was hiring him and withdraw his services.'

Langham looked across at Ryland and raised an eyebrow. 'Do you know if he actually broached this with whoever hired him?'

Bennett inclined his head in assent. 'On the morning of the Saturday before he set off, he told me that he'd written to his "employer" – who used a London PO Box number – and said that he would be unable to conduct the final event.'

He stopped suddenly and looked up. 'You don't think that . . .?'

'Yes?'

'I wonder if he did broach the subject of his ending his role with his employer, face-to-face, and whether this might have . . .?'

Langham took up the thought: 'Whether this might have brought about the attack?' He looked across at Ryland. 'What do you think?'

Ryland took a mouthful of tea and ballooned his cheeks in consideration. 'It's possible, I s'pose. Can't be ruled out. I think we'd be a lot nearer an answer if we could track down the cove who hired Cedric.'

Bennett smiled thinly. 'I only wish I could be of more help in that regard, gentlemen.'

Ryland drained his tea and said, 'I don't suppose Cedric owned a typewriter?'

'As a matter of fact, he did. But why do you ask?'

'It's just that we've come across some correspondence relating to the case, and we'd like to rule out the possibility that it was written on Cedric's typewriter.'

Bennett climbed to his feet and loomed over them. 'I'll show you to the cubby-hole that Cedric laughingly called his study. This way, please.'

They climbed the narrow, memorabilia-flanked staircase and Bennett opened a door to reveal a small room lined with books. A tiny desk stood before the window, a Remington portable upon it. Bennett stepped aside to allow Ryland to enter. Langham remained on the landing and watched the detective move to the desk, wind a sheet of paper into the Remington and tap the keyboard three times.

He pulled out the paper, examined the result and slipped it into his pocket.

He turned to Bennett. 'Do you know if Cedric kept the correspondence he had with the person or persons who hired him for the Stafford role?'

'I'm not at all sure, Mr Ryland. But if I could just squeeze by, I'll check.'

They performed a *pas-de-deux* shuffle on the threshold and Langham watched as Bennett walked his thin fingers through a drawer of correspondence. He looked up. 'There seems to be nothing here other than bills.'

Ryland shrugged his thin shoulders. 'Not to worry.'

They made their way downstairs and paused in the hall. Ryland thanked Bennett for his time and hospitality, and said they'd be in touch the moment they learned anything that might shed light on the affair.

'If you would, I should be more than grateful.'

After a round of handshakes they took their leave and returned to Ryland's sweltering Morris. Bennett stood in the open doorway, a valedictory hand raised beside his gaunt face.

'Well,' Langham said as Ryland released the clutch and pulled out into the quiet street, 'what did you make of that?'

The detective was smiling to himself as he clutched the steering wheel.

'What?' Langham said.

Ryland reached into his breast pocket with two fingers and withdrew the folded foolscap.

Langham straightened it out and stared at the row of letters: a series of d's with broken upstrokes.

'My God . . .'

'So,' Ryland said, 'it looks like old Cedric *was* our blackmailer.'

'It certainly does,' Langham said. He shook his head. 'But I just can't imagine Caroline . . .' he began.

'Nor me, Don. Of course, Cedric might not have limited his blackmailing to one victim. He might have had enemies all over the place.'

'Who followed him to Humble Barton and did the deed?'

Ryland shrugged. He stuck an arm through the window to indicate a right turn. 'The other possibility is what I was thinking back there.'

'Which is?'

'Cedric Hartwell wrote to whoever hired him to play the part, maybe arranged a meeting so he could hand in his cards. They meet, and our mystery man is more than a little disgruntled when Cedric says he's had enough – so disgruntled, in fact, that on the spur of the moment he takes the lawn-edger to Cedric's head.' He glanced at Langham. 'What do you think?'

Langham stared through the windscreen at an advertisement for Bovril on the back of a slow bus. 'It's a possibility, I suppose.'

They drove on in silence, and five minutes later they arrived at Wandsworth and the row of shops above which the detective agency was situated. Ryland pulled up behind Langham's Austin Healey.

'OK,' Langham said, 'just supposing the killer wasn't a blackmail victim but the person who hired Hartwell. Perhaps it was as you said – Hartwell wrote to whoever it was, arranged a meeting and said he was quitting. They argued, and . . .'

Ryland nodded. 'OK . . .'

'So who might have hired Hartwell to deceive Edward? Who disliked him so much that he decided to set up the deception? Who had the wherewithal – the money, the time, but more than that the *desire* to play on Endicott's incredulity?'

'Go on.'

'There's only one person who fits the bill, Ralph. This person despises Edward's world view, his irrationality. He once called him a fool in my company. And he owns Stafford Hall – so the logistics of setting up the occult event would have been simple.'

'You mean that Dent character?'

Langham nodded. 'Haverford Dent. Hartwell contacted Dent and said he wanted to quit. Perhaps he even said he was going to tell Edward Endicott about the deception. Dent attempts to stop him, follows him to the Chase. They argue, and Dent snatches up the lawn-edger . . .'

'And Dent's the type to fly into a rage like this?'

'Well, you saw him destroying the orrery,' Langham said. 'But where would Denbigh's death fit into this? You said it was too coincidental to be an accident. There's always the possibility that it was suicide, of course. But what if it

287

wasn't? Why might Dent have wanted the vicar dead?'

Ryland shrugged. 'Denbigh knew something? He found out that this Stafford was an impostor, hired by Dent? And when Hartwell was found dead he approached Dent with his suspicions and Dent decided to do away with him. That'd explain why Dent was wrecking that orrery.'

'Ah . . . destroying the evidence. It's a possibility . . . But we could speculate like this till the cows come home. What we need to do is find out for sure that Dent did hire Hartwell to pull the wool over Edward's eyes.'

'Can you arrange a meeting with Dent?'

Langham recalled winning the raffle – and he'd yet to claim his prize. 'I've got just the excuse,' he said, and told Ryland about the raffle.

'So while you're keeping Dent busy, I get into the hall and have a poke about. See if I can come up with any incriminating evidence – copies of letters to Hartwell, that kind of thing.'

'It's a big place, Ralph. Finding a letter or anything else in there might be like trying to find a needle in a haystack.'

'The bigger the better,' Ryland said. 'Dent's less likely to find me, right?'

'Don't worry, I'll keep him busy.'

Five minutes later Langham climbed into his own car and, with Ryland following in his trustworthy Morris, led the way from London.

He came to the crest of the lane, slowed down and stared across the vale where Humble Barton nestled. He made out the Chase amid the elms, the public house and the church next to the village green and, high on the hill above the village – ensconced in rolling parkland – Stafford Hall.

He drove down through the village and, minutes later, up the gravelled driveway of Endicott's Chase, Ryland close behind. He would bring Maria up to speed with what he and Ryland had found out in London then motor on to the hall.

Maria pulled open the front door as he braked before the house. She waved and said, 'The police have just been and taken Edward away for questioning again.'

Ryland shrugged his non-existent shoulders. 'Trust the boys in blue to bugger up the show, Don.'

Langham was about to tell her what conclusions he and Ralph had arrived at in London when the telephone rang in the hallway.

Maria gestured inside. 'Perhaps I had better . . .?' She hurried inside and Langham heard the faint sound of her voice as she answered the call.

She returned a minute later. 'That was Haverford Dent. He wants to see you, Donald. He said you have forgotten something.'

'Speak of the Devil,' Ryland laughed.

'Ah,' Langham said. 'The raffle prize. As it happens, Maria, Ralph and I were just on our way up to the hall to have a word with Dent.'

'He asked if you could pop round soon,' Maria said. 'He said he'll be busy later this afternoon.' She paused. 'Donald, Caroline was a bit down when the police took Edward. I think I should call in and make sure she is all right.'

He nodded. 'Come on, I'll drop you off.'

All three climbed into Langham's car and left the Chase, and on the way he gave Maria a condensed account of his and Ralph's meeting with Vincent Bennett that morning – and their suspicions concerning Haverford Dent.

As she climbed from the car outside Rosebud Cottage, she leaned towards Langham and said, 'Donald, do be careful up there, *oui*? If Dent *did* . . .' She faltered.

From the backseat, Ryland said, 'Don't worry about Don, Maria. I'll look after him.'

Langham kissed her on the lips, slipped the Austin into gear and accelerated along the lane towards Stafford Hall.

TWENTY-THREE

Maria stood in the lane and watched the car disappear up the hill and around the corner. She turned to the cottage, its white lime-wash brilliant in the light of the afternoon sun, and hurried up the garden path.

Boardman was sprawling in the shade of the porch when she pushed open the front door and called out, 'Caroline. It's me, Maria.'

'In the kitchen,' Caroline replied.

Maria made her way down the hall corridor and came to the kitchen. Caroline sat at the table, an empty glass on the table before her. Next to it was a full bottle of Gordon's gin.

'I was contemplating whether to get completely blotto,' Caroline said.

Maria crossed to the table and picked up the bottle. She placed it on the worktop beside the sink. 'Well,' she said, 'I'm glad you resisted the impulse.'

'It was a close thing, Maria. Oh, why do they have to hound him like this? And just when things between me and Edward were looking up.'

Maria sat down and took Caroline's hand. 'They were?'

The actress smiled. 'Edward came round yesterday, admitted what a fool he'd been neglecting me and Alasdair. He . . .' She smiled, tears in her eyes. 'Do you know what he said?

He said that I was the most beautiful woman in the world.'

Maria squeezed her hand. 'I have some good news,' she said. 'Well, good in the circumstances. Donald accompanied Ralph to London and interviewed the partner of this Hartwell character. Apparently it was Haverford Dent who hired Hartwell to play the part of Vivian Stafford.'

Caroline opened her eyes wide. 'But why? I mean, why would he do such a thing?'

Maria shrugged. 'Why else? To trick Edward. To make a mockery of his belief in the occult.'

'Why, the *evil* . . .' Caroline shook her head. 'I never did like Dent,' she murmured.

'Well, Donald thinks that it was Dent who killed Hartwell.'

The actress looked shocked. 'Dent?'

Maria relayed what Donald had told her – that Hartwell had told Dent that he no longer wished to go along with the deception, and was about to tell Edward about the duplicity: whereupon Dent, in rage, had attacked the actor.

'He is up at the hall at this moment,' she said. 'He had to collect his raffle prize, and Ralph intends to search the hall for incriminating evidence.'

'I do hope they'll be careful,' Caroline said. She smiled at Maria. 'I don't know about you, but I could do with a drink – and I don't mean gin. Tea?'

Maria smiled. 'That would be lovely, yes.'

They carried their cups out to the garden and sat on the bench beside the climbing rose bush.

The scent was overwhelming and a warm breeze blew as they sat and admired the garden.

Caroline said, 'Do you think it's silly to strive after happiness?'

Maria laid her head to one side and looked at the actress. 'I don't think so, no.'

'Only, it's never attainable, is it? We are never happy. There's always something that prevents true happiness.'

Maria stared at the older woman, feeling a little uncomfortable. She felt that, since meeting Donald, she had attained moments of very near perfection: on these occasions she had been blissfully happy. But . . . perhaps Caroline was right. Always there had been something to mar that perfection: her niggling doubts about whether Donald truly loved her, her father's less-than-enthusiastic response to her being in love with a writer of thrillers . . . the idea that Philippe Delacroix had crawled back on to the scene.

She smiled. 'I think it depends on the person, Caroline. I think if you are realistic, and don't wish for too much, then you can have happiness.'

'Too much?'

Maria shrugged. 'But I don't think it is too much to wish for someone to love you, do you?'

The actress smiled. 'No. No, I don't.'

'Well, perhaps now you and Edward will be happy.'

'Oh, I do hope so, Maria. Wouldn't that be wonderful?' She sighed. 'I don't know – I've never really known where I stood with Edward in the past. He blew so hot and cold. I mean, one week he'd call round a couple of times and we'd chat for an hour and everything seemed great, and then he wouldn't show up for a month and the next time he bumped into me he'd be all stiff and formal.'

'I think he is afraid of commitment, Caroline. And perhaps too set in his ways.'

'He could be so frustrating! I said that I'd come round to the Chase last weekend, on Sunday, and cook him a belated birthday lunch. It was all set, everything planned. He'd even put in his order: his favourite, beef Wellington and roast new potatoes – and then he took himself off on his blasted hike without even telling me. Imagine how that made me feel.'

Maria said, 'Things will be different now, believe me.'

Caroline sighed. 'Oh, I hope so.' She brightened. 'Anyway, yesterday he said that I must come round today and we'd have another meal before you went back to London. I could even cook the belated beef Wellington,' she laughed.

'That would be lovely.'

Caroline smiled. 'It's very nice of you to come round, you know? The villagers are friendly but I must admit that I miss being around . . . well, people like you and Donald. Creative, cosmopolitan. I hope that doesn't sound too snobbish?'

Maria laughed. 'Not at all, but I don't know if I would call myself cosmopolitan. And I'm sure Donald would run a mile at the label!'

'When all this is over, Maria, promise me that we'll meet up in London. Edward and I will come down for the occasional play and we could dine out, all four of us.'

'Of course we will,' Maria said. 'I would like nothing more.'

Caroline clapped her hands. 'Wonderful. Now, I don't know about you but I would love another cup of tea.'

Maria sat in the sunshine while Caroline busied herself in the kitchen. She was staring at the crimson blaze of azaleas in the border when Boardman came plodding around the corner and slumped to the ground at her feet. The hound made her think of Rasputin, and Edward Endicott, and she recalled something that Caroline had just told her.

Suddenly, despite the warmth of the sunlight, she felt very cold.

TWENTY-FOUR

Langham pulled up before the imposing gateposts and turned to Ryland.

'I'll get out here and walk,' the detective said. 'I'll wait until you enter the hall and then follow you in. You said he doesn't employ staff?'

'That's right.'

Ryland climbed out and gave a salute, and Langham eased the car past the gatehouse and up the winding drive. He told himself that, despite Maria's concern, he had nothing to worry about. All he had to do was to accept the raffle prize, keep Dent talking and Ryland would do the rest. Nevertheless, his heart was pounding as he approached the four-square pile of the hall.

He parked before the house, climbed out, and was about to ascend the steps when he was halted by a shouted summons. 'Langham! Hullo!'

He turned. Haverford Dent's tall figure was silhouetted against the sky on the rise beyond the main lawn. Langham waved and strode across the grass to meet him.

He climbed the bank and joined the artist on the crest. Down in the amphitheatre the orrery was in pieces, the tracks piled like jackstraws and the halved orbs nestled into each other like spoons. What had once been a bizarre work of art was now just so much scrap metal.

To their left, standing on a knoll overlooking the amphitheatre, the guillotine constructed from a car bonnet rose high into the summer sky. Langham glanced back at the hall; he made out Ryland's slight figure dart behind a stand of topiary before the building.

'I hear they've arrested Edward,' Dent said.

'Bad news travels fast.'

'Bad news?' Dent said. 'You don't think he did it?'

Langham looked at the artist's long, hollowed-out face, his skin the unhealthy shade of tallow. 'No, I don't. Do you?'

Dent shook his head. 'Edward might be many things . . . a bore, a gullible fool, a philistine . . . but he isn't a murderer.'

He gestured toward the dismantled orrery and Langham accompanied him down the incline. The artist came to the nestled orbs and laid a calloused hand on the hemisphere of Jupiter, almost lovingly.

'If Edward isn't the murderer,' Langham said, watching Dent closely, 'have you any idea who it might be?'

The artist looked at him with rheumy eyes set in deep wells of wrinkled flesh. He asked, 'Do you?'

Langham looked Dent in the eye and said, 'I've absolutely no idea.'

Dent moved on, caressing a halved Saturn, trailing a hand along a length of curved track. He stopped and stared up at the guillotine, then surprised Langham by asking, 'Do you believe in evil?'

Langham wondered at the question. 'Do you know something? I don't think I do.'

'Good man. Neither do I. It's a lazy word, a cliché beloved of lax leader-writers and addled judges. Words like evil and God and the Devil . . . all abstractions that have no real meaning in a sane world. Would you agree?'

'In principle, yes.'

'And what about people who are described as evil?'

Langham glanced at Dent as he replied, 'So called evil acts are the results of certain pressures, psychological and societal, to which . . . let's say weak or desperate individuals succumb.'

'And would you call me weak or desperate, Langham?'

The artist was still gazing up, his expression neutral, at the car bonnet guillotine on the hill.

'I think only you would be able to answer that question.'

'Perhaps I am weak. In fact, I most certainly am. I would draw the line at calling myself evil, but I am . . . weak *and* immoral, let's say.'

Langham felt his heart thud in his chest. He said, 'Immoral . . . in what way?'

The artist moved towards a pile of stacked half-orbs and sat down on the northern hemisphere of Mars, clasping his big hands and staring at them for a long time.

Langham leaned against the piled tracks, watching Dent.

'I possess the weakness of vanity,' the artist said at last. 'And anger, an all-consuming anger that is both an advantage, in that I have used it to fuel my better works, and a failing, when I direct it at those people whose views I despise. I have the failing of most egoists, in that I am also intolerant . . . and intolerance and anger and vanity can be a lethal combination.'

The silence stretched between them. Langham waited for Dent to continue.

'I met Edward Endicott in 'forty-nine,' Dent went on. 'I found him personable enough, though his gullibility rankled. He believed in a lot of occult malarkey, which I found objectionable – apparently he'd had some experience in Hollywood. I came to despise the man for his belief in the irrational. He had no proof on which to found his beliefs, of course – merely faith, which is all these believers have to hold on to.' He laughed. 'Also, I didn't like the way he derided my art. So I . . .'

Langham said, 'So you hired the actor, Cedric Hartwell, to play the role of Vivian Stafford, Victorian satanist.'

Dent stared at him, smiling. 'So you know all about that? I should have suspected you'd be on the ball, a scribbler of ingenious thrillers as you are.'

'What happened?'

'I ensured that I wouldn't be traced to Hartwell,' Dent said. 'We conducted all our negotiations by mail and I used an assumed name. I set up all the meetings, the séances, the "smoke and mirrors" hauntings . . . All Hartwell had to do was play the part – and he did so, brilliantly. Edward, the fool, fell for it hook, line and bloody sinker.' He laughed. 'It was wonderful to witness,

299

at first: his increasing belief in what "Stafford" told him about his life, his immortality. I honestly didn't think he'd buy it, didn't think he was so feeble-minded. And I must admit that I felt a twinge of guilt, but only a twinge. Then I rationalized that Edward deserved to be duped, deserved what was coming to him.'

'Which,' Langham interrupted, 'was to be the big reveal at the final occult evening – the occasion when you'd tell him everything, with Hartwell's help, and ask him where his belief in the occult stood then?'

Dent nodded, smiling as he said, 'Perspicacious of you, Langham. That's exactly what I *had* planned, yes.'

'But . . .' Langham said, 'then Hartwell contacted you, wrote to say he no longer wished to play the part you'd cast for him or appear at the final occult evening – scuppering your plans to humiliate Edward.'

Dent closed one eye and squinted at Langham. 'As a matter of fact he did contact me, yes.'

Langham ran a hand along a short length of track. He looked across at Dent, who was watching him. He was confident of besting the artist if it came to a fight, but *in extremis* the span of track could always be employed as a club.

He asked, 'Is that why you killed him, Dent?'

Dent's face was a convincing mask of surprise. 'What did you say?'

'You killed Cedric Hartwell. He contacted you, and in a bid to persuade him to continue the charade you broke with your anonymity and invited him up here. You met on Saturday but he refused to continue, then he set off to tell Edward how he'd duped him over the years. But you couldn't allow that, could you? You realized that it would enrage Edward when he found out – and perhaps you feared his anger. So you attacked Cedric Hartwell as he made his way to the Chase. Not a premeditated attack, perhaps, more a spur-of-the-moment act.'

Dent stared at Langham then flung back his head in an uproarious guffaw. 'You're way off the mark there, Langham. Way off! Go back to writing your detective stories!' He fixed Langham with a beady eye. 'I might be many things. I might be a fornicator, a deceiver, an egoist . . . but I am not a murderer. Whatever you might think, whatever clever plot you've concocted in that thriller writer's mind of yours, I never once harboured the desire to kill Hartwell.'

Langham stared at the man; Dent's show of indignation was convincing.

'You do realize,' Langham said, 'that the police must be informed about the deception?'

'Of course I bloody well realize, Langham!'

'After all, it did lead to a murder – perhaps more than one.' He paused, then said, 'Did you realize that Cedric Hartwell was a blackmailer?'

Dent stared at him, and he could tell from the artist's expression that this was news to him. 'A blackmailer?'

'He was extorting money from . . . someone in the village. For all I know, they weren't his only victim.' Langham watched the artist. 'Did you see him acting suspiciously with anyone? Do you recall anything at all that could shed any light on whether he might have been blackmailing anyone else?'

Dent said, 'You think he might have been killed by one of his victims?'

'It's a possibility.'

Dent opened his mouth to say something, but remained silent. Langham could almost see the cogs of his mind turning. 'What?'

Dent said, 'He was blackmailing Caroline Dequincy, wasn't he?'

Langham said, surprised, 'How did you know?'

The artist smote the hemisphere of Mars that was his seat, swearing out loud. 'It was my fault, Langham. But how was I to know?'

'What happened?'

Dent shook his head. 'It was the second occasion I'd met him. We were at the Three Horseshoes for an afternoon session and we met Caroline and the vicar and a few other locals. Then we came back here. We'd had a fair bit to drink, and there was something about Hartwell . . . I rather thought that he and I shared certain . . . proclivities. I saw in him a fellow sybarite who shied against the fetters of sexual convention, for want of a better expression. So I told him about my collection of erotica.'

'Ah,' Langham said, 'the blue films.'

'I prefer to call them erotica,' the artist said. 'And it turned out that Hartwell was an aficionado. His predilections ran to boys, but he didn't demur at watching the heterosexual act, and he was particularly excited by orgies. It was while

302

we were watching one of the latter that we espied . . .'

'Caroline,' Langham said.

Dent shrugged. 'I was surprised, to say the least. I mean, who would have thought it of our own Ice Maiden? But live and let live has always been my motto.' He laughed. 'It even gave me a certain grudging respect for the woman.' Then his smile turned to a grimace, and he said, 'But evidently Hartwell didn't think the same . . .'

'Evidently,' Langham echoed.

Dent stared at him. 'But . . . I mean to say, much as Caroline and I don't see eye to eye, she couldn't have killed the chap, could she?'

'I'm pretty certain she didn't do it. Or perhaps that's wishful thinking,' Langham said. 'But did you see Hartwell buttonhole anyone else in the village? Think, man. Did you see him acting in any way untoward with *anyone* . . .' He stopped as an expression – a quizzical frown – passed across the artist's rugged features. 'What?'

Dent stood up, walked a few paces and paused, staring up at the rearing shape of the guillotine. He turned. 'Well . . . It was perhaps the third or fourth time Hartwell was up here. We'd just had a long session at the Three Horseshoes. It was a nice night and we'd spilled out on to the green . . . It was late on, and dark, and I saw Hartwell and Alasdair . . . they seemed to be having an argument. Upshot was, young Endicott ran off like a frightened rabbit. I asked Hartwell what the hell he'd said, but Hartwell cut me dead, more or less told me to mind my own business . . .'

303

'You don't think . . .?'

Dent cocked an eye at Langham. 'Did you know that Endicott junior was a fruit?'

'I . . . suspected he was that way inclined, yes.'

'And if old Endicott had got to know about it . . . well, there's no telling which way Edward would have blown up. Not the most tolerant of chappies, old Edward.'

'But Alasdair . . .?' Langham said, his mind racing. 'I just can't see Alasdair committing violence on anyone.'

Dent looked at him. 'Not even some evil old bastard who's threatening to spill the beans about Alasdair's sexuality to his father?' Dent grunted a humourless laugh. 'Christ, what a business. And all because I had the hubris to think I could teach Endicott a lesson or two!'

Langham looked at his watch. He'd been with Dent for a little under fifteen minutes. He sighed. 'Look, I'd better be pushing off.'

Dent reached into the pocket of his tweeds. 'Oh – here you are. This is what you came up here for, after all.' He held out an envelope. 'The winning voucher. Well done, Langham.'

Langham shrugged, took the envelope and slipped it into his trouser pocket.

The artist sighed. 'And just when I thought the week couldn't get any worse . . .'

Langham had turned and was moving away from Dent, but something in the man's tone stopped him. He turned and stared at the artist.

Dent said, 'The Reverend . . . I should have bloody well seen that the orrery was an accident waiting to happen.' Dent shook his head. 'And then finding out that it was through me that Hartwell blackmailed poor Caroline . . . Do you know, despite the fact that she dressed me down in front of every bloody drinker in the village that time, and slapped my face into the bargain, there's something about the old gal I like.' His face darkened. 'And to find that Hartwell was blackmailing her . . .'

'Well, that's all water under the bridge now, Dent.'

'And if that wasn't bad enough, this morning I had word from the knobs at the gallery in London.'

'Bad news?'

'You could say that. The bastards don't want my work. Nothing, not a ruddy thing. Not a single sculpture. And I was relying on a fat cheque to make the hall half habitable.'

Langham gave a commiserating frown. 'I'm sorry, Dent.'

The artist sighed. 'Well, as you so wisely said, that's water under the bloody bridge, isn't it?'

Langham walked away from the dismantled orrery, paused at the foot of the grassy bank and looked back. The artist was gazing at the guillotine on the hill, his expression distant.

'Goodbye, Langham,' Dent said, with something in his tone that Langham understood only later.

He walked up the incline and down the other side, crossed the lawn to his car and sat in the driving seat. He glanced at the hall, but there was no sign of Ryland. He left the door open to cool down the stifling interior and was considering

Alasdair Endicott, and what he should do next, when he heard something.

A mechanical sound, a labouring grind that he had heard once before, and recently.

'No!' He leapt from the car, running across the lawn and up the incline. He could see the upper section of the guillotine now and the automobile bonnet as it started its swift descent.

He cried out again as he came to the crest of the rise and stared across at the work of art, and the artist, combined in the ultimate act.

He turned away a second before the bonnet impacted.

When it did, with a deafening crash, he flinched and froze with his back to the guillotine. He knew that he should turn, take one last look in case the artist had by some miracle survived and could be helped.

Bracing himself, he pivoted slowly and stared across at the macabre contraption, silent now, a ghastly epitaph to its creator who, Langham saw, was beyond all help.

Taking deep breaths, he returned to the car, slumped into the driving seat and closed his eyes.

He was startled, minutes later, when the passenger door was pulled open and Ryland slipped in.

'Not a bleeding thing,' the detective said. 'Turned his study upside down, for all the good it did.'

'It doesn't matter,' Langham said.

Ryland stared at him. 'What?'

Langham described his meeting with Dent, then told the detective that the artist was dead.

'Dead?' Ryland looked mystified, as if unable to comprehend the meaning of the word.

'By his own hand.' Langham gestured towards the guillotine. Ryland made to get out of the car, but Langham said, 'I wouldn't if I were you, Ralph. It's not a pretty sight.'

Ryland dropped back into the seat. 'So . . . what now?'

Langham thought about it then said, 'Dent thought that Hartwell might've been blackmailing Alasdair Endicott. If so . . .'

'What are you going to do, Don?'

'I think I'll go and see Alasdair now.'

'Want me to come with you?'

Langham smiled. 'I think I'll be able to handle him on my own.'

He started the engine and drove back into the village.

He parked outside the Chase, left Ryland in the car and entered the silent house. At the foot of the oak staircase he called out, 'Alasdair?'

He moved to the sitting room and saw, through the French windows, the young man sitting beneath the cherry tree at the far end of the garden. Rasputin was lying at his feet, and Alasdair appeared to be talking to the dog.

Langham stepped from the house and walked across the lawn.

Alasdair looked up, shielding his gaze from the sun. 'Oh, Donald. I was wondering where everyone was.'

Langham sat down on the grass beside Rasputin and scratched the dog's head. He looked up at

Alasdair. 'Did you know that your father has been taken in for questioning again?'

'No . . . I was out walking Rasputin. I've only just got back.'

Langham sighed. 'He'll be released, of course, when the police realize they don't have sufficient evidence.' He paused, then went on: 'I've heard about the altercation you had with Hartwell outside the pub a few weeks ago.' Langham hesitated. 'Look here, don't you think we'd better drive into town and tell the police everything? We'll get your father off the hook . . .'

Alasdair stared at him. 'Off the hook?' he echoed. 'What do you mean?'

'Hartwell was blackmailing you, wasn't he?'

Alasdair swallowed. He gazed down at the grass for a good minute, as if calculating, then looked up and said, 'Yes. Yes, he was.'

Langham asked, 'How did you work out that it was Hartwell who was . . .?'

'It wasn't that difficult. I received a typewritten note demanding a certain sum. I noticed a defect in one of the characters. A few days later I was at the Chase when my father received a letter from "Stafford". The address was typed, and it bore the same defective letter "d".'

'And you approached Hartwell outside the pub one evening, argued with him?'

'Yes, yes, I did. The galling thing was he was quite brazen about what he was doing. He laughed in my face and said that if I didn't pay up . . . well, that my secret would soon be public knowledge.'

Langham imagined Alasdair coming across the

308

actor on Sunday as Hartwell arrived at the Chase to tell Endicott senior of his part in the charade. Perhaps they had words again, and Hartwell made further demands . . . And then? Had Alasdair become enraged and, on the spur of the moment, snatched up the closest thing to hand, the lawn-edger, and swung it at the actor?

'What I can't work out,' Langham said, 'is why, after you attacked Hartwell on Sunday, you phoned and asked me to come up? Why did you say you wanted my help, and then on Monday draw attention to the blood?'

Alasdair stared at him, slowly shaking his head. 'What?' he said incredulously. 'But *I* didn't kill Hartwell.'

Langham blinked. 'You didn't?'

'Of course not . . .' He hesitated, then said, 'I didn't kill him, but I know who did.'

Langham's pulse felt loud in his ears. 'Go on.'

'On Wednesday . . . Marcus came to see me. He was in a hell of a state. He admitted what had happened, confessed . . .'

'Denbigh?' Langham said.

'It's terrible, isn't it, when you see someone you care for in such a terrible state, and you're absolutely powerless to help them in any way.'

Langham said, 'Alasdair . . . tell me, what happened?'

'Marcus was beside himself when I saw him on Wednesday, just before Dent's art show.' He paused, staring at Langham. 'Did you know that Marcus was on medication? Antidepressants. And all thanks to that bastard, Stafford . . . or rather, Hartwell.'

Langham opened his mouth in sudden understanding. 'Ah, so Hartwell was blackmailing Denbigh, too?'

Alasdair nodded. 'Marcus told me that he'd received a blackmail letter. I said I'd had one too, and we compared them. They were from the same person, of course. So the next time Hartwell was in the village, Marcus confronted him . . . not that that did much good. Marcus pleaded that he couldn't raise the money, but Hartwell was relentless and gave him two weeks in which to pay up. Then Hartwell arranged to meet Marcus in the woods on Saturday evening. He said that if Marcus didn't turn up with the first instalment of fifty pounds his bishop would get to know about his . . . his indiscretions.' Alasdair looked up. 'Well, Marcus was desperate. They met in the woods on Saturday. Marcus had managed to gather twenty-five pounds, but Hartwell was merciless. He wanted the rest, immediately. Marcus fled, followed by Hartwell . . .' Alasdair paused, taking a deep breath, then went on. 'He told me that he didn't know what to do, didn't know where he was going . . . he just wanted to be away from the malign man. But Hartwell dogged his steps, telling Marcus of the consequences if he didn't find the money. Marcus came to the bridge, crossed it . . . saw the Chase through the trees. He said that he thought of me, decided that he'd call in on my father and ask if he might phone me in London, ask me to come up . . . Oh, what a bloody awful situation he was in!'

'I'm sorry,' Langham said inadequately.

'Anyway . . . They hurried through the copse, Hartwell in pursuit, and something he said then made Marcus see red. He wasn't a violent man, Donald. He was a good, Christian man. But . . . but then Hartwell said he'd tell my father about Marcus's friendship with me – and Marcus saw the lawn-edger and . . . and in rage and desperation he took it up and swung it at Hartwell.'

'And killed him outright?'

Alasdair nodded. 'With a single, accidental, panicked blow . . .'

'And then?'

Alasdair shrugged. 'He hid the body in the woods and flung the lawn-edger in the river, then went back to his church and prayed for his mortal soul.'

Langham shook his head. 'The poor man.'

'Of course,' Alasdair said, 'when I came up here on Sunday and found the house empty, the study locked from the inside and my father missing . . .' He shrugged, unable to bring himself to meet Langham's gaze. 'That's when I rang you.'

Langham stood up, moved to the bench and sat beside Alasdair. He reached out, held his hand above the young man's shoulder for a second then brought it down in a futile, but necessary, gesture of consolation.

Alasdair pulled a handkerchief from his pocket and wiped his eyes.

'Come on, clean yourself up back at the house, then we'll motor into town.'

'Will they . . . I mean, will I be prosecuted for . . . what's the phrase? "Perverting the course of justice"? I should have gone to the police yesterday.'

'They'll probably just give you a good ticking off, that's all.'

Alasdair nodded, then said, 'But how did you find out that I was being blackmailed? Who told you about my argument with Hartwell outside the pub that evening?'

'I've just been up to see Haverford Dent. He told me.'

'He knows about me and Marcus? Oh, God! I wouldn't put it past Dent to let it be known . . .'

Langham sighed. 'Alasdair, Haverford Dent won't be telling anyone anything. He took his own life this afternoon.'

'Dent?' Alasdair looked shocked. 'He killed himself?'

'With one of his own bloody inventions.'

The young man stared at him, shaking his head. 'But why?'

'I think Dent didn't much like himself – himself or his fellow man. And he felt guilty about the orrery, and Marcus using it to . . .' He shrugged. 'Also, the gallery owners had just declined to buy his artwork. Taken all together, it just proved too much.'

They sat in silence for a while, before Alasdair spoke next. He looked at Langham. 'And need the police know about Marcus and me?'

Langham shook his head. 'I don't really see what good would come of the police knowing, Alasdair. If you come with me to the station and tell the inspector about Hartwell blackmailing Marcus . . .'

Langham looked up. The French windows of the study swung open and glinted in the sunlight. Edward Endicott appeared in the doorway, raised a hand in greeting then stepped back into the study.

'Your father's back,' Langham said. 'You'd better go and tell him what you've just told me, then we'll set off to the station.'

Alasdair nodded, and Langham watched the young man as he made his way back to the house, accompanied by Rasputin.

TWENTY-FIVE

Langham sat on the bench and stared at the Chase, attempting to forget the events of the past few days and appreciate the architectural beauty of the old house. Clad in ivy and Virginia creeper and basking in the sunlight, it appeared timeless – a building set apart from the concerns of those who called it home. It would be here still in another three centuries and more, the locale of further intrigue, perhaps, just as it had been the venue for murder in 1750 and the present day.

Maria appeared on the patio, waved and hurried across the lawn towards him.

He stood and she came into his arms. 'Well, you've missed a little drama,' he said.

'I have?'

Where to begin? he wondered. With Dent's suicide, his suspicions regarding Alasdair or the latter's explanation that it was Marcus Denbigh who had struck the blow that had killed Cedric Hartwell?

'Maria, the Reverend Denbigh confessed to Alasdair on Wednesday that he killed Hartwell. You see, Hartwell was blackmailing him . . .' And he went on to reprise what Alasdair had told him. 'Poor Denbigh was beside himself with guilt with what he'd done . . . Little wonder he threw himself at the orrery.'

314

She just stared at him and shook her head.

He took her hand. 'You look stunned.'

'Well, yes. I am . . .'

Endicott senior appeared at the French windows and called out, 'I say, I don't know about you, but I could do with a stiff drink.'

They moved to the house and entered the relative gloom of the study. Edward stood by the drinks' cabinet, decanter in hand. Alasdair sat on the edge of an armchair, staring down at the rug between his feet.

'Whisky, Donald?'

'Please.'

'And you, my dear?' Endicott asked Maria.

As if in a daze, Maria moved from the French windows and stood before the hearth, staring down at the grate.

'Whisky, m'dear?' Endicott asked.

'No . . . No, a little brandy, please.'

Endicott poured the drinks and Langham took a sip of his whisky; it coated his throat like velvet fire.

'Well,' Endicott said, passing Maria her drink, 'it looks like the damned affair is drawing to a close, and not before time. Alasdair just told me. Poor Denbigh. I can't imagine what he must have gone through.'

Langham looked at Maria. She was still staring down at the grate. 'I say, are you all right?' he asked.

She placed her brandy glass on the mantelshelf and reached out for the poker. Langham crossed the room and watched as she prodded through the small pile of ash with the fire iron.

'Maria?'

Standing up, Alasdair said, 'I think I'd better be on my way.' He pointed to Langham's full glass. 'No need to come with me, Donald. I'll take father's car.'

Maria returned the poker to its stand and turned to Alasdair. 'No, don't leave. Not yet.'

'Maria?' Langham said.

She stood with her back to the chimney breast and stared at Alasdair. 'Why don't you tell the truth, Alasdair? It wasn't Marcus who killed Hartwell, was it?'

Alasdair went white. Opened-mouthed, he stared at Maria like a petrified animal caught in the headlights of an onrushing car.

Langham shook his head. 'But you told me . . .' he said to Alasdair. He turned to Maria. 'What do you mean? How do you know?'

Alasdair slumped back into the armchair, ashen-faced.

'Maria?' Langham said, beseechingly.

'It was something Caroline said to me today,' Maria said, looking from Langham to Endicott senior. 'You didn't plan to go off hiking last weekend, did you, Edward? As you told Alasdair, it was next weekend that you planned to go.'

Langham turned to Edward Endicott, who was staring at Maria, speechless.

She went on: 'You'd arranged with Caroline to have her round for a birthday lunch on Sunday . . . But as things turned out you couldn't do that, could you?'

Endicott opened his mouth as if to speak, but no words came.

316

'Edward?' Langham asked. 'Maria? Would someone mind explaining . . .?'

In a controlled voice, though Langham could see that she was shaking with nerves, Maria said, 'I noticed the wood ash in the fire on Sunday, Donald. It didn't really strike me at the time: why would someone start a fire in the middle of a blazing summer? Later I saw the photographs of "Vivian Stafford" – and I noticed he was carrying a brass-topped cane in both pictures, but no one ever mentioned his cane being found.'

She paused, looking from Langham to Edward Endicott. 'While I was with Caroline, another thing struck me as odd. Rasputin, returning home from miles away . . . It just didn't ring true, when I thought about it. Dogs just don't leave their owners to run off home. And I recalled that Caroline, on our first meeting, said that she had found him near the folly. Surely, *if* Rasputin returned home, he would have come here, to the Chase, and you would have found him, Alasdair.'

Langham found a spare chair and sat down.

Maria went on, staring down at where Edward Endicott sat, deflated: 'What happened, Edward? Did Stafford – or rather, Hartwell – approach you and admit his part in the deception? Did you then fly into a rage and attack him?'

Edward Endicott sat in silence for a long time before replying. He shook his head, dazed. 'It wasn't like that at all, Maria. I didn't strike Hartwell because he and Dent had deceived me – I'm not that petty-minded, for God's sake. And I didn't even know about that at the time.'

317

'Then why did you attack him?' Langham asked.

Endicott sighed. 'Alasdair told me about . . . about Hartwell blackmailing him and Marcus. All because they were . . .' He stopped suddenly, gathered his thoughts, then went on: 'I might not be the most broadminded of men, but to blackmail someone because of their sexuality is despicable. I decided I'd confront Stafford – as I thought of him then – about what he was doing. Anyway, the opportunity arose on Sunday morning when he came here. We were in the garden . . . I asked him what the hell he was playing at, extorting money from my son and the vicar.'

'What did he say?'

'He was supercilious. He simply said that if Alasdair and Marcus didn't pay up . . . then their "little secret would be made public". Well, I saw red and grabbed him, took him by the lapels . . .' Endicott stopped, closed his eyes as if reliving the scene, then went on: 'He struck me with his brass-knobbed cane. Hell of a blow, just here . . .' He parted his grey hair to reveal a raised contusion. 'I reeled back, enraged, and . . . and I saw the lawn-edger and before I could stop myself . . . I snatched it up and swung it with all my strength. It was strange – the sudden desire to do the man harm, and then, the second I had done so, the instant and sickening regret as I stared down at the body. I'd killed him instantly.' He drew a deep sigh, slowly shaking his head. 'I should have informed the authorities there and then, gone into the house and phoned the police. Of course I should – I can see that,

318

now. Instead I panicked. I hauled the body through the copse and into the woods near the hall and concealed it there, then wiped my prints from the lawn-edger and threw it into the river. Only when I came back did I see the man's cane on the path. I thought that if the police noticed the bruise . . . So I broke the cane into three pieces and burned it in the fire. Should've removed the ashes, of course, at the same time as I retrieved the brass knob and buried it in the woods.'

A deep silence followed his words, broken only by the sedate ticking of the grandfather clock.

'And you never went hiking?' Maria asked.

Endicott shook his head. 'After I burned the cane I left the study by the French windows, intending to go back to where I'd attacked Stafford to see if I'd left any evidence. Then the door blew shut and the catch dropped, effectively locking me out. Then . . . then I heard Alasdair calling my name from inside the house . . .' He stared across at his son and smiled sadly. 'It was one hell of a shock,' he said to Langham and Maria. 'I wasn't expecting him until the following week . . . Then I recalled the lunch I'd arranged with Caroline. Well, there was no way I could face either Alasdair or Caroline after what I'd just done. I was in a hell of a state, believe me. So I took Rasputin and holed up in the folly. I keep a few provisions there, a camp bed and my staff and rucksack. I thought I'd wait a day until I'd calmed down a little, then emerge and face the world. Rasputin got out, and later I saw the police swarming around the place.'

He reached out for the decanter and poured himself another generous measure of whisky. He swallowed a mouthful and continued, 'Must admit I was in a bit of a funk. I decided to lie low until I thought it safe to come out with the pretence of returning from the hike.' He shook his head. 'I don't expect you to believe me, but I hate myself for the charade I've been playing these past few days, pulling the wool over the eyes of people I like and respect. But . . . good God, what else could I have done?'

Langham stared at Endicott, too stunned by the revelation to apportion blame. He turned to Alasdair and asked, 'So the story about Marcus coming to you on Wednesday, confessing to killing "Stafford" . . . it was all a lie.'

The young man could not bring himself to look Langham in the eye as he said, haltingly, 'Marcus was dead. He was past caring. He could no longer be hurt, by Hartwell, by the world, by what he was . . .' He paused, then went on: 'When my father returned on Wednesday, he confided in me, told me that he'd confronted Hartwell and . . .' He shrugged. 'You see, I felt guilty. If Hartwell hadn't blackmailed me and Marcus, then none of this would have happened. My father wouldn't have . . .' He shook his head and murmured, 'So when you turned up and thought *I'd* killed Hartwell . . . it came to me that there was a way to save my father. After all, the dead can no longer be hurt . . .' He looked across at his father and said, 'I'm so sorry.'

'Silly young pup,' Endicott said. 'I've told you again and again, don't go blaming yourself. You did nothing wrong, dammit. Hartwell was the criminal . . . and I was stupid enough to let rage get the better of me.'

Maria said, 'And Marcus? Why did he take his life?'

Alasdair stared at his hands in his lap and said softly, 'He did see me on Wednesday, and he was in a terrible state. He was petrified that the police might learn about Hartwell blackmailing him; he feared what would happen if the world knew.' He shrugged. 'But as I said earlier, I couldn't have foreseen that he'd . . . that Marcus would end his life like that.' He lifted his gaze and stared at Langham, 'And for what it's worth, Donald, I am sorry for lying to you. But I hope you understand what drove me to do so?'

Langham sighed. 'What a bloody business.'

'I . . .' the young man began, 'I don't suppose we could let the matter lie – say nothing?'

Langham looked across at Maria, who bit her bottom lip as if in contemplation.

Endicott senior interrupted: 'I'm not implicating Donald and Maria, Alasdair! I've lied enough. I'm going to the police now, as I should have done days ago, and I'll admit what I did. I'll claim self-defence, of course . . . and extreme provocation. I'll . . . I'll say I knew that Marcus was being blackmailed, I confronted Hartwell about it and he attacked me . . . You never know – I might get lucky and face a manslaughter charge instead of murder.'

Alasdair pressed his fingers to his eyes and wept in silence. Maria came to Langham and he held her.

Endicott brought his hands down on the arms of the chair and said, 'Right. I'll drive into Bury, seek out that Montgomery chappie and spill the damned beans. You stay here, Alasdair. No need your getting involved.'

Maria said, 'Edward, I'm sorry.'

Endicott smiled. 'No, *I'm* sorry, Maria . . . I'm sorry for stringing you along . . . sorry for not being man enough to confess at the time. I'm the one to blame. I've got broad shoulders, y'know, and I can take whatever's coming to me.'

He nodded to Langham, turned and strode from the room.

Alasdair stood, murmured his apologies again to Langham and followed his father from the study.

Langham remembered Ryland, and murmured, 'I'd better go and tell Ralph that you've solved the case.'

She looked up at Langham with tearful eyes. 'Oh, Donald, perhaps I should have said nothing?'

He squeezed her. 'No, you did the right thing. You couldn't have kept shtum about what you suspected. As Edward said, he's the one to blame.'

She shook in his arms and he realized that she was weeping. 'Oh, poor, poor Caroline,' she said, 'and just when things between her and Edward had taken a turn for the better!'

He kissed her forehead. 'She's a strong woman, Maria. And we'll make sure we're there for her, OK?'

She looked up at him and smiled. 'Oh, thank you, Donald. Thank you!'

'For what?' he asked, puzzled.

'For simply being Donald Langham,' she said.

He smiled at her and stroked a tress of hair from her face. 'I'll go and invite Ralph in,' he said. 'I don't know about you, but I could do with another stiff drink.'

EPILOGUE

Langham drove along the winding country lane towards the village of Meadford and his agent's stately home. Maria sat beside him, attending to her face with her compact – as if, he thought, she could make herself any more attractive.

A month had elapsed since the events at Humble Barton. Last week Caroline Dequincy had come up to London once for a dinner date. She had been subdued, but was facing the future with characteristic fortitude. On Maria's suggestion, Charles had invited her over to his place for the weekend, and Langham was delighted that she'd accepted.

'I'm looking forward to seeing Caroline again,' he said. 'She was rather down last week, though she did put a brave face on things.'

'I like Caroline a lot,' Maria said. 'I admire her strength, her courage.'

'She's a remarkable woman,' Langham said. 'I just hope . . .'

'Yes?'

He shrugged. 'That Edward's lawyer can convince a jury that he did attack Hartwell in self-defence. He *might* not face a murder charge then.'

'Oh, I do hope so, Donald!'

He glanced at Maria. 'It's strange, isn't it . . .?'

'What is?'

'You think you know someone, believe what they tell you . . . don't think for a minute that they're lying . . .'

'Ah, you mean Edward.'

'He was pretty convincing, wasn't he? The thing is I like the man. I could see myself doing exactly the same thing in his position. "There but for the hand of fate . . ." I thought to myself.'

She frowned. 'I'm not sure you would have attacked someone like that, Donald.'

'Oh, I don't know. If someone threatened a loved one, as Hartwell was threatening Alasdair . . . Who knows what you might be driven to in that position?'

They drove along in silence for a minute, then he said, 'You know, that was pretty dashed clever of you, Maria. There I was, thinking Alasdair had done for Hartwell, and you were streets ahead.'

She bit her lip. 'I don't know . . . I sometimes wonder if I did the right thing. Perhaps . . . perhaps I should have said nothing, Donald? It is unlikely that Edward would have committed violence again, isn't it? The police would have believed Alasdair's story about Marcus Denbigh, and Edward and Caroline would be together now.'

'You did the right thing, old girl. And do you know what? I think that on some level Edward was relieved when you uncovered the truth. He's an honest man, essentially, and I think living a lie would have troubled him deeply. This way, perhaps, he can atone . . .'

'For his sins?' she said, smiling archly.

'Atone for his crime,' he said.

'I hope so,' Maria murmured.

Langham slowed down as he took a sharp corner. Maria finished her make-up, snapped shut her compact and replaced it in her handbag.

He was looking forward to the weekend at Charles's. He would bide his time until the opportune moment, wait until they were alone, and then ask the all-important question. Events of late had rather kicked thoughts of marriage into the backseat, but now the way was clear to settle the matter once and for all.

'And how is your chest, Donald?'

'Do you know something? It's fine. Haven't had any gyp for a week or so.'

She smiled. 'And the nightmares?'

'I took your advice.'

'My advice?'

'About writing of my wartime experiences. In the new novel I have a character reliving his. He's pretty much going through what I'd experienced. Killed a man . . .'

'And?'

'Early days, but we'll see, won't we?'

They rolled through the sun-soaked Suffolk countryside, skirted Bury St Edmunds and took the road to Meadford. Langham reflected that it was good to be away from London and in the country again.

'Oh, and my father phoned this morning. He's invited us to dinner next week.'

'So I didn't blot my copybook with him last time?' he laughed.

'He thought you charming,' she said, 'and very English.'

'Hmm. Should I take that as a compliment?'

'Of course! My father rather likes the English, though he wouldn't admit as much outright. He says you were the perfect gentleman, and he's very happy that I am happy, too.'

'My word.'

'And he has read another one of your books.'

'Well, I hope he liked it more than the first one he read.'

'He did. He said he quite liked it. Of course, it's not his preferred reading.'

'Of course not.'

'But he did think it better than the average English thriller.'

'Well, commendation indeed. I'll have that plastered across the cover of my next one: "Langham pens better than average thrillers", the French Cultural Attaché.'

Twenty minutes later they passed through Meadford, turned right at the church and soon came to the turning that led to Charles's country pile.

Langham pulled up beside his agent's silver Bentley. Half-a-dozen other cars filled the gravelled forecourt and Langham spotted guests on the side lawn. He lifted the Fortnum and Mason's hamper from the backseat and carried it to the imposing front door.

Charles Elder, resplendent in loud checked tweeds, emerged from the house to greet them.

'You're here! And such a wonderful day! I have it all planned – once you've settled in and we've had a little drink in the library, just the four of us.'

'Four?' Maria asked.

'I have been chatting to your lovely friend, Caroline Dequincy. We get along like the proverbial blazing house.' He hesitated, then said, 'I didn't ask her about Edward, of course. That would be *too* indelicate. Have you heard anything regarding that little matter?'

'Edward has a good lawyer,' Langham said, 'but it all depends on the strength of the prosecution's case. If they convince the jury that it was premeditated murder, then . . . then I'm afraid there's no hope for Edward.'

'My word,' Charles said. 'Poor Caroline.'

Langham deposited the hamper on a side table in the hallway and opened the lid.

Charles said, 'But what is this, my boy?'

'Straight from Fortnum and Mason's,' Langham said.

Charles exclaimed, 'But no expense spared. Champagne. Parma ham. And is that a jar of caviar? My word . . . such largesse!'

'To get the weekend off to a good start,' Maria said.

'But I won't keep you,' Charles said. 'Off you go and fetch your luggage. I'll see you in the library in twenty minutes.'

Langham carried their cases from the car and followed Maria up the grand staircase. She led the way to the west wing, opened a bedroom door and paused. 'Yes,' she sang to him. 'I think this one will do nicely.'

He followed her into the room, noticing that the bed beside the large window was a double.

She turned to him. 'And you can leave your case in here, Donald. Next to mine.'

His heart began a laboured thudding. 'I can?'

Silhouetted against the sunlight falling through the window at her back, she looked like an angel.

'Come here,' she said.

He obeyed, and held her in his arms. 'I think, Donald,' she said, with a playful expression on her face, 'that you have something to ask me, *non*?'

He stammered. 'I do . . .? I mean, yes. Yes, I *do*.'

'Well, then . . .'

He gazed into her big brown eyes, swallowed, and said, 'Maria . . .'

'Yes?'

'I . . . that is . . . Dammit – I never thought I'd be so dashed nervous!'

She raised her fingers to her lips and laughed. 'Out with it, Donald!'

He laughed with her. 'Very well, Maria. Look here, you know how much I love you.'

'You do?'

'More than anything, and . . . and I was wondering – well, that is . . . would you . . .?'

'Yes?'

'Would you care to marry me?'

She pursed her lips, clearly in an attempt to stop herself from crying. She nodded and kissed him again and again. 'Oh, of course I would, you funny man! Of course I would!'

Ten minutes later they descended to the library and found Charles busying himself at the drinks table.

Maria cleared her throat and said, 'Charles,

Donald has an announcement to make, and we would like you to be the first to know.'

Charles turned, brandy glass in hand, and stared at them, puzzlement on his large face. 'An announcement?'

Langham beamed and took Maria's hand. 'Maria has agreed, just minutes ago, to become my wife.'

Charles stood open-mouthed, as if in shock, then burst out: 'But my dears! My children! This is the most . . . the most wonderful news . . . and you have almost, *almost*, succeeded in rendering me speechless! This calls for champagne,' he went on, reaching for the ice bucket and withdrawing a magnum of bubbly.

He hurried to the French windows and called out to his guests to come and share in the good news.

Minutes later a dozen smiling guests – friends of Charles's from London and beyond – stood in a semicircle with glasses in hand. Caroline Dequincy, looking wonderful in a beige summer dress and sunhat, smiled across at Maria and Langham.

Charles raised his glass and proposed a toast.

Langham looked into Maria's eyes and squeezed her hand.

'To Donald and Maria,' Charles said. 'May you find all the happiness you deserve!'

'To Donald and Maria!' the guests chorused.

They raised their glasses and drank.